THE GUARDIANS

What Reviewers Say About Sheri Lewis Wohl's Work

Drawing Down the Mist

"Vampires loving humans. Vampires hating vampires. Vampires killing humans. Vampires killing vampires. Good vampires. Evil vampires. Internet-savvy vampires. Lovers turning enemies. Nurturing revenge for a century. Kindness. Cruelty. Love. Action. Fights. Insta-love. This one has everything for a true drama."—*reviewer@large*

Cause of Death

"I really liked these characters, all of them, and wouldn't say no to a sequel, or more."—*Jude in the Stars*

"*CSI* meets *Ghost Whisperer*. ...The pace was brilliantly done, the suspense was just enough, and I'm not ashamed to admit that I had no idea who the serial killer was until almost the end."—*Words and Worlds*

"*Cause of Death* by Sheri Lewis Wohl is one creepy and well-written murder mystery. It is one of the best psychological thrillers I've read in a while."—*Rainbow Reflections*

"[A] light paranormal romance with a psycho-killer and some great dogs."—*C-Spot Reviews*

"There's a ton of stuff in here that I enjoy very much, such as the light paranormal aspect of the book, and the relationship between our two leads is very nice if a bit of a slow burn. The case was engaging enough that I didn't really set this title down once I started it." —Colleen Corgel, Librarian, Queens Public Library

"Totally disturbing, and very, very awesome. ...The characters were amazing. The supernatural tint was never overdone, and even the stuff from the killer's point of view, while disturbing, was awesomely done as well. It was a great book and a fun (and intense) read."—Danielle Kimerer, Librarian (Nevins Memorial Library, Massachusetts)

"This thriller has spooky undertones that make it an intense page turner. You won't be able to put this book down."—*Istoria Lit*

The Talebearer

"As a crime story, it is a good read that had me turning pages quickly. ...The book is well written and the characters are well-developed." —*Reviews by Amos Lassen*

She Wolf

"I really enjoyed this book—I couldn't put it down once I started it. The author's style of writing was very good and engaging. All characters, including the supporting characters, were multi-layered and interesting."—Melina Bickard, Librarian, Waterloo Library (UK)

Twisted Screams

"[A] cast of well-developed characters leads you through a maze of complex emotions."—*Lunar Rainbow Reviewz*

Twisted Echoes

"A very unusual blend of lesbian romance and horror. ...[W]oven throughout this modern romance is a neatly plotted horror story from the past, which bleeds ever increasingly into the present of the two main characters. Lorna and Renee are well matched, and face ever-increasing danger from spirits from the past. An unusual story that gets tenser and more interesting as it progresses."—Pippa Wischer, Manager at Berkelouw Books, Armadale

Vermilion Justice

"[T]he characters are so dynamic and well-written that this becomes more than just another vampire story. It's probably impossible to read this book and not come across a character who reminds you of someone you actually know. Wohl takes something as fictional as vampires and makes them feel real. Highly recommended."—*GLBT Reviews: The ALA's GLBT Round Table*

Visit us at www.boldstrokesbooks.com

By the Author

Crimson Vengeance

Burgundy Betrayal

Scarlet Revenge

Vermillion Justice

Twisted Echoes

Twisted Whispers

Twisted Screams

Necromantia

She Wolf

Walking Through Shadows

Drawing Down the Mist

The Talebearer

Cause of Death

Avenging Avery

All that Remains

The Artist

Witch Finder

Buried Secrets

The Guardians

THE GUARDIANS

by

Sheri Lewis Wohl

2024

THE GUARDIANS
© 2024 By Sheri Lewis Wohl. All Rights Reserved.

ISBN 13: 978-1-63679-681-9

This Trade Paperback Original Is Published By
Bold Strokes Books, Inc.
P.O. Box 249
Valley Falls, NY 12185

First Edition: December 2024

Credits
Editor: Shelley Thrasher
Production Design: Susan Ramundo
Cover Design By Tammy Seidick

Dedication

For Rogan. I miss your smile, your laugh, your hugs.
Flying squirrels and cheesy corn. Taken far too soon,
the light and love you brought into the world can
never be erased. I'll see you on the other side.

Lest Satan should get
an advantage of us:
For we are not
ignorant of his devices

2 Corinthians 2:11
The Holy Bible
King James Version

CHAPTER ONE

A radia Burke knelt next to the birthing pen and stroked the beautiful Anatolian shepherd's head. With her pale fawn hair and black face, Gia was a classic, and she'd just delivered a healthy litter of seven. Four boys and three girls. Puppy number three turned out to be the special one. As he cuddled close to his mother and siblings, the shine appeared. Not every litter produced a shine, but Gia had given her the perfect little guy today. "Oh, sweet mama, you gave me a winner." Her mind already whirled with a training plan and a potential placement.

"How's it going?" Lizzy Christopher, her kennel assistant and Jackie-of-all-trades, dropped down next to her. "I swear, they're so stinking cute. These dogs make the best puppies."

She smiled. "Yeah. They are adorable for little lumps." At this moment, they were tiny and round. Their personalities, coloring, and temperament would show themselves in the coming weeks. "He's my guy." She pointed to number three. He might be a lump like the rest of the litter, but the Guardians always showed themselves from the moment of birth. He'd stay with his mama and siblings until week nine and then move to the special kennel.

"I wish I could see it." Lizzy frowned and bit her lower lip, her blue eyes sad. "I don't have anything special about me."

Aradia rocked back on her heels. "Now you're talking crazy. You are a dog whisperer if I've ever met one. They all love you—good, bad, high-drive, or tentative. That's a true gift, my friend, so don't ever talk down to yourself. You're as special as they come."

A smile brightened Lizzy's face. "See. This is why I love working here. You spot the bright and shiny in everyone, and not just the ones born with the extra. You make me and the dogs feel good. What are you going to call him?"

A good question. Aradia had been thinking about a name since she realized what he was. "He's beautiful and dark, and will be a warrior, so I think Duncan fits him." As a general rule, she didn't name the pups in a litter. They had different color baby collars and were referred to by each one's color. Except when it came to the Guardians. Those pups were named on day one.

Lizzy nodded. "He looks like a Duncan."

"Really? He looks like a ball of fur to me, shine aside." While she did name them immediately, personalities didn't emerge for weeks. Naming a pup on day one meant going with her instinct.

"Totally a Duncan. I might not be able to see the shine in him, but I can see personality, and I don't care if you say it's too early. That little man is going to be a strong Guardian."

Aradia laughed. "Fair enough. How about we give Mama and her babies some peace and quiet? She's done a lot of work today."

"Good job, Gia," Lizzy said. "You're a very good girl and a most excellent mama."

Both of them stood and walked outside, where the sun shone warm on Aradia's face. The air was fresh, a gentle breeze picking up her hair to blow it into her face. "You heading out?" She pulled a band out of her pocket and smoothed her long hair back into a ponytail. Better.

Since it was hard enough to get good, competent help she could trust with her secrets, she didn't like to impose on the staff she did have too hard. Aradia might be pushing her luck if she asked her to stay now, at well past four. If Lizzy left now, she'd be home before the traffic picked up, and that might not seem like a big deal, but it was. She didn't want anyone who worked for her to spend time fighting through rush hour just to get back and forth to work. The little things made a big difference.

"I promised Sammy I'd throw the ball for him before I left today. Can't break a promise to my favorite guy. Don't tell Henry I said that.

He's convinced I'll dump him for a dog one day." She laughed as she ran her hands through her short, curly hair.

"He might not be wrong." Aradia spoke from experience. She'd done exactly that to her husband after only two years of marriage. She'd felt guilty for a long time until she realized both of them were happier this way. He'd found someone who loved him the way he deserved to be loved, and she felt free to find love with whomever she wanted, whether that be another man or a woman. She'd realized a long time ago that love for her wasn't about gender. Well, in theory anyway. Not like she'd put herself out there to even look for a forever partner.

Lizzy laughed harder. "Never say never."

"I'd make a bet that being a wise man, Henry will simply get you a dog, and then you'll all live happily ever after." Aradia focused once more on Lizzy, pushing aside troubling memories of her past.

"That's a plan I can totally support." She turned full circle, looking around. "Where is Sammy anyway?"

The resident old man, Sammy held a place of honor in the Burkehaus Kennels. Fourteen years old, he had a white muzzle, and his hearing wasn't even close to what it used to be. Having sired a number of fantastic litters, he now kept watch over the entire operation. He could no longer run like a pup or even hear an intruder. Neither dampened his enthusiasm for the job. Talk about a big heart.

"There he is." Aradia pointed to the large dog as he ambled their way. Sammy probably thought he was racing toward them. How she loved her resident grandpa, a little tug at her heart reminding her their time together was growing short. "Thanks for everything, and I'll see you Monday morning. Have a fun weekend."

Lizza pulled a ball on a rope from her back pocket as she walked toward Sammy. "That I will. Henry and I are going to Sandpoint for the weekend. He's got a gig up there."

Sandpoint, Idaho was an easy, scenic drive from her place between Chewelah and Deer Park in eastern Washington State. Then again, one of her dogs, along with his handler, was stationed up there. Any place where her Guardians worked called for extra vigilance, and that made it super hard for her to relax in areas of known portals.

Even though she had confidence in their abilities, it was important not to get lax. Not that she ever truly relaxed.

"You guys will have a good time." She smiled, not wanting her always-on-guard mentality to rub off on Lizzy. Her tendency to go above and beyond around the farm had more than earned her time to just have fun, and if she caught a whiff or hint of trouble, she'd cancel her Sandpoint plans and stay with Aradia.

Lizzy's eyes sparkled as she glanced back over her shoulder at Aradia. Love could do that. "One of these days, he's gonna break through. I feel it coming. Maybe that's my something special. I feel things."

Ardia smiled. "I have my fingers crossed for him and his music. If you feel it, I believe it too. Besides, I've heard him, and I think you're right. He's not just good. He's very good. He has that rare something that will put him over the top." Henry had real talent, and she'd be sad when Lizzie had to leave her to help him follow the dream. It wasn't a case of *if* she left with him to pursue musical success, only a matter of *when*. No ability to see the future, only the ability to recognize true talent.

"Appreciate the good vibes. See you Monday," Lizzy turned her attention to Sammy while swinging the ball on the rope.

The game of fetch would last about five minutes, about all Sammy could handle these days, and then Lizzy would be on her way. Sammy would be super happy, and Lizzy would have a fun-filled weekend. She watched the short game of fetch, and after Lizzy's car rolled down the driveway, Aradia picked up her phone, found the contact she wanted, and tapped the number. "We have a winner."

Mercy Boroughs could already tell the answer to this request would be a hard no. While the potential client was vague on the phone, the moment Mercy put eyes on her, she understood the true purpose for her visit.

"I can't do that for you." She kept her voice calm and even, her words firm. Her feet hip-width apart, arms crossed over her chest, Mercy silently assessed her latest visitor.

Seattle socialite Della Tollare pleaded. "I'm not asking you to do it. I'm asking you to provide me with the herbs, and I'll take care of the rest. You won't be doing anything wrong."

"Except providing you with the means to kill your husband." How stupid and gullible did people think she was?

Blue eyes met hers, bright and hopeful. They didn't appear to be the eyes of a killer, yet that's exactly what this woman would be if Mercy handed over what she asked for. "He's not a good person. I'm asking for something untraceable that will keep everyone safe. Nothing unreasonable."

"I'm a healer." *Also, not stupid.* She kept that comment to herself.

"Think of it as healing everyone he's hurt. He needs to be brought face-to-face with justice. This is bigger than me or you."

She'd heard that particular argument more than once. Didn't work any other time someone used it on her. "The answer is still no. I will not give you what you're asking for."

"Come on. Please. I don't have anywhere else to turn." Tears began to pool in Della's eyes. She blinked again and again, obviously not to hold back the tears but to make her entreaty look sincere. Something else Mercy had seen more times than she cared to count. She might live in a largely rural area—didn't mean she'd just fallen off the turnip truck. She'd learned very early how to read people, which was easy with this woman.

"If it's that bad, call the police." The law could handle an abuser, if he truly was one. More than likely just a rich guy she didn't want to be married to anymore and a prenup that would cut her out of the money. Same old story. Different face.

"Oh, hell no. I would never go to the police. You have to understand. He's too powerful, so they're useless to me. You're my only hope." The unfallen tears dried up.

Yawn. "I refuse to help you take someone's life, whether they're a horrible person or not. I don't do murder."

"You're not." The pleading in her voice took on a high, unpleasant tone.

"If I give you what you're asking for, then yes. I'll be an accessory to murder. For the last time, no."

For a long moment, the blue eyes held her gaze. Recognition dawned, and Della sighed. "Fine, but you're losing out on a lot. I can pay you well, and you'd be doing a service to the world by taking him out of it."

"I don't want your money." Blood money didn't do it for her regardless of the amount, and through the years, Mercy had been offered numbers followed by a whole lot of zeros.

Della sneered as she glanced around. "Pretty clear on that. This place is a dump."

"Good-bye." Della had overstayed her welcome.

As Della walked to the door, she muttered, "Self-righteous bitch."

Taking no chances, she followed Della outside, thinking, not for the first time, that it might be better if she had a big dog around. Typically, she worked alone here at the farm, although most of the time, the people who did business with her were good and honest, the kind who came looking for ways to heal or to maintain good health, not to kill. Hands in her pockets, her long hair tucked up inside her straw hat, she enjoyed the light breeze that both carried the scent of hundreds of lavender plants and made her dangling amber earrings sway. Once Della's car disappeared down her driveway, she pulled her phone out of her pocket. "Ken, I just had another one."

"Name?" She could picture Detective Ken Groth sitting at his desk while reaching for a pen, his black hair, streaked with gray, hanging over his collar.

"Della Tollare. About five-ten with blue eyes and expensively dyed red hair. She's set on getting rid of her husband because, as she explained, he's abusive and dangerous." They always used that reason, and she often wondered why someone didn't come up with a more creative one.

"Tollare," he muttered and she could hear the click of the laptop keys. "Oh, right. The guy does have a reputation for being an asshole. He's a developer who owns about half of downtown Bellevue. I'm sure his net worth has nothing to do with her request."

"Or a prenup that cuts her out of everything if she divorces him."

"They really hate those prenups."

"Ain't it the truth."

"Not exactly a bright bulb if she gave you her real name."

Ken's comment echoed Mercy's earlier thoughts. "She obviously didn't really think this all the way through."

"Copy that. Well, thanks for the info. We'll keep an eye on this situation."

She ended the call, slipped the phone back into her pocket, and closed her eyes. Her reputation as an herbalist had grown over the years. Few knew her ability to heal came from more than just her skill with herbs. She didn't want people to know that her magic played a role. Most wouldn't believe it anyway. They were content to accept that her ability to cultivate top-notch healing plants ensured her success.

A dark side accompanied her reputation for healing. Every now and again someone sought her out for other purposes. One after another, she shut them down. Funny how unsophisticated these wanna-be killers were. They asked for her help, she turned them down, and then they walked away. What did they think she'd do? Pretend they didn't just ask her to help them kill someone? Each time, she called Ken and passed the inquiry along. If they got a no from her, they'd most likely keep searching until they found someone who would say yes. Mercy wasn't the only one skilled with both healing and deadly plants. Ken thwarted their plans even if their intended victims were assholes.

At least she hadn't had any blowback. So far. Maybe the magic that surrounded her kept her safe. Good enough for her. She opened her eyes and took long, even breaths.

Mercy had wanted to send the latest assassin on her way. Something wasn't right in her world. Not because Della had asked her to help her murder a supposedly bad man. No. It went deeper than that. Vibrations roiled beneath Mercy's feet, and they didn't come from living near an active volcano. She'd lived with those since Mom had adopted her and brought her to this farm. This was something much different. Now, they whispered that evil came Mercy's way. Not of the Della Tollare variety either. No, this felt far different. Darker. More dangerous.

Hard to just ignore it and continue with business as usual. Not her style, so once more, she pulled her phone out of her pocket and, this time, selected a different number. The moment the call was picked up, she said, "You get the feeling trouble is coming?"

❖

August Fian sat at the table sipping on a glass of bourbon while he pored over the texts. The 24 × 36 inch map of the United States tacked up on the corkboard had five markers. If he interpreted the texts correctly, and he did, three more remained in North America. Given the patterns of the markers, at least one would be in the Pacific Northwest. Another likely spot, northern Canada. Number three had him scratching his head. Not a real big deal. Open a major portal and the rest would take care of themselves. Sort of the hole-in-a-dam thing. Once the barrier had been breached, there'd be no holding them back. A wave would start, and portals would open all over the world.

His phone rang, and he put it on speaker. "Ama, what's up?"

"Any luck?" Her voice, unusually deep for a woman, blasted through the phone. He liked that about her. Confidence and strength.

"Still looking for the last three." He squinted as he continued to study the map. If he studied it long enough, something would come to him.

"I think I've got a lead for you."

"Spit it out." She should have led with that. While he liked Ama, as much as he liked anyone, that is, this wasn't the time for casual chitchat. The urgency came from another little piece of trivia he'd mined from the ancient texts. The optimum moment for breach would be here soon. The night of the Black Moon, a rare occurrence that held incredible power for the underworld. Now he just had to find the biggest portal to open on the night the Black Moon hit center sky. Ama could go with him to assist, as she'd proved herself useful on more than one occasion. He suspected he'd have to explain the assist part to her in detail. There would only be room for one leader.

"Washington State."

He nodded even though she couldn't see him. That tracked with his belief that a major portal existed in the Northwest. Right as always. "Not really narrowing it down. I need something more specific. Washington is too big, with too many mountains, to run around just looking for a portal." He put his finger on the map. Plenty of mountains, a plethora of places where a portal might exist. Correction. *Did* exist.

"Oh, come on. With the work you've been doing, I'm surprised you haven't gotten it yet. So obvious." Her teasing tone did not amuse him. Humor in general didn't land well with August. His parents had always said he had a serious demeanor. They had declared it to be a personality deficit. He disagreed.

As he frowned and stared at the map, it hit him. "Bingo." He tapped the southwest corner of the state with his finger.

She laughed. "Knew you'd get it if you gave yourself a few to check out the geography. So obvious."

He stuck a red pin in the town of Cougar. Or, rather, what passed for a town. More like a spot on the map than a thriving community. A population that consisted of three digits. Three low digits. The second he put that pin in the name Cougar, the floor rumbled beneath his feet. Actual town or not, the universe had just sent him a solid. "Got it."

"We're almost there." Her voice took on a triumphant tone as if she'd actually accomplished something. No need to correct her. He'd let her have her delusions.

"Call me if you get anything else." He had plans to make, and as Ama might want to talk more, he hit the end button on his phone before she could blather on.

August stood, linked his fingers together behind his back, and began to pace. Something about that last pin got to him. Important in a way that others were not. That wasn't to say the others didn't matter. They did. It would take maximum effort to breach the barriers that had kept the rightful heirs unfairly confined to the underworld. He'd spent his entire life preparing for the day he could free the demons from confinement, then bind them to himself—an army to protect and elevate him to a position of power never before seen. He was more than ready for the moment, and it beckoned just beyond the sunset.

In the bedroom, he went to the closet and grabbed his ready kit—the black leather bag on the floor. No need to pack anything else. Nor did he worry if he would return. Those kinds of details were unimportant. A new world order awaited, with him at the helm. Ordinary things like this house, the furniture, the clothing—none of it would hold any appeal or value in his future. Everything in his world would be shiny and new once he harnessed what rightfully belonged to him.

Out in the garage, he studied the vehicles. The appropriate mode of transportation held great importance. As much as he'd love to take the Jag because of the speed, the smooth ride, and the coolness factor, it lacked the room he needed for additional tools. Those might become essential once he reached Cougar. Better to be prepared for battle ahead than to be caught short. No one would ever be able to say that about him in any sense, and he laughed at his own little joke.

He finally settled on the GMC Yukon. Jet-black with plenty of cargo space. Stealth and utility rolled into one, exactly what the job called for. In the back he loaded his weapons of choice. A carbon-steel dagger made by the world's premier blacksmith. Weighted perfectly with a mother-of-pearl hilt, the dagger had been custom-made for him. A shame it had to be the last weapon said blacksmith made. Blessed by a mage, it remained one of his most powerful weapons and critical to what was to come.

Next came a razor-sharp ax, three tarps, just in case—a holdover from his Boy Scout days—and from the garage freezer, a Ziplock bag of hamburger. Not just any bag of meat. Specially prepared for the kind of hunt he would be undertaking. He put it inside the travel cooler, plugged into the auxiliary power. Handy little gadget, guaranteeing the ground beef would stay unspoiled throughout the trip. The last item, a leather bag to carry all his necessary tools when he arrived on-site. He always left a few items inside. Salt. Several sealed vials holding various toxic substances that could come in handy. A case holding half-a-dozen filled and ready syringes. And his own grimoire, where he kept the most important spells and ancient knowledge he amassed and consolidated. He didn't need the grimoire for reference, as once he learned the magic, he remembered it word-for-word. More a comfort to know that the grimoire was close to him at all times.

In the backyard he walked the perimeter. The locks on the two walk-gates and a twelve-foot sliding gate needed to be checked. At the garden, he stopped briefly. He had meticulously planned and executed everything. The plants were hearty and healthy, with his pride, the oleander, a profusion of red blossoms. A stone path snaked around the flowers, bushes, and trees, creating a soothing oasis for a warrior who needed to be battle-ready all the time. Not that he minded being on alert 24/7. He'd been born to the job and embraced it with utter, complete devotion.

The sun had begun its descent to the west by the time he had checked and double-checked everything. While it might be better to start the drive tomorrow, the urge to get on the road now hit him hard. By leaving at this time of day, he could drive until he got tired, then find a nice hotel for the night. Every mile he conquered today would put him closer to this goal. No fault with his logic.

He climbed into the Yukon, hit the button to open the garage door, and started the engine. He glanced in the rearview mirror as he drove out of the driveway, turning onto the street. Fifteen minutes later, he merged onto the freeway and smiled as he whispered, "Ready or not, here I come."

CHAPTER TWO

Aradia didn't feel bad that she'd awakened her sister, Sabina, even though it clocked in at well past midnight in Bucharest. Payback could be a bitch, and given Sabina's tendency to call Aradia at all hours just to say hello meant she had it coming. "You catch what I just told you?" She fingered the ring on the fine chain. Sabina's random calls weren't just to say hello. The whole family seemed to think Aradia had isolated herself after the divorce, and she let them believe that.

"Geez, Aradia. Give me a sec. I was sound asleep." Definitely not quite awake yet.

She smiled picturing her sister sitting up in bed, her long hair a tangled mess, blinking in the darkness of the bedroom. Sabina lived in a small cottage on the outskirts of the city, and it didn't lack for charm. Aradia didn't get to visit often, but when she did, she soaked it all in. More important than its charm, the little cottage sat near one of the known portals. Like Aradia, nothing—her life, her location, or her vocation—came about due to chance. A time and purpose for everything, even where they lived.

"I know, I know, and I'd say that I feel bad for waking you up, but that would be a lie. It's very satisfying to drag your butt out of sleep. This little guy is special." They'd been super close growing up and had shared every important moment. Adulthood and life in different parts of the world hadn't changed a thing about their sibling relationship.

"You've had special pups before." Her voice sounded less sleepy and not at all irritated. Sabina's congenial personality cloaked a strong inner warrior. "You didn't wake me up in the middle of the night to tell me about him. Spit out whatever you really called to tell me."

"It's more than the pup." That part she hadn't shared with Lizzy earlier.

"What's happening?" No trace of sleepiness now.

"Two things. First, tremors in the earth. Subtle but getting stronger. Tells me they're getting ready and pushing up as close as possible." Aradia rubbed her thumb and forefinger over and over the gold band that hung from a chain around her neck.

"Well, we've had that before and were able to push them back."

"This is different." Both Aradia and Sabina had experienced near-breaches before. Always preceded by things like tremors. If her sister were with her now, she'd pick up on the distinction as quickly as Aradia had.

"Fair enough. Tell me." Background noises let her know Sabina had moved to the kitchen and was possibly making some tea.

"It's the pup. At first, the litter birth wasn't anything different. You know how it is. Usually, when a special one is born, it shows up the second the pups arrive. This time, it came maybe half an hour later, as if powers had gathered to make sure he would be exceptionally mighty."

"All right. I agree with you. That's not the norm, and I've never seen that happen before." Sabina, like Aradia, bred Guardians. The world saw them as exceptional breeders of Anatolian shepherds, which wasn't inaccurate. Their true calling, hidden beneath the façade, was to nurture and train the Guardians. Sabina's teams were placed strategically throughout Europe and Asia. Aradia's dogs were fantastic, keeping the unsuspecting safe from the dark forces in North America.

"Are you noticing anything there?" Vibrations still whispered beneath Aradia's feet. She frowned as she stared out the window.

Sabina's answer came quickly. "No. Business as usual here." The sound of water. Definitely making tea.

"Then the breach is looking to happen in this part of the world." Not that she'd really had any doubt. She'd been around this type of situation long enough to be able to read the signs. Still, talking it through with her sister made her feel better. Power in numbers, she supposed, and wished Sabina could be sitting at her table drinking her tea. Most of the time, Aradia didn't mind being alone and, in fact, preferred it. Right now, not so much.

"Do you need me to come?" Sabina always had an uncanny ability to almost read her mind, their connection as strong as if they'd been born twins.

Yes, yes, yes, she wanted to say. *Come now.* She didn't. The practical, self-sufficient Aradia said, "I'd love for you to fly over, but I don't think it would be a good idea. It could be part of the plan. Draw us away so they can breach portals without backup." The forces they might have to deal with were cunning and awful. To underestimate them could prove a recipe for disaster. As much as she'd love to have Sabina at her side, it wasn't worth the risk.

"I agree. I'll reach out to my teams and see what, if anything, has been noticed here. I'll let you know."

Her sister understood as well as Aradia both what was at stake and how to do the best job they could to protect as many as possible. Ideally, everyone. Sometimes they succeeded in that goal. Sometimes they didn't.

"Same here. I'll keep you posted." Already mentally considering the list of teams she'd want to contact, Aradia reached for a pen to jot down names and locations.

"Hey, sis. Could you do it not in the middle of the night? I mean, at my age, a girl needs her beauty sleep." She was a whopping fourteen months older than Aradia, and a flat-out stunner. Her husband, Paulo, always looked at her with an expression that said he knew he'd won the lottery.

Now she smiled and set the pen on the counter. "Yes, big sister, unless I absolutely have to wake you up, I'll call during more civilized hours. Wouldn't want lack of sleep to make you all wrinkly and crone-like."

"You wish. I still make this age look good."

"Sure. We'll go with that." The familiar banter warmed her. Sabina did it on purpose. Her sister never failed to make her feel better. Filled her with such gratitude to have a sibling this wonderful. How she wished she could pull her close for a big hug.

"Love you."

"Back at you."

Tears pooled in her eyes. "Stay safe. You know I don't have any spare sisters."

"I'll do my best." True enough. They only had each other.

"Keep me posted."

"Count on it." She held her phone for a long time after the call ended. Made her feel closer to Sabina. Finally, she slipped it back into her pocket. Chores to do before darkness fell.

First things first, she checked on Gia and the newest members of the family. Gia slept in her pen, the pups also sound asleep except for Duncan. Eyes still closed, he held his tiny head high as though he listened to the sounds of the universe. As if he waited for her to come in and talk to him.

She knelt and touched a finger to the top of his head. "Thank you, pretty boy. Rest now, and gather your strength. Grow big and powerful. Your day will come soon enough. Tonight, you sleep." At the sounds of her soft words, he settled next to his litter mates and stilled, his tiny chest rising and falling. Time to go outside and check on everyone else.

As Aradia checked each kennel, she touched the fences and spoke to every dog. The kennels were spotless, thank you, Lizzie, and tails wagged as she went by. Though her operation was big and producing some of the best Anatolian shepherds in the country, if not the world, she made sure all her dogs had plenty of socialization and affection. She bred for high energy and perfect structure. She also worked for the kind of dogs that could be trusted in any situation, whether that be protection or family pet. For the most part, she'd been successful. Once in a while, a dog came back to her, with very few exceptions the failure of the humans, not the canine. She always reassured the dog, made sure its confidence wasn't damaged, and then found it somewhere it would flourish. Thankfully, a returned dog happened rarely. She prided herself on placing each in the appropriate home.

Set apart from the regular operation were her special kennels and training facility, and she walked there now. "Hello, my beauties," she said as she stepped inside the building. Ten individual kennels lined the walls, flanking a large, central training arena. Seven sets of dark eyes stared back at her. Not one dog barked.

"You feel it, don't you?" This time, low whines answered her. Yes, indeed, they felt it. No surprise. Each and every dog in this kennel possessed the shine. Each and every dog, a Guardian.

She walked from pen to pen and opened each gate. The massive dogs stepped out. No rushing, no growling, no aggression, only deep concentration and anticipation.

"All right, ladies and gents. Let's get to it." They ran to the center training area. Not only did they all know that meant get to work, but they also loved it. Working dogs by breed, the Guardians embodied an incredible drive. They were a true joy to work with, and that's what she did now.

An hour later, Aradia put six of the happy dogs back into their kennels. All seven had performed very well. One had performed exceptionally well, and it hadn't surprised her. "Come, Tara."

At ninety pounds, Tara was the smallest of the seven. Her diminutive size for the breed didn't reflect the warrior that lived inside her. Special from the moment of her birth, Tara appeared to have been born prepared for the battle ahead. No surprise there. Tara was the dog Aradia wanted at her side for the looming conflict. The Guardians were all special, Tara even more so, even though Aradia wouldn't say it out loud. Some dogs were of the heart, and she'd recognized that about Tara on day one.

She knelt and put her hands on Tara's head. Looking into her dark eyes, she said, "Let's get ready for the bastards, shall we?"

Tara barked.

❖

Mercy ended the call with Timothy Knutsen, feeling most validated. Eight miles from her farm, Tim and his dog, Clemons, were what constituted a close neighbor around here. According to Tim, Clemons had been acting agitated for the last week. It had started slowly and, today, clearly ramped up. He wouldn't leave his post on a line that tracked right straight to the base of Mt. St. Helens. The uninformed would say Clemons was merely responding to the small series of earthquakes that happened in the area not infrequently. Mercy didn't believe that to be true.

However, she didn't have all the facts. Tim and Clemons were different. That much had been clear right from the moment she'd met them. When Mercy had pressed him on his background and the training Clemons had gone through, he got very tight-lipped. He'd say only that Clemons could sense disturbance on the mountain. That he possessed a very sensitive nature. No matter what he said, he clearly held back. About himself. About Clemons.

Fair enough, considering she didn't share everything with him either, and that's why she never called him on it. Mercy might be the leading herbalist in the western United States. She might also be a whole lot more. They were grand friends, the kind who kept parts of themselves very close to the vest.

The sound of the doorbell interrupted her racing thoughts. "You got here fast." Mercy opened the door, and Rufus Delgado stepped inside. He set his leather fedora on the table just inside the entryway. His long, black hair was tied back in a ponytail that reached mid-back. She'd never seen his hair any other way and always wondered what it would look like once freed from the leather tie. Tim had been her second call. Rufus, her first.

"Got a lot of the same vibes as you and decided it would be a good idea to get closer sooner rather than later." He dropped into a chair next to the fireplace, stretching out his long legs and crossing his cowboy-boot-clad feet. She didn't have to tell him to get comfortable. They'd been close since the moment they met. Some who spent time around them made it clear they thought the two of them were more than just friends. They were wrong. Tight, without question. They'd never be more for a reason that didn't seem to be obvious to everyone. He liked men. She liked women. How people missed that about them she didn't know. Wasn't like either one of them made it secret. She guessed a lot of people saw only what they wanted to.

"That was a quick three hours." It was almost two hundred miles from his home in Yakima. Big shocker. The guy did like speed, and she wondered how many speeding tickets he'd racked up over the years.

"None," he said as if she'd asked the question out loud. Sort of worked that way with people like them.

She shook her head. "Good to know and glad the weather stayed decent if you're going to drive like a bat out of hell." Not getting a ticket didn't mean he'd adhered to posted speed limits. She knew him better than that. He might like to drive fast, but at least he did it clean and sober. Might have been a good idea for Rufus to go into racing rather than counseling. Thing is, as much as he liked to drive fast, he liked helping people more.

"Don't tell my father." He winked.

She laughed. "What? He'll take your keys away and send you to your room?" She had met the senior Delgado several times, a short, stocky man who still retained his heavy Mexican accent and who headed a large agricultural business in the Yakima Valley. She liked him a lot, but she'd sure never cross him. She wasn't related, and no question about it, if she misbehaved, he'd send her to her room as though she were another of his children.

"Ha. Maybe when I was sixteen. These days, he's more likely to have my mother ask an officer to talk with me about my driving habits. Again."

Mercy liked his mother as much as she liked his father. A member of the Yakama Nation, Elaine Olney Delgado currently served as an officer for the tribal police. "She wants you to represent your people in a law-abiding manner, and who can blame her? Can't have the child of an upstanding member of the force turning into a scofflaw."

He nodded. "True enough, and while I can appreciate the sentiment, she forgets what I can do. I won't embarrass her. Probably."

"You'll know." Didn't really need to be said. For both of them, a given.

He nodded slowly. "You got it, sister. I'll know if a stater is going to pull me over. I'll know about the radar way before it has a chance to pick me up."

"Can't dismiss the perks to what we can do." A burden in some respects. A blessing in others. Good and bad went hand-in-hand.

"Some perks, yeah. A shitload of bad too." A darkness flashed over his face, and she wished she could do something to ease the pain in his heart. He'd used his gift to help find some of the missing and murdered Indigenous women. The heartbreak of what he'd seen couldn't be erased. The only solace came with bringing them home and giving answers to their families.

Mercy brought the conversation back to the here and now. "Something bad's waiting to happen. I just can't put my finger on what kind of bad or where it's coming from."

Now he leaned forward in the chair, his elbows on his knees, his fingers steepled. His expression cleared, and his gaze met hers. "You think maybe the mountain's going to blow again? Put a whole lot of people in danger?"

Not a bad guess, given where she lived. The mountain had blown forty-some-odd years ago and created a major catastrophe across the state. Those who'd been around when it happened and made it out safely still talked about it. While she'd tried to search for some kind of clarity to what she'd been sensing, it refused to come. "It's not clear enough for me to figure it out, but truthfully, that's not what it feels like. The mountain isn't reaching out to me. Seems darker than mother nature flexing her muscles." Goosebumps rose on her arms, and she shuddered.

Rufus pressed his lips together in a frown. For a few seconds he stared at her before saying, "I sure don't like that."

"That makes two of us."

❖

As much as he wanted to drive straight through, August chose wisdom over desire. Besides, they'd been anticipating an opportunity like this for centuries, and waiting a day or two more wouldn't be the worst thing to happen. Had to wait on the moon anyway. Better to take his time, pick up reinforcements, and arrive at the battlefield rested and ready to claim what rightfully belonged to him the moment the Black Moon hit center sky.

He pressed a button on his steering wheel and said, "Call Ama." A lot to be said for the tech in the newer vehicles. A few seconds later, the call connected.

"How close are you?" Ama's deep voice filled the car.

"Just on the other side of the bridge." A short drive once he crossed the Golden Gate Bridge to reach her house. The lights on the suspension cables were pretty impressive this time of night.

"Good. I'll leave the door unlocked for you."

He disconnected the call without responding. Never did quite understand the appeal of the famous landmark. Interesting, sure. Lights at night were cool, but really, no big deal. Lots of interesting bridges across the country. All it really did was span the water and make it easy to get from one side to the other. So many more interesting things in the area, like the old prison. Alcatraz, while not the home of a portal, appealed to him a great deal. The energy on the island never failed to fill him up. Each time he came here, he took time to ride the ferry over and soak it all in. If he had time, he'd make a trip over now just to grab the buzz. Sadly, no time to reap that benefit. He'd have plenty of opportunity for it once this all ended.

Ama's house, like most in the area, sucked when it came to parking. Took him all of twenty minutes to find a spot and almost ten to walk to her front door. This would be one of the last places he'd choose to live. At least she always had the good sense to hand him a martini, dirty, as he walked through the open doorway. She did know him well enough to anticipate what would make him happy. Or at least happier. True happiness waited on the other side of this particular mission.

It took only a few seconds once he rang the doorbell for her to fling open the front door and hand him the anticipated drink. She grimaced. "What's with the hair? You trying for a Jesus look?"

"What? You jealous I look better with long hair than you do?" He knew exactly how good he looked. Women were drawn to his pale hair that fell past his shoulders. A balanced diet and consistent use of excellent hair products ensured it stayed healthy and shiny. Had the body to go with it too, not that he bragged about it.

"Sure. That's what it is. I'm jealous of your model good looks." She shook her head and turned away from the door, heading down the hallway. "Quite sure I'll get over it."

"Bitch," he said under his breath. She didn't appear to have heard him or, if she had, ignored him. Worked for him either way. He followed her down the hall right after he took a drink of the martini. Pretty good.

"Take a load off and tell me the plan." She'd settled into the living room with her feet up on an oversized ottoman. A glass of red wine sat on the side table next to her chair. She'd started without him. First or second?

He sat across from her, feet on the floor. Somehow, he didn't have the urge to relax. "Three words. Rule the darkness."

"Oh, please. Guys like you have been saying that for centuries and, so far, nyet. What makes you think it will be different for you?"

Ama disappointed him, and did she just roll her eyes? How she failed to recognize his greatness stunned him. Someone with her experience and knowledge should be able to see it without much effort. Saddened him that he'd have to explain. "I will open the most powerful portal in the northern hemisphere, and I will seize the power. After that, well, let's just say, the world will be my oyster."

She picked up her wineglass and took a long drink, her gaze on his face the whole time. "What the hell does that mean? The world *is* your oyster. Bro, come into the twenty-first century."

His fingers tightened around the glass, and he resisted the urge to down the drink in one pull. "Oh, I'm all here, *sweetheart*. I know exactly what century we're living in, and I know exactly what I'm going to be able to accomplish. You're going to want to keep close or…" He smiled. Now, he did take a big drink, downing half of the martini. He'd give her credit, it was good.

Her eyes narrowed as she studied his face. The way she looked at him made him think his smile didn't come close to making it to his eyes. Good. Better she be on alert. More than that, she needed to understand exactly who sat across from her. "Or what?"

He shrugged. "Figure it out. Shouldn't be hard for a smart woman like you."

She pressed her lips together and, for a moment, said nothing. Then, her expression cleared. "Let's talk about where we're going."

Good decision on her part. He could use her help. If she'd made a different one, doing it alone would have been okay too. Important to be flexible. "That's simple. We're heading for Mt. St. Helens."

"It's still active." Ama's gaze stayed on his face as she turned the wineglass in her hands.

"Of course it is. Funny to me how the scientists think that one of these days it's going to explode in a way that will make eastern Washington oceanfront property." He finished off the martini, appreciating the tiny buzz it gave him.

"The uninformed." She seemed to be following along well. Good. Would make this easier, and he wasn't in the mood for complications.

"The stupid. All ignorant of the power just beneath their feet pulsing to be free. I understand it well, and their time below has dragged on far too long. They're longing for a leader to bring them back into the world."

"A leader like you, Jesus-man."

He ignored her dig. In fact, he kind of liked that his appearance seemed to bother her. Too close to the truth maybe? Fitting, in his mind. Several thousand years later people still followed Jesus. He planned to be in the same position several thousand years down the road. "Most definitely like me. I will open the portal, and they will bow to me as the new Demon King."

She smacked her now-empty wineglass onto the side table. "Seriously, the Demon King? What in the world do you think makes you different from those who've tried in the past? I mean, granted, you're smart, but you're not the first smart guy I've dealt with who had grand ideas of ruling over the demons. They failed. Many, many have crashed and burned. You really think you're that different?"

Failure would never come to him. With far too much to live for, he couldn't be unsuccessful in this mission. To not succeed meant the ultimate sacrifice, and death was most definitely not on his agenda. One more reason to open the portal and call forth loyalty. Darkness would be his to rule for eternity. The point Ama had missed. He'd be around forever, though ultimately, she'd be reduced to dust.

"None who came before me were me. That plain and simple." Again, she missed the obvious.

"Yeah, plain and simple. That's gonna work." She rolled her eyes, and his hands curled into fists. Not now, he repeated in his mind.

"Are you always this big a pain in the ass?" At least he tempered his comment and didn't punch her very smart mouth.

Her smile lit up her face. "Most definitely." She stood and picked up her glass. "Another drink?"

Chapter Three

Aradia had spent an additional two hours with Tara last night. The first hour, she'd taken her into the local farm store, where dogs were always welcome inside. As they walked down all the aisles, she introduced her to the strangers who asked if they might pet her and had Tara do a few down-stays as Aradia waited some yards away. The socialization exercises completed, they returned home to run a few scenarios and work on their joint fitness. After she'd put Tara up, Aradia's confidence in her choice of a fellow warrior solidified. She could and would do the job. Together, they'd be ready for whatever came their way.

When she'd first lain down last night, the shadows on the ceiling had danced and swayed, an entertaining waltz she worried would keep her awake far too long. Reminded her of the many sleepless nights wondering how she'd ended up married to a man she would never be able to love as a wife should, and how to walk away. Those were not good nights. As it turned out, she dropped into sleep pretty quickly, the ghosts of her past leaving her in peace. A nice surprise when she woke up rested and ready for the day. Easier to be on high alert when not bone tired.

Over coffee, she looked at the route from her house to Cougar, or at least a nearby town where she might be able to find a hotel room that would allow Tara to stay with her. Tim had offered to let them stay at his house, but she'd politely turned him down. She liked him a lot, and Clemons was a well-behaved giant. But Tim's house was tiny, and she liked her space. Other than a few nights with Sabina, she'd not spent a single night with anyone since her divorce. Alone time suited her well.

She and Tara could sleep in her SUV if necessary. With the backseats folded down, she'd have plenty of room for her and a dog, and that way she'd be able to stay near the mountain. But just because she could didn't mean she wanted to sleep in there. A real bed held much more appeal, except at the moment, she wasn't having much success tracking down traditional lodging. Time to shift gears, and she smiled when she found the perfect non-traditional option. A small house only a few miles from Cougar was available, and the host allowed dogs. Perfect place to land. She had it secured within five minutes. Things were coming together for this mission.

Now, to make arrangements for the dogs. Lizzy wouldn't be around for the weekend, and she wouldn't ask her. Her normal schedule would resume on Monday, and Aradia wanted to keep it that way. Routine worked best for the dogs, and Lizzy knew it well. Kept the dogs happy and content. Someone, however, needed to be here around the clock and to cover the weekend while Lizzy and Henry were up in Sandpoint. That someone needed to understand her special dogs, which narrowed the options. She crossed her fingers as she phoned her cousin Mona.

"Been waiting for you to give me a ringy-dingy." Mona's voice was deep and raspy, as though she smoked a hundred cigarettes a day. But she didn't smoke or indulge in any other substance she deemed unhealthy. Mona just happened to have one of those voices. Probably could have made a hell of a blues singer.

Not much of a stretch to figure out how Mona knew she'd be calling. "Sabina alerted you, didn't she?" She didn't doubt for a second that, as soon as finished talking with her sister last night, she'd turned around and called their cousin. That's how their family rolled. They might all be thousands of miles apart and even in different countries, but they were close just the same. Distance couldn't take that away from them.

"Nah. Had a dream."

It surprised her that Sabina hadn't called her this morning, though it didn't surprise her that Mona knew anyway. She sometimes forgot that Mona's gift didn't involve the Guardians. Instead, she had dreams, or visions, or whatever someone wanted to call them. Bottom line, she saw things, and usually they involved family. Not a big stretch to believe she'd had a dream about Aradia. "That figures. You packed yet?"

"Of course. Catching a flight that will put me in Spokane this afternoon. I'll be at your place in time to get everyone dinner." Though Mona wasn't a dog breeder/handler/trainer, she still knew how to handle a kennel, and that made her one person Aradia would trust with her dogs a hundred percent of the time. A comfort to know Mona would be on-site in a matter of hours.

"I really appreciate it. Thing is, I don't know how long I'll be gone, and we have a litter born yesterday." Wouldn't be fair to not give her a heads-up. Puppies were a lot of work.

"No worries, little one. The hubby can take care of the farm while I'm gone, and you know me. I love the babies."

Mona's husband was an all-around good guy. The fact that he was a veterinarian made him Aradia's favorite cousin-in-law. All her dogs loved him, not that they visited often. Their home in Toronto wasn't exactly close.

"Good man."

She could hear the smile in Mona's voice. "Yeah, he is. How bad is it there?"

"Don't know yet. The rumblings are mild at the moment, though I sure can feel them, and so can the dogs. I'm anxious to get over to Mt. St. Helens. It appears that's where they're originating, and I want to be boots-on-the-ground as an assist to the team stationed there. Something bad is trying hard to breach the portal. The tremors are substantial enough to feel them all the way over here."

"Well, that's messed up and doesn't bode well. Haven't had a major breach attempt in decades." Mona might not be front and center in the legacy business, but she kept a finger on the pulse just the same. A hazard of being born into their family. Nobody escaped the family business entirely.

"No, and I've thanked the gods for that. Something has changed, and it's making itself known. I need to get there to help Tim sooner rather than later." A tremor rumbled beneath her feet. *Yes, I feel you.*

"I agree that you should probably get rolling. Are any others coming?" Aradia could hear Mona moving around, most likely packing.

Mona wasn't asking about someone coming to help Aradia and Tim. Any breach attempt took work on both sides of the portal. Demons below sent the tremors through the earth as they pushed against the magic that kept them confined. And humans above longed for the darkness and power of the demons promised in the deep of the night when their whispers filtered through the veil separating the worlds. People from one generation to the next waited to hear those whispers and then acted upon them. A very old story.

"Pretty sure someone's on the way. Can't tell yet if it's a lone warrior or an army of them." She didn't have anything to base her belief on, just a gut feeling that someone with darkness in their heart raced toward the potential portal breach. Like the Guardians and their handlers, they heard the demon calls.

"Are you sure you don't want to call in for more help? Sabina could make it in a couple of days. I don't like the idea of you working this alone."

"I need to assess first, and frankly, I'm not sure we have that long. I'm hoping there hasn't already been a breach."

"Okay, but I'd feel more comfortable if you had backup."

Tim and Clemons were good, and she had great faith in their abilities. "I will have backup. A strong team is stationed in the town nearest the mountain, although we haven't pinpointed the exact location of the portal yet. I'm bringing my best dog, and I'm fairly confident the other team and I will get there before the breach can release any of them into the world." She prayed she wasn't wrong and that they wouldn't be too late.

"If you're sure, because, cousin, I gotta tell ya, I'm not." Mona's tone conveyed her skepticism as much as her words did. Given what had happened to her mother, who could blame her?

"Trust me. They're a very good team. We can stop this without having to call in our own legions." By the time additional teams could reach the location, it would most likely be too late. Whatever brewed out there moved fast. The vibrations grew a bit stronger each hour. They weren't messing around. Aradia didn't plan to either.

She ended the call and sat back in her chair. Mona had a right to be concerned, even if she hadn't wanted to admit it. Mona's mother had lost her life at an attempted portal breach twenty-seven years earlier. Aradia's aunt, her mother's sister, had been alone at the portal. She'd stopped the breach but had been killed doing so. That reality lived with them all, as well as the forever question of what could have been done differently in order to save her aunt's life.

The memory did make her question if going alone might not be her best decision. Someone was heading toward Cougar, and she could feel its approach whispering along her nerves. It didn't feel like an army, more a warning to be prepared. That she could do. She'd been trained her whole life for an event such as this. Besides, she wouldn't be going completely alone. She'd have Tara with her. With a dog at her side, she never felt alone. Tim and Clemons would be there too. Far from alone.

Aradia stood and stared out the window. "All I need are my dogs," she said softly, and a tear slid down her cheek. Maybe it was the truth, and maybe it wasn't.

Last night, Mercy had helped Rufus settle into the guest room. They'd compared notes over dinner, agreeing that something weird was going on, and decided to see what the new day brought. Perhaps what they were feeling would turn out to be nothing more than a quirk of nature. Or, maybe it would turn out to be something much worse. She hoped for the former. Her instincts leaned toward the latter.

In the kitchen, she stood in front of the open cupboard lined with small glass jars, carefully labeled with her own tidy handwriting. No need to read them to know what each jar held. The labels were a sort of better-safe-than-sorry exercise. Used by those with skill and knowledge, the plants and herbs could do magical things. Used by those without such skill and knowledge, the end result could be deadly. Important not to take the chance of the uneducated grabbing a jar that could cause harm.

She reached into the far back of the cupboard for the small bottle of thorn apple. The universe was trying to talk to her, yet the message came in garbled. Time to clear it up a bit, and if that meant using a little something to boost the message, she could work with that. It took real skill to utilize something like thorn apple, and fortunately, Mercy possessed those skills. With Rufus here to amplify the psychic energy, more information would likely come to her without the need to amplify with organics. The minute he walked into the house, the air had changed. Always loved having a kindred soul close by, and there were so few of them. She didn't put the bottle back into the cupboard.

It took only a few minutes to boil the water she poured over the thorn-apple-augmented tea leaves. Some in her line of work preferred to smoke the leaves, and she'd done that once and only once. Never again. A bit too dangerous for her liking, the potential for inadvertent poisoning always a concern, and the effects after smoking it lasting far too long. Using a precise amount in her tea worked well for what she hoped to achieve without the risk.

Setting the strainer in the sink, she took the cup to the table and sat. For probably a minute, she held the cup between her hands and stared down into the steaming liquid. Taking a deep breath, she brought the cup to her lips, and after several sips of the tea, Mercy rested her head on her arms. Her vision blurred, and the sounds of the morning faded away.

The ground shook, and she stumbled, landing hard on her hands and knees. Sharp rocks cut the tender flesh of her palms, the hot flow of blood immediate. Mercy pushed up and stared as she wiped her hands on her jeans, leaving dark, damp streaks in the denim. Trees had toppled, boulders rolled past, and a gap widened in the side of the mountain as if a large curtain were being pulled aside.

The air grew hot, and as she inhaled, heat pressed against her chest, pushing the breath from her lungs. As it had done decades earlier, once more the mountain readied to erupt with lava, molten and destructive. She stepped backward, putting distance between her and the shuddering mountain.

All those years ago, it had tried and failed to destroy what had been her family's home for a hundred years. She would retreat, but she wouldn't run. She would see those friends who supported her and her family to safety.

She took one more step back, her gaze on the widening crack in the mountain, and slapped a sticky hand over her mouth. They stepped out of the yawning chasm, a deep-red glow behind them, their faces hard and dark, their eyes sending chills down her back. One by one, they emerged from between the stones, the crunch of their feet on the wilderness floor as loud as gunshots. She couldn't stop staring at the faces she recognized. The faces of the demons that had haunted her dreams since that dark night when she'd been young and alone in the park. She screamed.

Mercy popped up from the table, the scream from inside her vision bursting from her throat, raw and loud. When her racing heart settled, she sat back down and laid her trembling hands on the tabletop. She wiped away tears with the back of her hand and then pushed the cup of tea to the other side of the table.

Rufus rushed into the kitchen, dressed in sweats and a T-shirt, his long hair wet and loose. Must have just stepped out of the shower. "What's wrong, Mercy? Are you hurt? What's happening?" His gaze swept the kitchen as if looking for an intruder.

Her words were soft because that was all she could manage. "We're in deep shit."

He sat across from her and put his big, warm hands over hers. His gaze dropped to the almost-empty, delicate teacup with the tiny blue flowers painted on the side and then moved back up to her face. He studied her for a moment through narrowed eyes, picked up the teacup and sniffed, then held it out in her direction. "What did you drink? I have a pretty good idea, but tell me anyway."

She looked away. He wouldn't like her answer. He also wouldn't give her a pass. "Thorn apple."

"Jesus H. Christ, Mercy. What in the actual hell were you thinking? That is seriously dangerous stuff, and you know it better than anybody. Lord almighty, I can't leave you alone even long enough to take a shower."

She couldn't blame him for being irritated, and she also wouldn't lie to him. "Even with you here, I don't feel like we have time to wait. I had to force it." Mostly true.

"Force what?" He took the teacup to the sink and poured the remaining contents down the drain, an expression of distaste on his handsome face.

"Something evil is happening nearby, and I need to know what it is. We might be a small community, but we all need to be safe, and I believe the mountain is trying to tell us. Or warn us. Or something. I had to do what I needed to in order to hear." Like the darkness, not knowing scared her, and so she'd use whatever she needed to for answers.

He pointed to the cup he'd set in the sink and frowned. "So, you decided drinking a potentially fatal cup of tea was worth the risk?"

Again, she went straight for the truth. "Yes."

He sat back down at the table, closed his eyes and shook his head. "You know you make me crazy, right?"

"I'm sorry I scared you." Supposed she did owe him an apology for that part, although she wasn't sorry for trying to discover the truth using the skills she knew best. Frightening as it had been, important information had come from her experience. "It's not getting ready to erupt." He had to understand this wasn't Mother Nature at work.

"What?" Surprise, not disbelief, crossed his face. He pushed wet hair over his shoulder as he leaned near.

"Mt. St. Helens. It's not a repeat of 1980, and it's not getting ready to erupt again, at least not now." She began to braid her hair, the rhythmic motion helping her concentrate.

He leaned forward, his arms on the table. She had his interest now, all traces of his former irritation gone. "Okay. So tell me what the mountain shared with you."

She loved how he listened and accepted her. Outside of her mom, she'd always been leery of sharing with anyone the things she could see. Rufus never failed to make her feel safe. She stopped braiding and stared into his eyes. "Demons." Might as well get right to it.

His eyes narrowed as he glanced out the window. "I don't want to sound stupid, but demons? What exactly do you mean by demons? I need more."

She'd needed more too, which is why she drank the tea. Probably best not to point that out to him right now. "The mountain is opening, and demons are getting ready to spill out. That's what I saw anyway and the best I can interpret."

"That's messed up."

She loved that Rufus didn't say her vision was fantasy or that it resulted from imagination. He took it at face value. "We have to make a plan to stop them. We can't let evil like that emerge around here. Well, or anywhere, for that matter."

Rufus ran his hands through his damp hair, combing through it with his fingers. "Any ideas? I haven't come up against anything like demons before. Some evil bastards, yeah. Walking, talking demons? No."

She started to say she had no idea. Then, all of a sudden, a puzzle piece that had been eluding her for a very long time dropped into place. She reached over and took his hands. "I do, as a matter of fact. Get dressed, because we need to go talk to a man about his dog."

August managed to sleep five hours. Pretty damn good for him. Anything over four hours, he considered a win. He'd been this way his whole life, and even though the studies he'd read reported that people who slept fewer than seven to eight hours a night would have shorter life spans, he never let that worry him. He wasn't exactly the norm. The way he saw it, he'd live a long and fruitful life. An eternal life.

That thought made him anxious for Ama to haul herself out of bed. Time to get on the road. They'd be able to make it up north before sunset only if they left soon. Darkness had yet to fully fade from the morning, a detail Ama would be sure to point out. She'd want to wait until the sun came all the way up before they started their drive. What? Did she think she needed her beauty sleep? When would she realize things like slumber weren't important?

For August, the draw to the portal grew stronger with each mile he drove north. He could feel it here in northern California. By the time they reached Washington, he figured it would be like the pull of a rare earth magnet.

Sipping on his coffee, August gazed out the kitchen window. As much as he wanted to go pound on Ama's door and yell at her to get her rolling, he'd give her another hour. The exercise of startling her wide awake would be satisfying but not particularly useful in the big picture. He had to wait for the night of the Black Moon anyway. That would be the difference between success and failure. Dragging her out of bed to race up there now wouldn't hurry that particular lunar event. Patience and grace wouldn't hurt him either. Irritate him, maybe. Hurt him, no.

He carried both his coffee and his backpack to the table and sat down. The scrape of his chair across the tile floor screamed. From an inside zipper pocket of the pack, he took out the silver ring with the ruby center stone. He slipped it on and, as always, closed his eyes as a rush of energy pulsed through him. Never got tired of the feeling. He opened his eyes and reached back into the pack. He took out a box and opened the clasp that kept it secure. Squares of old parchment with frayed edges were stacked inside. Some blank. Some not. He chose a blank piece.

For a few moments, he stared at it and considered what to write. Images flashed through his mind, fast yet clear. He picked up his pen and began. Five letters across, five down below, each creating a perfect square of twenty-five. They came quickly, as always, which told him they were the right ones.

Finished, he picked up the small piece of parchment and held it against his forehead. Another rush of energy flowed through him. Eyes closed, he breathed evenly and waited. As expected, it took only a few seconds. Yes, yes, and yes. He opened his eyes, dropped his hand, and smiled. After a couple of breaths, he tucked the parchment back into the box, snapped the lid shut, and slid it into his backpack once more.

"What did you see?" Ama's question made him jump, his pack tumbling to the tile. That pissed him off. He didn't like his things getting dirty. Who knew when she'd last cleaned her floor.

He turned and snapped. "Could have given me some warning that you were up and spying on me."

"Bro, it's not like I tiptoed in here, and to say I was spying on you is a pretty big stretch. You were so wrapped up in your little ritual, you didn't hear me. Not my fault you were oblivious. That's on you." She reached for a coffee mug out of the cupboard next to the sink.

He leaned down and retrieved his pack, brushing it off before setting it on the chair next to him. "Sometimes you're kind of a bitch." It would be impossible to spend any length of time with Ama. She'd drive him to drink.

From the pot he'd brewed earlier, she poured coffee into her mug. She turned to look at him. "And you're a bastard, so I guess that makes us even."

"Fair enough." Not really, although agreeing with her should shut her up. He reached over to his backpack, pulled out a leather-bound notebook, flipped open the cover, and wrote: *Flauros, Ashroth.* He would add more names later. For now, these first two were a fitting lead. Great potential for assignment as his generals.

Ama leaned over his shoulder and read. Rude, but he didn't call her out on it. "You've called on the magic of the light?"

A touch surprising she'd pick up on that point. The ancient magic wasn't common knowledge, and that she might have been taught any of the old ways more than a little unusual. Historically, the teachings were limited to males. He contemplated lying to her and decided it didn't matter. "Yes."

"Is that a good idea?" She sat across from him, sipping her coffee and staring at him over the rim of the mug. "It could get away from you."

He smiled as he thought about what he'd just seen while choosing to ignore what sounded like an intentional dig at him. "It's the very best of ideas." Putting it mildly anyway. Ama wouldn't understand it at any other level.

"Are they the demons that are coming?" She pointed to the two names he'd jotted down.

August ran his finger over the names he'd written down. "Only a couple of the demons who will bow to me. More will arrive, and they will all serve me as their king."

"Bow to you is what you really mean." Her fingers now tapped on her mug.

He frowned. Her tone bordered on snarky. Maybe he shouldn't have let her previous dig slide. "What exactly did you think would happen once I open the portal? We'd all be buddies singing songs around the campfire and toasting marshmallows?" Seriously, he'd have given her more credit than that.

"I guess…" She dropped her gaze to her mug. At least she had the good sense to acknowledge her lapse.

"You guess? You didn't really think it through, did you? I don't know what you thought I'd be doing up north. Why I'd leave my home to drive to a mountain several states away?"

She shrugged as if it were no big deal and looked him in the eyes, her expression bordering on defiant. "I'm not in left field. Pretty grounded, if you ask me, because nobody has been able to open any of the major portals in the past. So, if you get right down to it, no. I've never thought it all the way through. If I pondered the situation, it makes sense they'd need a leader."

He tucked his notebook into the backpack and stood. Maybe she'd be able to see the big picture after all. "And they'll have one."

Chapter Four

A radia put the last bag into the truck and shut the tailgate on the loaded bed. Amazing how much more stuff needed to be packed when traveling with a dog, not that she minded. The best trips always included at least one dog, whether it was an adventure for pleasure or a mission that included stopping demons from invading the earth. Could be the unconditional love of a dog spoke to her soul. Could be that she could always be her true self with them and they always forgave her mistakes. No judgment, only love.

Out in her kennel, Tara paced. Couldn't fool her. She sensed they were about to embark on the kind of journey she'd trained for her entire life. The dogs always knew. They possessed that little something extra necessary to help keep the world safe, even if the rest of the world had no clue they were facing danger. People looked at her dogs and believed them to be nothing more than well-trained canines ready for patrol or search-and-rescue or family security. Okay with her, as many of her dogs excelled at those jobs. They were the pups without the shine. Her special dogs, like Tara, embraced their true vocations. Most didn't realize what Tara and the other Guardians were capable of. More of a need-to-know basis, and most people didn't need to know.

Before she headed out, she made sure all the occupied kennels were stocked with fresh water. They'd all be fine until Mona arrived. She'd feed them dinner and refresh their water after she arrived so no need for Aradia to fill food bowls before she left. Never a moment of worry when Mona took control of the kennels. Made it easier, though not easy, to leave her precious pack. Especially hard with a new litter to think about. She liked to keep a close eye on them, particularly when said litter produced a pup with the shine.

When Aradia opened the gate, Tara raced out of her kennel and out the door to the driveway, where she jumped into the backseat of the truck. If she hadn't left the back door ajar, there'd have been a whole lot of barking. When Tara wanted to go, she wanted to go now. She stood steady as Aradia slipped her into a harness that hooked into the seatbelt and then shut the door. One last thing to do before they got on the road. She couldn't leave without checking on the newest members of the family again. Inside, the mama and babies were doing well. They'd be fine until she got back. Aradia ignored the whisper in the back of her mind: *if you get back.* "See you soon," she said to them and to the little voice in her head.

Tara waited in the backseat of the crew-cab truck, her nose on the window. Good thing Aradia wasn't OCD or she'd be driven to drink with the constant nose prints on the truck windows. "You ready for this, girlfriend?" she asked as she slid behind the wheel. As soon as Aradia started the truck, Tara lay down, and she took that as a solid yes. Good plan to make herself comfortable given they had almost a six-hour drive ahead of them. About as far apart as they could get and still be in the same state. "Let's roll."

Easy drive from the farm into Spokane. Pain in the butt once she got into town. Boy, would it be nice when they finally finished the north-south freeway expansion. Pieces were done, which helped speed up the time it took to get to I-90. Not enough to avoid sitting at a bunch of stoplights. A good reason not to live in the city. She sighed in relief when she reached the on-ramp at Division Street. The merge, always a pain, wasn't bad this time of day. Finally, as they drove up the Sunset Hill, she began to feel as though they were on the way. From here on out, a fairly straight shot to the west side.

She'd just passed Moses Lake when her phone rang. A familiar name popped up on the display, and she tapped the button on her steering wheel to enable hands-free answering. Easy technology made her happy and a whole lot safer. "Hey, Tim. What's up?"

"Are you on the road yet?" His deep voice, filled with an undercurrent of urgency, echoed her own feelings.

"West of Moses Lake and heading toward Vantage." The tiny town sat on the west side of the bridge that spanned the Columbia River. A gorgeous view of the massive basalt cliff walls, known as the gorge. Impressive as it was, the frequent high winds that could rock the truck when crossing the bridge across the river kept her on high alert. She looked forward to seeing the "Grandfather Cuts Loose the Ponies" each time she neared the area. A sculpture consisting of fifteen ponies, two hundred feet long, sat on the hillside about two miles east of the Vantage Bridge. Made her smile every time she saw it. "I'll be to the ponies in no time."

"Good." She heard an edge in that single word that made her increase her speed, hopefully not enough to earn a ticket. "Is something wrong?"

"Clemons is really twitchy. Something big is going on. I've never seen him like this."

A charge went up her spine, and she sat up taller in her seat. "I don't like that." Okay. Maybe getting there faster would be worth a ticket. The speedometer crept up and, in the back, Tara whined.

"Right back atcha. We've had rumblings now and again, but they've been slight. Whatever's been going on the last few days, it's not good. And, before you say it, not the volcano. Deeper. Darker. I can tell the difference between the mountain talking and unnatural origins."

"Demons."

She could hear the breath he blew out. "That would be my bet."

Her mind went right to the lessons she'd learned from the texts passed down through generations of her family. She hadn't chosen this job. She'd been born into it. "Who's calling them?"

"Million-dollar question. It's been relatively quiet since we were posted here. This seems like it came out of the blue. Or someone really powerful discovered the secret of this mountain."

"I'll drive faster." She ended the call and reached back to pat Tara on the head. "You hear that, girlfriend? We have to be ready. Bad boys and girls are heading our way." Tara licked her hand.

She pressed a call button on the car screen. Sabina picked up on the first ring, even though it would be dinnertime for her. "What's wrong?"

"Any chance you can do research on activity in the southwest corner of Washington State? Given the strength, I have to think this is an old one." Someone didn't have to be right at the portal to make it start. A bit like a siren's call. Shout out the right words, send out the dark vibes, and see what happened. The only question became which of them would make it there first. Good or evil. Light or dark. That Tim and Clemons were nearby put the odds on the side of good. She hoped.

"That bad?"

"It's beginning to shape up that way, and I'm looking to find out if anything has happened here in the past."

"You know, given the age of the region, I may not be able to dig out much." The sounds of a keyboard told Adriana her sister was already digging in.

Sabina wasn't wrong. The West, in the big picture, was relatively young in terms of settlement. A portal might have existed for hundreds or even thousands of years. Cities and towns, only a few hundred. "I'll take whatever I can get, and it might be a good idea to check with local tribal authorities to see if they have any history that could help. Besides, you know what Mom used to say."

"Any knowledge is a tool in the arsenal."

"Bingo." When she was a kid, she'd thought her mother's kernels of wisdom trite. The older she'd gotten, the more experienced she'd become, the more she appreciated everything her mother had passed down.

"I'm on it and will call you with what I find."

"Perfect, thanks. And, well, I guess I am sorry I interrupted your dinner."

Sabina laughed. "No worries, sister. I'll get to return the favor someday. You know, like maybe when you're out on a date." Sabina's laugh was soft. "Talk soon. Love you."

"Love you too." She ended the call and blinked back tears. Sometimes the distance between them loomed large. Even with such a great network of friends, Aradia missed being around someone who loved her. Couldn't be though. The universe had a different plan for her, and she had to make peace with being alone. There'd be no call interrupting her on a date. One tear slid down her cheek. She wiped it away and sat up taller in the seat.

With Sabina researching, she ticked that task off the list forming in her head. As good as Tim was, his skills ended at dog handling. She'd really welcome knowledge from the elders who'd seen and experienced so much more than she had. The only issue that remained was time. Sabina's task wasn't small. It would take days to comb through the database. At least modern technology had allowed them to take the old texts and convert them into electronic resources. Made the research job a lot faster.

To her left, the wild horses came into view, and she smiled. Something about the raw power the sculpture evoked pushed back the melancholy and filled her with resolve. Wild horses had roamed the cliffs of the Columbia River Gorge for so many years, and while only the sculpture remained to remind those who passed by that they had once lived here wild and free, their beauty could never be erased. Their strength of spirit filled the air she breathed in. It gave her courage.

Her eyes on the road, she pushed her speed just a bit more. The horses fading in her rearview mirror, she drove the curve that took them onto the bridge, the white caps on the Columbia River attesting to the strength of the wind. A few more hours of driving, and when she arrived at the mountain, Clemons and Tara would do their jobs, which could mean the difference between retaining the beauty or losing it to darkness.

Her shoulders stiffened as the miles passed, and Tara whined in the back. Neither had anything to do with the hours in the truck. Someone was coming, and the darkness they sought to release into the world undoubtedly accounted for what both she and Tara were feeling and what Clemons sensed. Armed with skill and knowledge, two solid Guardian teams would stop one with evil intent—she hoped only one anyway—the portal protected once more.

Rufus stopped Mercy before she left the house to go tend her crops. "This may sound weird, but I had a dream and think it's important." He had his hands in his pockets, his hair now tied back as usual, and his fedora on his head. The Rufus she knew and counted on. Except not quite.

"A vision?" He'd poured out the thorn apple tea earlier. Then again, his gift didn't require the assistance of organics. Mercy studied his face. His eyes had a sort of haunted look. He tended to be one of the most upbeat people she knew, so if he was concerned, so was she.

He shook his head slightly. "Not really a vision. More like the spirits are trying to help through me. Kind of tapping me on the shoulder to make sure I'm paying attention."

"I'll take it. What did they tell you?" With an open mind and open soul, he'd be exactly the person who could receive messages from beyond the veil. At least that's what Mom had taught her.

He adjusted his hat. "A little unclear, but the gist of it seemed to be that someone is coming, and you need to work with her. She's important."

"Important how?" That wasn't what she'd expected him to say. Why would the spirits be worried about who she worked with? She wanted more along the lines of an exact location of the gaping hole in the mountain she'd glimpsed in her vision.

"Didn't get the Cliffs Notes on it, more an impression. In other words, open the door when she knocks."

Confusing at first, it made a bit of sense when she thought about her most recent booking. "Well, I do have someone coming with her dog to rent the cottage." She'd been working on the property since inheriting it from her mother, and besides some serious upgrades to her greenhouses, she'd renovated the rundown cottage near the road into a short-term rental property. An easy income stream, and folks who liked to visit Mt. St. Helens often booked it. Climbers, researchers, and the plain old curious. They all came to see the mountain that held the distinction of being the deadliest volcanic eruption in United States history. The healthy passive income it brought in offset the work it required to keep it clean and ready for the visitors. Knock on wood, but so far it had been a great experience with only minor hiccups.

The visitors who came all asked her the same question as they stared at the splendor of the mountain: "Aren't you scared to live so close?" Maybe she should be. She wasn't. Always felt like destiny that she should be here. Besides, Mom had left it all to her, and that meant everything to her. It would take something incredible and unimaginable to get her to ever leave here.

"Yeah. I think maybe that's her. There was something about a dog in it. In fact, the more I think about it, the dog seemed almost as important as the woman." Rufus glanced out toward the rental cottage.

"Maybe your spirits are suggesting something more along the lines of warning us to be discreet when someone else is nearby and the dog might be aggressive?" She hoped not, at least as far it concerned the dog. Generally speaking, she loved dogs, which is why she allowed them in her rental. They seemed to like her too.

He shook his head as he returned his gaze to her face. "Nope. That's not it."

"How do you know?" It actually made a lot of sense to her, so what was his problem with it?

"Can't really put a finger on it. I just know that we shouldn't hide anything from her, but more like we need to share with her. Yeah, that's it. Share." Now he nodded as if it all fell into place as he spoke.

His guidance might be muddled, and it didn't track for her, but she had no doubt that what he saw would turn out to be important. He possessed that kind of gift, and she respected it whether she understood it or not. Others might say both she and Rufus were freaks. She disagreed. They were both fortunate to have a world full of mystery and magic. When someone began life like she did, they didn't discount a single blessing that came their way, even if it labeled them as different. "All right, message received, and I will try my best to follow it."

"Me too." Rufus shoved his hands into his pockets and smiled. "We have to stick together, you and me."

She put her hand on his shoulder. "Always."

The sound of a car in the driveway caused her to turn toward the window. It would be hours before her guest renting the cottage would arrive, and the car coming their way wasn't unfamiliar. The day just kept getting more interesting. "Well, that's a surprise."

Rufus frowned as he followed her gaze. "Why would a sheriff be showing up here? Come on, now. We're model citizens. Pretty much anyway."

Said in jest. True nonetheless. "That we are." She gave him a sideways glance before she stepped outside. "Pretty much anyway."

"Hi, Mercy." Frank Long stood next to the open door of his patrol car, his arm resting on it. In uniform and vest, he looked big and imposing. "Got a minute?"

"For you, Frank, always." She knew him, while not well, enough to be comfortable with him. He always came across as a stand-up guy, and she liked that about him. Couldn't say that about everyone she met in law enforcement. To be fair, most were good, and she blamed only one for the character opinion she reserved toward any officer she met.

Tapping his fingers against the open car door, he said, "I'm gonna get right to it. Some hikers discovered a body near the mountain." His brows drew together as his lips turned down into a frown.

He didn't need to specify which mountain. In this area, it meant Mt. St. Helens. "Climbing accident? A fall?" Wouldn't be the first time someone suffered a fatality there. Once in a while, rather than a fall, it turned out to be a health issue. A little odd that he'd come to her for either one.

He looked down before bringing his gaze back up to her face. His dark eyes narrowed. "Can't get into a bunch of details, but the short answer is no."

An uneasy sensation settled in the pit of her stomach. She didn't like the direction of this conversation. "A murder?" Pretty rare in their corner of the world. Even if it was a small community, it remained a very safe one. Another reason she loved living in this area.

He shook his head. "I want to say no. Truth is, I don't know. That's why I'm here."

Okay. Now they were getting to it. "How can I help?" She assumed he came for some type of assistance. Her particular skill set ran to the natural world and her work as an herbalist. Sure, she did see things, with the aid of special plants, and her intuition tended to be pretty astute. Death investigation? That went way behind anything she'd ever been called upon to do.

"You've lived here a long time."

"Since I was five." No need for the details of how she came to live with Mom here at the farm. Most knew she'd been adopted. Few knew how or why. At her age, she didn't feel embarrassed about her past. What her brain knew and her heart felt were two very different things. The whole truth she held close.

"You know I've been here for only the last fifteen years, so I'm hoping to pick your brain as someone who can take it back further."

History she could help with. "Pick away."

"Have you ever heard of someone succumbing to plant bacteria or something along those lines?"

She narrowed her eyes as she studied his face. What an odd question, considering the kind of things that would typically happen out by the mountain. It also didn't track with any other death she'd heard of out there. Definitely needed more here. "You need to elaborate."

He closed the car door and stepped closer, shoving his hands into his pockets. He looked down for a moment and then raised his gaze to her face. "Here's the thing. It's nothing I've ever seen before, and I've done this for a really long time. I think you know I was a cop in Seattle before I came here, and through the years, I've seen a lot."

All of that made sense. It didn't give her any more background on his question. "Keep going." She had a bad feeling about what he'd say next.

"The body's legs were completely discolored with veins black and spidering up to the face, as if he'd stepped into something and it raced through him. No other signs of trauma or force. Eyes and mouth open. Almost as if whatever it was caught him by surprise and took him down fast. All I can think of is perhaps a toxin traveling to his heart."

Maybe. Maybe something darker. "How old, do you guess?"

He pressed his lips together and tilted his head. "Hard to say with all the discoloration, but I'm going with not old. Thirties, maybe forties. Looked to be in good shape otherwise. Typical mountain hiker. Medical examiner will be able to fill in that blank."

"That's pretty weird." Rufus stepped up behind her and put a hand on her shoulder. The warmth of his touch never failed to fill her. He was as close to a brother as she'd ever get, and she treasured him with his long hair, well-worn fedora, and eternal optimism.

"And you are?" Frank's eyes narrowed as he frowned.

"Rufus Delgado." He stuck out his hand. "Friend and confidant."

Frank's eyes cut to Mercy. She gave him a subtle nod. "He's one of the good guys, and he might be able to help."

"Another herbalist?" Frank's expression cleared as if that thought appealed to him.

Rufus shrugged. "Naw. I'm a psychic. Plants are cool and all, but my superpower is looking beyond the veil. Me and the old ones are like this." He held up his clasped hands.

Mercy didn't miss the subtle shift in Frank's body and pretty sure Rufus didn't either. It wouldn't bother her friend. Unshakable confidence in his abilities meant the skepticism of non-believers bounced right off him. Funny thing how he more often than not turned those skeptics into believers. Another thing she loved about him.

"I need to speak with Mercy." Frank stood up taller, as if that might intimidate Rufus.

"No problem." Rufus didn't get rattled or intimidated. "I'll be inside if you need me." He turned and disappeared into the house, likely heading straight for the coffeemaker. The man did love his java.

"Tell him to keep what he heard to himself." His gaze cut to her house. "What I've told you is not ready for release to the public at large."

"Frank." She waited until he looked at her, a light breeze picking up the gray-streaked hair off his forehead. 'You can trust Rufus. He's not a flake, and he really can see things others can't. He has a gift, and whether or not you believe, it's real. Nothing you confide in either of us will be shared."

"All right. I'll hold you to that. Right now, I want to know if you've seen any strangers lately or if you're aware of anything like this happening in the past. Maybe something your mom might have mentioned? Somebody who might have come to you asking for a special kind of herb?"

She ran through recent visits or requests and came up with nothing. Same with her memories of her mother's lessons. "Sorry. I don't have anything useful right now. I had one rich bitch show up asking for something to kill her husband, and I turned that one over to the Seattle PD. Nothing else that raised an alarm for me."

His expression soured. "What is it with the money people? They always think they can do whatever they want."

Didn't she know it. "Well, she'll find out pretty quick she can't. The Seattle PD will make sure of that. As to your victim on the mountain, I wish I could help, but I've got nothing."

His frown deepened. "Damn. Was hoping you'd have heard something. This is so out of the norm."

Mercy had a thought and blurted it out. "Can I visit the site? If I can see the vegetation, perhaps I'll come up with something that might explain it. There are some dangerous plants in the region, though, to be honest, this area isn't a breeding ground for something that dangerous. Still, might be worth a look."

Frank's facial expression didn't look encouraging. For a second anyway. He shrugged and said, "Once the techs have cleared out, I'll send you the coordinates. If you could look around and see if anything piques your interest, I'd appreciate any help."

Someone dying out there wasn't good, and her heart ached. The mystery of the vegetation piqued her interest too much to ignore. "Great. Send it to me, and I'll take a look. I'll shoot you my assessment of the vegetation."

"Talk soon." Frank got into his car and backed out.

After he left, she filled Rufus in over his freshly brewed coffee. Unlike Frank's jump to judgment of him, he possessed a level of professionalism that meant the information wouldn't go beyond the two of them. Rufus had ethics. Besides, once Frank sent her the coordinates, they'd both go. She would do her thing, and he would do his. They made a great team.

"He's kinda cute, don't you think?" Rufus took a sip of his coffee and stared out at the empty driveway. Did she hear a bit of a sigh in his voice?

She laughed and patted his shoulder. "Barking up the wrong tree, my two-spirited friend. He's married to a lovely woman, and they have four kids. One a six-foot-seven local basketball star on his way to the University of Washington next year."

Rufus shrugged and sighed. "I mean, that uniform. A guy sure can dream."

She thought of the Seattle patrol officer she'd met a couple of years ago. Almost six feet tall, with curly black hair and brown eyes. How she'd wanted to ask for her number. Still kicked herself for not asking. Hard to shake decades of protecting herself from being hurt. Nothing ventured, no heartbreak. Would she ever meet someone who could break through her walls? "Can't we all?"

❖

The weather cooperated, providing blue skies and plenty of sunshine. August knew it had more to do with his mission than luck. The universe would not disappoint him, for it understood the hold he would soon possess on the world. Beneath his palms, the steering wheel vibrated. Nothing wrong with the car. Something else pulsed with energy, and it grew stronger and more persistent the farther north they drove. Ama rode in silence for at least half an hour, sipping coffee from her trendy travel mug and staring out the window at the passing landscape. She put her coffee in the holder and pulled at her phone.

"What's the plan when we get there?" Ama had her head bent as she swiped again and again at her phone. "I'm not finding much for hotels."

"I pulled up plenty of places to stay." When he'd realized where they were headed, he'd made a quick check himself. He hadn't booked anything, as he wanted to leave his options open. The events would unfold as they needed to, and he wanted to remain flexible. It often paid off to be ready to turn on a dime.

Ama made a face as she glanced over at him. "I kind of like having decent amenities. Oh, wait, 'no kind' of about it. I won't stay in some crappy motel. You may go for cheap and easy, but not me."

"Don't be a snob. This isn't a vacation." The decor at Ama's house made a loud statement as to the level of luxury she preferred. Not that he liked cheap motels either. He just didn't plan to share that fact with her.

"Like I'd forget that. Still have to sleep though, and I'm not real fond of bed bugs."

"Snobby."

"Practical." She returned her attention to her phone, her hair swinging down to obscure her profile.

He almost laughed at her. He suspected her idea of practical meant a suite at a five-star hotel. Too bad for her. Where they headed, nature could very well end up being their beds for the night, if he even bothered with sleep. Rest wasn't all that important to him. A shower, sure, but sleep he didn't need. "How about we just travel in silence?"

Ama waved a hand, not even glancing up. "I'm going to keep looking for a decent place to stay."

He kept his speed steady as he drove, not wanting to risk getting pulled over. Any delays in their journey would be on his terms, not some state trooper's. His hands wrapped around the steering wheel, warmth began to build in the red-stone ring, spreading into his fingers. He smiled and broke the lovely silence that had thankfully lasted a good ten minutes. "We got one."

Ama looked up. "We got one what?"

He took a deep breath. This would be a long trip if she insisted on being so stupid about everything. She should be able to feel and follow. What kind of hunter lacked the sensitivity for the job? It wasn't just reading texts, studying grimoires, and learning spells. A sensitivity to the universe factored in as well. A tuning in to the forces unseen. "We created a crack, and it took a soul. All is progressing nicely." He explained it as simply as possible so she could follow.

Ama frowned, and her eyes narrowed. "How do you know? Nobody's called you."

Gods help him. If he could open the passenger door and shove her out while driving seventy miles an hour, he sure would. "Seriously, who do you think you're traveling with?"

"Blah, blah, blah. We all know the great and powerful August Fian."

He really didn't appreciate the sarcasm but controlled his own words. No need for her to believe she got to him. Her obvious efforts to annoy him were not going to work. "Then you know I'm not a regular man."

"Again, great and powerful."

Enough of her impertinence. "Not a joke, Ama."

At last, she set her phone in her lap. "All right, fine. From a professional standpoint, how do you know a crack has opened and taken a soul?"

Again, he shouldn't have to explain this. She wasn't a newbie who needed training in their arts. "I felt it. It's like a wave, or perhaps more like an aftershock. My magic is getting stronger, another sign we're on the right track."

She folded her hands in her lap and looked straight ahead. "I thought you were certain already." He wasn't particularly fond of the tone of her voice.

Why on earth did he agree to Ama coming with him? Tiresome under the best of circumstances. Downright insulting now. "I am certain. Simply sharing the news with you."

"Sounds more like bragging." She glanced sideways at him. He had the feeling she poked the bear with intention.

"We need to go back to silence." His hands tightened on the steering wheel, the heat from the red stone fading.

"Fine." Her tone of voice sounded like that of a hormonal teenager.

The quiet lasted for maybe two minutes before she hit the button to slide the passenger-side window down. Cool air blasted through the SUV. "What about the Guardians?" The road noise from the open window had her almost yelling the question.

He'd wondered how long before she brought them up. Her fear of the massive dogs was well-known within their ranks. The story went that she'd been bitten on the neck by a very large mixed breed as a teenager and had feared all dogs since. He suspected the guilt for that unfortunate event fell more on her shoulders than the dog. Probably irritated the hell out of it, and it resorted to the only option it had to get rid of her—its teeth. Sure couldn't blame the dog.

"I've got that handled."

"How?"

Here they went again. "Does it really matter?" Some details weren't necessary to share.

She turned her head to stare out the open window. The wind whipped her hair around her face, and he wondered why it didn't bother her. "Yeah, it matters. I don't want to get caught off guard again."

"Don't blame me for your lack of preparation. You should have known what you were walking into." Like August, Ama had been training since childhood. She really didn't have a good excuse for what had happened to create such a fear of canines. By now, she should have gotten over it. The Guardians were an unavoidable reality in their world.

Her fingers went to her neck, obscured by the collared shirt, something she always wore. "Let's not go down that road. I've heard it a thousand times, and I can't change what occurred. But I don't want it to go through it again."

"Again, I've got it covered." How many more times would he have to repeat himself?

"Guns don't work."

"Ama!" He got her fear. If he'd had a hundred-plus-pound dog take him down by the neck, maybe he'd be twitchy too. That wasn't the case with him, and he knew everything he needed to know about the Guardians. They weren't just dogs. They were born with something special, and anyone worth their salt respected it. He not only respected them, but he also prepared for them. Conventional weapons were useless against these animals gifted by God or some other magical source. A bubble of protection existed around them, with very few ways to penetrate it and stop them. Good thing he didn't rely on the conventional.

"Okay, fine. You got this." Now she sounded petulant, like the teenager who'd been bitten all those years back.

"For the last time, trust me, and if you can't do that, I can drop you at the closest airport for a flight home." *Please, please, please, let her take that option.*

She turned and stared at him, the only sound in the interior the whoosh of the air pouring through her open window. Finally, her hand dropped away from her neck, and she said softly, "I trust you."

About damn time. If they had to make the entire trip with her crappy attitude, he'd lose his mind, and she'd lose her life. "Great. Now do me a favor."

She pushed the button to bring the window back up. "Whatever you need."

"Close that damn window, and shut the fuck up."

CHAPTER FIVE

"What do you think, girlfriend?" Aradia drove slowly down a long driveway, following the directions of her GPS app. The little house that came into view looked exactly as it did on the website she'd booked through. Nice. Homey. "Think this will work for us?"

Tara had started pacing in the backseat at least a hundred miles ago and now stared out the window through narrowed eyes. Aradia wasn't sure how close they were to a portal but pretty darned sure one wasn't very far away. The fact that Tara had tensed as though she readied to chase prey let her know that more than a portal entrance might be nearby. It would be one with a spiderweb of cracks.

Or, rather, she hoped only riddled with spiderweb cracks. If more than that, then trouble came their way racehorse fast. Didn't want to consider what they might mean. Not just for her and Tara, but for everyone. Evil of the magnitude of what waited on the other side of those cracks defied explanation. She wouldn't be the one responsible for allowing it to enter the world. She might have failed in her personal life, but she refused to fail at her God-given duty.

All those thoughts turned over and over in her mind as the miles had rolled by. She stopped in Ellensburg for gas, let Tara out for a break, and grabbed an iced tea at the fast-food restaurant just down the street from the service station. She shared an order of French fries with Tara, even though neither of them should have been eating the junk food. They'd work it off once they arrived. Less than half an hour later they were back on the freeway headed to ground zero.

When they'd arrived, her navigation app had her turning into a wide, well-maintained driveway. From the road, the only thing visible had been a sign with the address. Other than that, thick trees and tall underbrush. Not exactly wild, more a definite privacy vibe. About a quarter mile down, the trees gave way to a beautiful open space with several large greenhouses, acres of planted fields, and two houses. One smaller house sat closer to the edge of the trees, a larger home much farther down the drive, far enough away that the temporary tenants of the short-term rental wouldn't be bumping into the homeowners. Impressive setup, and she never would have guessed it would be this beautiful after she'd turned off the main road.

As instructed, she parked at the smaller house, and a code provided in the email allowed her access to the house via a cipher lock. "What do you think, girl?" Tara moved through the rooms sniffing and checking, her tail wagging. A good sign. The Tara seal of approval. "Yeah. I like it too. Who would have guessed accommodations this nice were available out here in the middle of nowhere?"

Tara jumped up on the sofa and lay down, but Aradia shook her head. "You know we have to go out there." Tara closed her eyes.

"Fine. I'll get our bags." She laughed and walked back out to the truck. Aradia had their things inside within a few minutes, while Tara continued to sleep. Didn't much surprise her, given the way she'd paced on the trip over. It might seem odd that she slept so hard right now, but not to Aradia. Tara took the time to recharge in anticipation of what would come next. The real work would begin once they approached the mountain.

Standing at the window, sipping a bottle of water, Aradia studied their temporary digs. A working farm, though from here she couldn't tell exactly what crops they grew. Not a weed operation, which she might have suspected, given the forest-like barrier that prevented prying eyes from viewing the crops. Of course, that said, she had no idea what might be inside the massive greenhouses. Still could be one of the licensed marijuana farms that existed all over the state. A question to explore later. Right now, something else weighed heavy on her heart and mind.

She turned away from the window and looked at the napping Tara. "What do you think, beautiful? Are you ready to go see Tim?"

Tara raised her head and looked at Aradia as she put her phone to her ear. The call rang only once, which didn't surprise her. He'd been waiting for her to reach out.

"You're here." A note of relief in his voice, and she understood. This would be his first encounter with a potential portal breach. She remembered her first experience vividly, as well as the lessons she'd learned. Those things tended to stay with a person.

"We are."

Tara finally opened her eyes and looked at Aradia. She sat up and her posture said ready.

"Good." He gave her directions and she jotted them down.

"Got it. We'll be on our way in five minutes." Tara jumped down from the sofa and stood next to the front door.

"Hurry," Tim said. "There's been a development."

Her finger hovered over the "end" button. "What do you mean?" She didn't like the undertone in his voice. She glanced at Tara, who had put her nose on the door as if to push it open. Her body language screamed urgency.

"We have a dead man."

❖

As promised, Frank had texted Mercy the coordinates about an hour after he left her house. "Come on," she'd said to Rufus. "We have the location so let's go see what, if anything, we can pick up."

Rufus hadn't needed to be asked twice. He'd been in the truck and buckled up before she even reached the driveway. It hadn't been a long drive to the location Frank sent, and now they bushwhacked their way to the point she'd entered into her GPS. Quite a ways off the marked path, though the responding personnel had tramped down enough of the grasses and bushes to make it easy to follow the informal path.

"How much farther?" Rufus, like Mercy, spent a fair amount of time in the wilderness and wasn't struggling. Still, the coordinates Frank had sent put them a good mile or so from their vehicle. Made her wonder what the dead guy had been doing all the way out here. Then again, the local search-and-rescue team could tell lots of stories about people who got themselves turned around and properly lost. Way too many folks overestimated their navigation abilities and wandered off marked trails thinking they'd be fine. Often, they weren't.

She glanced down at the handheld GPS unit. "We're about a quarter mile out."

Rufus looked around at the trees, wild grass, and low bushes. "What made the guy come out here? It's kind of blah."

She agreed. The area didn't lack scenic views and interesting landscapes, but where they hiked now didn't hold as much appeal. Then again, no accounting for what people wanted to see and experience. Could have been bird-watching. Could have been searching for a specific variety of moss. Could have been nothing more than just traipsing off the trail for peace and solitude. "A very good question with no good answer."

"You picking anything up?" He held his head high, as if by doing so he could capture messages on the wind. Knowing Rufus, that's exactly what he could do, if there were any. She kind of hoped there were.

Mercy pressed her lips together and breathed in deeply. Slowly, she blew the breath out between her lips. "A little vibration, and that's about it so far. Not exactly normal. Not exactly weird either. You?"

"Same. Tiny rumble under my feet, but honestly, nothing that shouts danger. No whispers from the universe either. Kind of letting me down." He took his hat off and rubbed his forehead.

It wasn't hard to find the spot where it had happened. The undergrowth had been trampled even worse by the responding officers and techs. More concerning than the crushed and broken vegetation, which always made her heart hurt, was the slash of blackness in the shape of a man that marred the earth. That sight made her stomach roll.

"Oh, hell," Rufus muttered as he put his hat back on. He might not be an herbalist, but he knew bad when he saw it. One of the reasons she'd been trying for quite a while to make him an apprentice. With the gifts he already possessed, he'd be a powerhouse.

"I see it." She narrowed her eyes and once more breathed in deeply to see if she could pick up the scent of anything telling.

His face darkened, and he frowned as he stared at the ground. "I'm feeling it now. How about you?"

"Big-time." While Mercy didn't pick up a particular scent on the breeze, she'd never before experienced the buzz that filtered up from the earth and into her legs. She wholly embraced the idea of unseen forces that could affect the world both good and bad. This felt decidedly bad. "Let's take a closer look."

Rufus had stopped about twenty yards away. His hands were clasped behind his back, and he leaned away. "That's a big nope for me. I have a distinct do-not-touch sense about this. Whatever it is, it killed that guy, and I'm not ready to go to the great beyond yet. I can wait quite a bit longer to meet my ancestors."

She nodded. In contrast to Rufus, Mercy leaned forward. "I understand, but I need to see it up close. I don't recognize anything from here, and I'm not getting a specific scent that could narrow it down." The same curiosity that she'd had as a child standing at Mom's side filled her now. Mystery drew her to find answers.

Her steps were slow as she closed the distance. Her vibes tracked with Rufus, and while his caution was wise, her compulsive need to understand eclipsed the take-care sensations. The ground cover confused her. Pretty standard for the region, yet as she closed in on the darkened section where the body had been found, it grew increasingly black. More than unusual. Even as the wild grasses died, they normally turned more golden and then brown as they disintegrated. They didn't turn black and hold their shape.

From her pocket, Mercy pulled out a small paper bag and some tweezers. Easier and more efficient to study the black matter more carefully back at the farm. Kneeling close, she leaned near, vaguely aware of an odd sound coming from her left. She didn't look up and screamed when a massive dog hit her, knocking her to the ground and away from the scarred earth.

August had been enjoying the peace and quiet as they drove north, his mind running through the lessons he'd learned and the practice he'd done preparing for the day he'd claim his rightful place. His teachers through the years had been good. Helpful and encouraging. None truly understood his potential, though, and to this day, that bothered him. He had deserved recognition back then and demanded it now. Vain, yes. He knew that. Didn't change a thing. They should have acknowledged the greatness within him, and by God, they all would before the Black Moon set.

He cut his eyes to Ama and wondered what she saw in him. The earlier digs were a clue that she, too, didn't quite grasp the totality of what destiny held for him. What it held for her, if she kept true to the course and loyal to him. Not so sure she could do that. Her mouth tended to run away with her, and that didn't work for him. Obedience, unquestioned and immediate, would be her strongest tie. A lot more miles under their wheels would give him time to see if she would fit into his new order.

Warmth spread through him again, the red stone of his ring hot to the touch. Just went to prove the strength of the changes soon to occur. The ring let him know he remained the rightful wearer. He glanced down at his left hand as it held onto the steering wheel. The beauty of the stone made him smile. The ring should have come to him directly, and things would probably have gone down much differently. Like so many challenges in his life, he'd been forced to step up and orchestrate his own trajectory. Dad had been a major obstacle. At least until a family barbeque. Oleander worked as well on humans as he anticipated it would work on the Guardians. Dear old Dad never even suspected his grilled burger had been spiked. Neither did anyone else at the party. The official cause of death: a cardiac event. It had been hard not to smile when he got that word from the ME's office. Dad's bad heart meant they never even bothered to run a toxicology search for poisons.

Early in his life, he'd learned how important broad-based knowledge could be. It gave him a skillset that set him far apart from his peers. It also provided him with the ability to pivot in any situation. He never knew when he might need to change directions in a hurry. August could assess a situation in seconds and determine what had to happen for the best outcome. Best outcome for him, that is. He prided himself on that skill, and to date, he'd been one-hundred-percent successful.

He glanced at the gas gauge. Time to make a quick stop. Some guys liked to see how close to empty they could run a vehicle. Not

August. Foolhardy, in his opinion. The gauge sat at half a tank. Optimal to top it off and make sure he had plenty of fuel. He put on the blinker and pulled off at the nearest exit.

"Where are we going?" Ama looked up from her phone. She spent hours with her nose in that thing. She'd probably break out in hives if he took it and tossed it out the window. Tempting. Very, very tempting.

"Gas and restroom."

"Cool. I could use a soda."

"That crap will kill you."

Ama patted him on the shoulder. "Life is short, man. Live it large."

He shifted away from her touch. "You live it large your way, and I'll live it large my way." They were miles apart on what that meant. He pulled the SUV up to a gas pump and got out.

Ama headed to the C-store restroom and, presumably, the soda machine. Watch her come out with one of those horrid hot dogs that sat on the warmers for a day or three. No respect for the sanctity of her body. He shuddered.

August finished topping off the tank and had moved to a parking spot outside the C-store to wait for Ama when his phone rang. He almost ignored it. No one he really wanted to talk to right at the moment. He glanced at the display and shook his head as he answered. "Well, this is a surprise."

"I know what you're up to, August."

His ex-wife's shrill voice had that note of disdain that never failed to make his fingers curl into fists. "It has nothing to do with you." He should have ignored the call. Sometimes, he was a glutton for punishment.

"It has everything to do with me. By rights, it's all mine." The arrogance that he'd found so tedious while they'd been together echoed in her words.

"Willa, I'm not having this discussion with you again, and how did you get my number?" He'd changed it at least twice since the last time she'd tracked him down. She was like a bad rash that kept popping up. A poison rash, no less.

"When are you going to figure out that you'll never get away from me. I have friends in high places." She'd be smiling at that declaration while whipping her long black hair as shiny as high-gloss paint over her shoulder, her makeup model perfect. Willa believed in perfection in all things. Her only mistake had been marrying him. She hadn't understood that his accession to perfection meant she had to take a backseat.

"Which translates to I-fuck-everyone-to-get-what-I-want." He'd learned that lesson mere weeks into their short marriage. However, all that practice had made her skilled in the bedroom, and at least for a little while, he'd availed himself of her skills. A classic take-the-good-with-the-bad scenario. Until he just couldn't anymore. He deserved better than Willa, and he'd have it soon.

"Vulgar as always. You never have respected my position in the world."

"I don't have time for this, Willa." Bad enough he shared the SUV with the smart-mouthed Ama. Having to listen to the same old song and dance from his ex-wife stretched his patience beyond bearing.

"You won't beat me." Such misplaced confidence. Not for much longer.

He kept his voice calm and even. She hated it when he didn't rise to her bait, which made it a fun game for him. "I don't have to beat you. It's mine, and you know it as well I do. You're just pissed that I've beat you to it."

"And that's where you're wrong, hubby. When this all goes down, you won't be able to say that I didn't warn you. Get out of my way."

"Or what?" He rolled his eyes, sorry she couldn't see him.

"Or I'll kill you."

August pushed the end button so she didn't hear him say, "Fuck you, bitch."

CHAPTER SIX

Aradia raced behind Tara and Clemons. Both of the Guardians worked hard and fast, not waiting to see if their partners followed them. She and Tim understood that the dogs trusted their handlers would follow. Right now, they did their best to keep up with two very athletic canines.

They'd been searching since they left their temporary digs and met up with Tim and Clemons. All of a sudden, Tara's and Clemons's heads came up as if to catch something on the wind. Their black noses twitched, and then they took off like the proverbial bats out of hell. Aradia understood that evil reached out to breach the barriers. Tim had warned her something dangerous lurked far too close to the surface, and watching Tara's reaction now made her believe he hadn't been wrong.

She caught up with Tara just in time to see her body-slam a woman who'd knelt close to the ground where the grass and weeds were black as night. Didn't need to know why either the ground was discolored or Tara took her down. She already knew. A few seconds after the hit, Aradia reached the woman now safely out of range of the disturbed ground. Reaching out a hand, she helped her up while using her body to move her back even farther from the slash of black. Kinda of a safety-first sort of thing.

"What in the actual hell?" The woman's eyes were full of fire, and who could blame her? If a dog the size of Tara did a SmackDown on her without warning, she'd be a bit testy herself.

She kept her voice even and calm. "I'm sorry if Tara hurt you. It wasn't her intent. She was actually trying to protect you." Absolute truth. Not a single Guardian would ever harm an innocent.

The woman brushed at her clothes as she gave Tara a side-eye. "Protect me from what?"

"Everyone okay?" Tim and Clemons came running in their direction.

"Tim?" The woman turned and stared. "You know this person? That dog?" She pushed strands of long, silver hair out of her eyes. Brown eyes, Aradia noticed now. The color of dark chocolate. She loved dark chocolate.

"Yeah, yeah, Mercy. They're good folks, and trust me, Tara *was* trying to protect you." Tim stopped and, like Mercy, pushed his hair out of his eyes. Either he needed a haircut or he was going for a pop-star look.

"I know my plants." Her words were defiant, her hands on her hips. "I don't need anyone to protect me."

"That's a given, but trust me when I say more is going on here than you know." Tim stepped next to her and brushed bits of grass off her shirt.

"I am sorry for the aggressive takedown, but she truly was looking out for you. Touching that—" Aradia pointed to the blackened slash—"could have, probably would have, killed you."

Her gaze slid down to the black plants, and she visibly shuddered. She put her hands on her hips and stared at Aradia. "I know my way around deadly plants. I don't need protection from you or your dog."

Aradia looked to Tim. "Does she realize?"

"Maybe somebody could fill us in?" A man with long black hair and dark eyes stepped up next to Mercy and put an arm around her as if to protect her from Tim and Aradia. "Are you all right?" He frowned as he glanced from her face to Tara, who still stood guard just in case someone might be thinking about touching the spoiled ground.

Aradia wondered where he came from. Until he spoke, she hadn't even noticed him. Focusing on Tara and her beeline for the woman had put her into tunnel-vision mode, and he had to have been close by. Not good. She needed to be more situationally aware, or she could have an ugly surprise. Surprises could be fatal.

"Fine, though irritated at being knocked on my ass." She cut her gaze to Tara and then back to the problem area. "I need samples of that." She pointed. "I can't analyze without a sample. You might not be aware of it, but a man died right there, and we need to determine what killed him."

"It's not the plants." It might be easier to let her believe it to be a tragic accident with a very explainable cause. Then again, when did she ever settle for easy?

Mercy put her hands on her hips and stared. "And you would know that how?"

Aradia didn't break the gaze. "It's my job to know—and theirs." She pointed to Tara and Clemons, who remained on high alert, staring at the ground.

Mercy's gaze softened as she looked at the two dogs once more. "Okay. That's a little unnerving."

"A little?" Rufus was shaking his head. "That's a lot unnerving. What are they seeing, or are they hearing something?"

Tim stepped up. "You don't really want to know."

Mercy clearly thought differently. "You're wrong on that one. I want to know who you are." She pointed to Aradia. "And I want to know what those two are sensing. Someone died right there, and we need to know how and why."

Tim looked to Aradia, then said, "The explanation could take not just some time but a pretty good leap of faith."

This time Mercy cut her eyes away to her companion. "What do you think, Rufus? Are we up for a conversation that requires a big old open mind?"

"If we weren't, that handsome cop would never have asked us to take a look at this." He nodded toward the dark earth.

That remark got Aradia's attention. "What cop? What did he ask you to do?" She had a bad feeling there was more to the story here than just scorched earth.

"Is she cool, Tim?" This Mercy didn't seem all that convinced Aradia could be trustworthy. Fair enough. She wasn't so sure about this Mercy either.

Tim nodded. "As cool as they get. How about we go back to your place and talk this out? She's the one booked into your rental, by the way."

Mercy's gaze sharpened. "You're the guest bringing a dog?" She glanced over at Tara again.

Aradia wondered if their reservation was about to be canceled.

"If you live on a big farm with some righteous greenhouses, then yes, that would be correct. I'm the lady bringing the dog. Specifically, that dog." She nodded in Tara's direction.

No one spoke for maybe thirty uncomfortable seconds. Then Mercy said, "Let's go. This situation—" She waved her arms to encompass their surroundings—"can't be mere coincidence. Let's all head to the farm so we can get to the bottom of this. Before we go, I really need a sample of that." She pointed to the ground again.

Once more, Aradia shook her head. "That's a big, fat no. We'll cleanse this before we go, but you don't dare touch it. I realize you don't know me, but Tim does, and he'll back me up. It's important to trust me on this."

Mercy's expression said a lot. She didn't like being told what to do. Too bad. In this instance, her life depended on it. Aradia really thought she'd push back and braced for more argument. Instead, after a few seconds, Mercy nodded. "All right. I don't like it, but if Tim says to let you do whatever it is you two do, then fine. But I expect an explanation once we get back to the house. Come on, Rufus." She spun and walked away. Her friend, Rufus, followed her after a glance over his shoulder. Interestingly, that glance wasn't for her but landed squarely on Tim.

To say that the woman pissed Mercy off would be putting it mildly. In her own backyard, no less. Took a lot of gall to push her and Rufus out of the way like a couple of little kids who were trying to intrude on a big-people conversation. Not too much insulting about that. Later, she'd come back for her samples. While she might grant the woman a win for the immediate skirmish, the battle still waged. She'd get her samples one way or the other.

"Did you happen to catch her name by any chance?" Rufus asked as they drove away from the mountain and back toward the farm.

Until he asked, it hadn't dawned on Mercy that during the course of the entire exchange, no one had mentioned the stranger's name. Wasn't exactly the scenario for polite introductions, but still, it seemed like Tim would at least tell them who she was. Back at the house, she could pull up the rental information, so in truth, she likely already had her contact info. First order of business once they got home: find the identity of lady brown hair and blue eyes.

She parked and immediately sprinted inside the house. Didn't wait for Rufus. He knew the way and would be right behind her. In the kitchen, she logged onto her laptop and pulled up the rental information. Rufus peered over her shoulder as she said, "Aradia Burke. No name on the dog, just a note that she's large and well-trained."

"Trained enough to knock you over like a locomotive. Her name's kind of cool, don't you think? I've never met anyone named Aradia." He walked to her fridge and opened it. After surveying the contents, he pulled out a bottle of iced tea. Unsweet. The sweetened version made her gag.

Mercy sat back and thought more about the unexpected collision. Without question, it had shocked her when the dog slammed into her, and it happened so fast, she hadn't had time to brace herself. She'd tumbled backward like the time she'd fallen from the tire swing, landing on a rock and putting a three-inch gash in her head. No hole in her head this time, only the same kind of surprise about finding herself on the ground. The dog hadn't been violent, only protective in a way that seemed to extend to her. She'd kept Mercy from moving back to the scarred earth to collect her sample. Actually, kind of impressive, though she'd keep that thought to herself.

"More like she was performing a job. It felt more protective than hurtful." The more she thought about the realization, the more it fit. That dog hadn't been aggressive; she'd been working. What kind of working dog kept people away from danger out in the wilderness?

Rufus appeared to be thinking along the same lines. "How would the dog sense a problem with the ground? I mean, I'll be the first to admit the intelligence of dogs is often underappreciated. Still, a stranger protecting you from what? Blackened vegetation? That's weird. Did it smell something bad? Hear something? I don't know about you, but I want to learn more about those giants."

"Definitely weird, and I'm going out on a limb here and say the lady and her dog have a story. Did you also notice that Tim and Clemons were totally familiar with them? The dogs worked in tandem like they'd been together their whole lives. Don't tell me that's not weird too."

"Oh, you mean the second cute guy I've seen today?" Rufus leaned against the counter and smiled.

She stared at him. "Really? My friend, you're overdue for a date. We've got a guy dead from some strange reaction to the environment, a mysterious woman with a dog that has an equally mysterious job, and you're pining over a couple of handsome men?"

"A guy in a uniform and a guy with a big dog—what's not to pine for?" He smiled as he sipped on his bottle of iced tea.

She couldn't help herself. She chuckled. "You are too much."

"Maybe just enough for one of them?" He winked.

"I can't..." She laughed again.

"Seriously, though. Good vibes off both the cop and the dog handler. Also, the lady. Words on the wind whisper good souls." His expression had turned serious. "Those are two people we can trust."

She sobered. "I like hearing that. I've known Tim since he settled here and have always been sure he was one of the good ones. Didn't get to know Frank until a few years ago, though always hoped for a pure soul. Now, the woman? Time will tell." She hoped time would tell her something positive.

"Oh, she's good. I feel it." He patted his chest and winked.

Mercy shook her head. "I trust your feelings, except in this case, your judgment might be clouded by, and I quote, the second cute guy."

"Oh, come on. I'm a little insulted. Give me more credit than that. Not that I can't be swayed by good looks, but really. That's not what's going on here. I promise." He used his index finger to draw a cross on his chest.

Now she nodded. "Point taken."

He winked again. "Not that the second guy isn't cute."

Their conversation ended at the knock on the front door. They looked at each other before she spun and headed to the entryway. As she expected, Tim and the woman, sans both dogs, stood on her front porch. She opened the door and waved them in. Nobody moved.

"Tell me you brought some samples of the plants?" She directed her question to both of them, though she didn't expect the woman to respond. At least Tim would be sympathetic to her cause. She hoped. Helping was what they were about, or so they'd proclaimed, and they'd effectively shut her down out there. Pretty rude when she thought about it. Who were they to tell her she couldn't take a sample? Frank had asked her to help understand what happened out there, and the woman stopped her. The more Mercy thought about it, the more it irritated her.

"No." The woman answered this time.

"What is your problem, Aradia Burke?" She looked surprised that Mercy knew her name. No psychic abilities needed for that one. "I found your name on the booking form." She might be a looker, but her personality thus far dimmed that light.

Aradia tilted her head and sighed. "Just Aradia, please, and my problem has nothing to do with you. I apologize for coming across as aggressive. There's just a lot going on, and I didn't want you to get hurt. Tara only made sure you were clear of the danger. She would never have harmed you."

Not what she expected to hear. A tiny bit of her resistance faded. "Why don't you come in, and let's chat. I'm curious about what's happening that has you out there patrolling my mountain." Oh, yes. She made it territorial. She'd lived here a long time, and this lady waltzes in and tries to push her around. Not going over well at all. "You have some explaining to do."

For a few moments, Aradia stared into her eyes. Then she cut her gaze to Tim. He nodded slightly. "Tell them," he said. "They need to know what's coming."

Mercy glanced over her shoulder at Rufus, who shrugged, and then her gaze went back to Tim and his friend. "What's coming?"

Aradia stared once more into Mercy's eyes. "Demons."

❖

A bolt of lightning shot up August's back as he drove north, and he gripped the steering wheel hard enough to make his hands grow pale. He blew out a breath and allowed himself to feel the power.

Listen for the message. Since childhood, the universe had spoken to him. That was one reason why he'd known he would someday rule the forces that waited below. It had been whispered in his ear. The first time, he'd been six years old and sound asleep in his little bed, the moonlight spilling into his tiny room, and the whispers drawing him out of slumber. Any other child would have been scared.

"We're waiting." That's what he'd heard. "We're waiting."

Barefoot, he'd stood at the window, the moonlight on his face, and he'd understood. Somewhere out there they waited for him to show them the way. A first-grader who didn't stand out in the classroom, yet he'd understood.

"Be ready." The whispers had continued, and with an understanding that went far beyond his six years of life, he'd known in that instant what destiny held for him. He'd begun his mission to learn all he'd need to grab it with both hands when the day arrived.

That same night he'd left his little room to get a drink of water in the kitchen. There on the table he saw his father's ring. The red stone glowed in the dark room, as though it beckoned to him. He didn't resist the call and picked it up. Warm and pulsing, it too seemed to whisper to him. "I will be yours." He set it back on the table, not wanting his father to walk in and see him touching it. Someday it would be his, and he would wait for that day. He walked to the sink, got his drink of water, and then went back to bed. Within minutes, he fell asleep again, and when daylight dawned, the rest of his life began. He didn't think anyone else in his family noticed the difference in him. He knew, and that's all that mattered.

His current feelings as he drove down the highway reminded him of what he'd felt that night all those years ago. The guidance of those whispers filled him with purpose, and he made sure to be ready. At the end of this trip his reward waited. The ring pulsed on his finger, a palpable reassurance that he walked the right path. The ground trembled. The wind spoke. The forces aligned as they waited for him to destroy the divide between the worlds. "Soon," he whispered.

He pulled off at a rest stop in the middle of Oregon. For a few minutes, he needed to get out and walk around. That and, frankly, the drive had started to bore the crap out of him. On this stretch of the journey, flat with low-growing vegetation and only sporadic stands of trees, the only thing that broke up the boring view were the wind farms. Lots and lots of those giant, white windmills that looked like three-armed monsters. The most interesting thing about them was to catch if the arms were actually turning, and, well, that wasn't all that engaging either. Good thing he'd gotten some rest last night, or he'd be falling asleep at the wheel.

"Boring, boring, boring," he muttered under his breath. Ama didn't hear, as she had earbuds in listening to who knows what, her head tilted back, her eyes closed. She didn't seem to notice he'd veered off. At least she'd finally stopped constantly scrolling on her phone. Skilled as she might be, the more time he spent with her, the more he wondered about her long-term usefulness.

Ama looked up only when the car came to a stop in front of a low brown building with large signs sporting bright-yellow lettering that served to direct them to the men's and women's restrooms. Men on left. Women on the right. Sad-looking grass grew, sort of, on either side of the concrete paths leading to the restrooms, and behind the building was more sad grass with signs designating it as the pet area. Knowing how so many pet owners didn't bother to pick up after their animals, he had zero plans to get anywhere close to that stretch of quasi-green.

Ama's head tilted up only when he turned the engine off. She took the earbuds out and looked around. "Wow. I don't know if I've ever pulled into a rest area and found it empty. Won't have to wait for a stall in the bathroom." She laughed at her own crappy joke.

He got out, stretched his arms, and breathed in deeply. The wind blew with intention here, his hair flying around his face. He pulled a band out of his pocket and tied his hair back. Undoubtedly, Ama would have another Jesus joke about it. Her snarky comments tested his patience, and they still had a long way to go.

She slammed her door and, as he'd done, stretched her arms, and rolled her head. "Oh, man, that feels good. Didn't realize until now how stiff I'm getting sitting in that seat. Been a while since I've been on a big road trip. Planes are more my style."

"Take advantage. We might not stop again." He would, but she didn't need to know that. He could be snarky too.

"Yeah, yeah. Still weird that we're the only ones here. Where are all the truckers? They always hang out at rest stops." She did a three-sixty turn.

An idea trickled into this head only after Ama pointed out their solitude here along the Oregon highway. It took on more life and promise as he watched her walk into the ladies' room, the door swinging shut behind her. He made it halfway to the men's room before he turned around and sprinted back to his SUV. He could pee anywhere, and the strong wind seemed to be talking to him. He liked what it suggested.

He was just beginning to merge into traffic when he glanced in the rearview mirror. Ama stood in the middle of the empty parking lot, her arm raised and her middle finger pointed toward the sky. He pressed the accelerator and watched his speed increase. Fifty. Sixty. Seventy. His laughter filled the car, and his mood immediately improved.

CHAPTER SEVEN

A radia stepped inside the big house and looked around. Nice. Not a big surprise, considering how pleasant the rental turned out to be. Someone who had that much pride in a dwelling they rented out to strangers surely kept their own home at the same or better standard. That was definitely the case here, or at least as much as she could see. Not that Mercy appeared to be a clean freak. More about dignity and attention to detail. She appreciated those traits. Echoed her own way of living.

Tim had called her during the drive back to the farm and filled her in at least somewhat. From his description, she sensed Mercy Burroughs would turn out to be an interesting woman in a lot of ways. More than an herbalist, one who used the gifts of nature to do good work. Healers were important and amazing, and from what Tim said, Mercy was a healer of the highest order. Something else, too, although as yet Aradia couldn't put a finger on it, and he either wasn't divulging more or legitimately didn't know more.

Mercy's friend so far was a mystery. Tim didn't know Rufus and couldn't give her much background about him. He, too, had the vibe of an intuitive. Given his clear Native-American heritage, she would be interested in his take on the ground where the man had died.

She felt a little bad that she'd driven them away from the site. They possibly could have provided some interesting and helpful additional information if they'd had time to study the location more closely. The risk wasn't worth the benefit. That slash of darkness against the beautiful natural habitat spoke volumes to her. The spider cracks were beginning, and they provided evil an avenue out of the underworld. Both Tara and Clemons gave off what amounted to a five-alarm warning. The poison that leached out, an ominous sign of what headed their way.

Before leaving, she'd sealed the crack and burned the poison that seeped through. No one else would lose their life on that particular patch of ground. Her worries didn't lessen, and she suspected Mercy would be angry that Aradia had destroyed any chance for her to study the vegetation. It had to be that way, and Mercy would have to accept it. One of those times when it had to be what it had to be.

"You want to expand upon the demons thing?" Mercy motioned for her to have a seat in the living room.

Sunlight streamed into the room, warm and inviting. The large windows provided a beautiful view of the farm's flourishing fields. A light breeze outside had the acres and acres of plants swaying as if in tune with a lovely melody. Inside, colorful paintings graced the walls and gave the room a homey feel. "This is a beautiful place." Aradia sat.

"Yeah, it is." Mercy's voice was all business. "Demons?" Mercy's long, silver hair caught the sunlight, almost glowing. The beauty of her thick mane of hair didn't diminish the intensity of her gaze. Her brown eyes didn't waver from Aradia's face. The woman had focus and something else. One word came to mind: magic. That's what she'd been sensing since out there on the mountain.

"What are you?" The words came out without much thought. Sometimes her mouth worked before her brain engaged.

Tall and lean, Mercy stood at the fireplace, her feet shoulder-width apart, her hands behind her back. On the outside, a confident woman. Exteriors didn't always capture the whole person. Something she knew firsthand. "You tell me what you are, and I'll tell you what I am."

She started as she always did. Most of the world couldn't embrace her reality. "I'm a dog breeder and trainer."

Mercy nodded, and a tiny smile turned up the corners of her mouth. Aradia had the feeling she was being humored. "Fair enough. I'm an herbalist."

Definitely being humored. "What else are you?"

Mercy's expression didn't change. "What else are you?"

For a few seconds Aradia studied her face. Strength. Grace. Intelligence. All right, she'd let it fly. "I also breed, train, and work the Guardians."

"And they are?"

Aradia glanced at Tim. As he'd done earlier, he nodded slightly. Her gut agreed with Tim's approval. Mercy and Rufus were trustworthy. "They guard the portals to the underworld and keep everyone safe from the demons that want to take over and fill the world with evil and darkness." Under different circumstances, a statement like that would get her referred to a licensed professional.

Mercy stared at her. "Demons." It wasn't really a question, more a repetition, as if to let the information settle. Another thing she liked about her.

Tim spoke up. "Mercy, she's for real, and so are the Guardians. Clemons and I have been patrolling this area since he became field-ready seven years ago. Clemons is a Guardian, and I'm his handler. It might sound crazy. Trust me, it's not. We've been on the alert for demons at the mountain for going on a decade."

Aradia jumped in, her instinct pushing her to share. "Portals exist all over the world, and those like me have been breeding and training the dogs for centuries. I come from a very long line of those responsible for the Guardians. My kennel is north of Spokane, but I have dogs placed everywhere."

Now Mercy looked to her friend. "Rufus, what sayeth you?"

Rufus walked over to where Aradia sat and knelt in front of her. "May I?" He held out his hands.

Though she'd never had to bring in outsiders before, the oddness of his request didn't faze her. No protocol existed for this situation. Besides, she had a really good feeling about both Mercy and Rufus. She gave him her hands, his grip light yet intense. She hadn't been wrong about him. He had that something-something that couldn't quite be explained. To her, it needed no explanation. She could accept it as is, and she liked him already. His life force glowed clear and true.

As they touched, energy pulsed between them, warm and, more important, pure. A very good soul. An old soul. For maybe ten seconds, he closed his eyes and breathed evenly, in and out, in and out. A calmness settled over them both. Then he opened his eyes, smiled at her, and let go of her hands, rocking back on his heels. He gave her a tiny nod. She nodded back.

He stood and turned to Mercy. "She's the real deal."

❖

Mercy wasn't sure why the confirmation from Rufus made her happy, but it did. The urge to share with this woman washed over her as strong as a tidal wave. Standard operating procedure for her always involved remaining very private. Childhood trauma had a way of doing that to people, even as they became adults and knew better. In this moment, she set aside her usual protocol. No rational explanation for her need to open up to Aradia, yet there it was. She held Aradia's gaze, her eyes as blue as the sky outside. Like Mercy, she too wore her hair long. Dark, flowing, and beautiful. How many times had she heard that women their age shouldn't wear long hair? Screw them all. She'd do whatever she damn well pleased. It appeared her newest acquaintance subscribed to the same philosophy. The only difference was that Mercy's hair had gone silver at least five years ago, while Aradia's had stayed a deep, shiny brown.

"I'm Wiccan." There, she'd said it out loud, not something she did often. Or ever.

"Wiccan?" Aradia's question was easy and not filled with disbelief.

"My mother taught me the old ways, and I've practiced for decades. It gives me comfort and keeps me grounded." A simple answer that didn't capture all the nuances of what Wicca gave her. Simple worked in this instance.

Aradia nodded. "Wiccan is good. Your knowledge could really come in helpful."

Mercy smiled as warmth flushed through her. Not often she ran into someone this accepting. Most people rolled their eyes and, though they might not say it out loud, thought her a bit of a freak. Not Aradia. Maybe she was a sister? As she studied her, she decided Aradia wasn't a witch but perhaps a sister of another kind? That thought intrigued her even more.

"My mother's family has practiced and believed for centuries. I'm an herbalist because of this farm and the healing I can do through nature and my Wiccan beliefs. Mom gave me an amazing education."

"Is your mom here?" Aradia looked around as if expecting Mom to walk through the door.

"I lost her three years ago." It still brought a rush of emotion to talk about her. Made her wonder if she'd ever get through the pain of her death.

"I'm sorry." Not just words. Emotion threaded through Aradia's voice, and Mercy appreciated it. Someone who understood loss.

"Thank you. She was an amazing woman, and I thank her every day for the life she gave me." A lot more to that particular story that she rarely, if ever, shared. No reason to be ashamed of any part of her journey. The reality didn't make a difference, and a little piece of her still felt shame. Mom always knew when those emotions rose within her and would keep her from dropping into the darkness. The light she gifted to Mercy had to have come from heaven. She missed her so. "I carry on with the old ways the best I can to honor her memory."

Aradia nodded. "I get it. We've been around a long time too, and we teach each new generation as we were taught. Right, Tim?"

"You know it. Aradia is one hell of a teacher. She's the only reason Clemons and I can do what we do."

The admiration in Tim's face mirrored his words. A special bond existed between him and Aradia. Told her more than any of the words that had thus far been spoken.

Mercy shifted gears. "Now, how about you fill me and Rufus in on what you two were doing out there. You sort of explained the dogs and your roles as their handlers. That makes sense, except I suspect there's more you're not telling us."

Aradia leaned forward, her expression calm. If Mercy's comments offended her, it didn't show. "Fair enough. Here's the down-and-dirty version."

Mercy sat across from Aradia as she explained about the portals, sealed for centuries to contain the demons, and how Clemons had alerted them to an impending breach. Though Aradia had raced across the state to assist him in closing the chasm, she'd been too late to save the man who'd lost his life. She and Tim were going to do their best to make certain no one else was harmed.

After she finished, Mercy digested the information. She had no problem believing what Aradia had explained. Those whose lives didn't involve an understanding of an unseen world might have found the story fantastical. That wasn't her. The majority of people might not want to believe it, but forces existed both seen and unseen. Most were good. Others were very, very bad. Whatever had turned the vegetation lethal fell into the latter category.

A single question kept rolling through Mercy's mind after Aradia finished her fairly detailed explanation. "What makes this one different from attempted breaches through the years? You said portals exist all over the world. Surely this has happened before."

Aradia and Tim glanced at each other. Tim answered first. "In a lot of ways, it's not different."

"But…" They were still holding back. Why? She would have thought Tim, someone she considered a friend, would be more open to sharing, and it seemed as though, up to now, they'd been pretty forthcoming.

Aradia dropped her head for a second and then looked back up at Mercy. "Tim's right in that in many ways it's similar to past breaches. At the same time, in many ways it's very different. Starting with the man's death. Very few documented instances of a spider crack resulting in a death like that exist."

At least this piece of information tracked somewhat with Mercy's instincts. "I have thoughts on that subject. It might look like a fatal reaction to something poisonous, but that doesn't really make sense. I know my plants, and that shouldn't have happened, even with a rare toxic variety."

"I agree." Aradia nodded. "I've read about something similar in old texts. But I haven't seen an incident like this in my time."

"Okay, so if it wasn't like that, what did the texts say happened the other times?"

Something flickered in Aradia's beautiful eyes as she paused before answering. Fear? "At least one demon escaped."

❖

August grinned. Abandoning Ama at the rest stop had to be hands-down the most fun he'd had in years. Kind of like the time he'd punched his little sister in the stomach and successfully blamed it on their older cousin. Because of the innocent expression on his cute little face, everyone had believed him. That had been a good day too, though his cousin rarely talked to him after that, no loss, and his sister gave him a wide berth, much appreciated.

Now he raced north, ignoring posted speed limits. More recommendations than requirement, as far as he was concerned. August needed to get there, access the timeline for the total breach, and get himself ready. He mentally rolled through the spells required to harness the energy that pulsed beneath the earth. Not many could control the activity below like he could. He'd learned from the masters and then taken that knowledge to another level. His sister liked to think she had the skills needed for what loomed on the horizon. He had news for her. Not in the ballpark. Not even in the parking lot.

His smile warmed as he drove, at least until his phone rang. "Oh, for the love of God, Willa. What do you want now?"

"Just giving you fair warning. I'm going to beat you on this one." The sugar in her voice didn't cover up the venom.

"Oh, please, like you've ever bested me at anything."

"All a matter of opinion and perspective. Your perspective has always been skewed."

"I have a very clear vision, which you simply never understood. Wrapped up too tight in your visions of grandeur." He waited for her explosion. She didn't like to be called on her own bullshit. Really detested it when it came from him.

Her laugh was light, cheerful. The sound made him uneasy. Not like her at all. She typically leaned on anger and indignation, especially when it came to their interactions. "We shall see, won't we?"

She ended the call, cutting off any response from him. Bitch always did like to have the last word. Probably pissed off that he'd hung up on her earlier before she could say anything else. Okay today to let her think she'd bested him. Soon enough, things would end very differently for her, and her ability to get the last word in any disagreement would abruptly and permanently halt. A price to be paid for her constant refusal to respect one greater than herself. Her blinders would finally come off, and he looked forward to that moment.

So many things to look forward to. The future shone bright for him, and he smiled as he squinted against the bright sunlight streaming through the windshield. Warming sunshine at the moment. Wouldn't last too much longer. He looked forward to the darkness that would fall once the portal opened all the way. When he commanded the demons of the underworld, everything would change. He would reap the rewards due him after decades of hard work.

August pushed the accelerator a little harder, anxious to complete his journey as well as put more miles between himself and the rest stop where Ama had learned it didn't do well to piss him off. Not that he really cared if she ended up stuck there, but since her phone wasn't in the console, she obviously had it with her. She could call someone to come get her. Made him smile to think how long she'd have to sit there waiting for rescue.

When his phone rang, August glanced at the display, expecting it to be Ama. No plan to pick up. Way more entertaining to let her sit in that windy, isolated rest stop and stew. Except it wasn't Ama. It wasn't Willa again either, though it wouldn't have surprised him if she called back to rage at him some more. He didn't think Willa ever got tired of hearing herself talk.

"June?" His younger sister rarely called. They weren't what one would call close. Barely tolerant of each other would be a more apt description of their relationship, which had been that way since the day of her birth. At five, he'd been disappointed in his parents for bringing her into the fold. His feelings toward June hadn't changed in all the decades since, and she'd never forgotten the punch in the stomach.

"Why would you do that to Ama?" Anger rippled beneath her tight words. Always in control, little sister never gave in to extreme displays of emotion. "That was low, even for you."

He shook his head. Seems like she'd know him better than that by now. "Figures she'd call you."

"Why not? We're friends, and when my brother does her wrong, why the hell not call me? Someone who knows you well and can commiserate."

"What? You going to run home and tell Mommy on me?" Big freaking deal if she did. His mother wasn't a big fan of his anyway.

She liked to say he had a bad attitude. He'd heard the same song and dance his whole life. Didn't bother him as a kid. Really didn't bother him as an adult. "If you insist on getting involved, just go pick her up and take her home. The rest of this has nothing to do with you or Ama."

"It has everything to do with me, and you're the one who brought Ama into it. I know what you're up to, August, and it can't be. You need to back the hell off. You don't have big enough balls to pull this off. You'll just end up making a mess like you always do."

His fingers tightened on the steering wheel. "This belongs to me, and face it, sister. You can't stop me." She always tried to push the theory that she was the faster and smarter of the two of them. The favored child with the most excellent education in their craft. He always let her believe that lie.

"Watch me." The call went dead.

Bad enough that Willa wanted to beat him to the portal, but now June had jumped into the mix too. Women. Such a pain in the ass ninety-nine percent of the time. He wasn't going to let the two biggest pains derail either his plans or his future. Neither one of them had the kind of knowledge and power it would take to control what would happen soon enough. He'd been preparing for this his entire life, and to say he was ready put it mildly. Locked, loaded, and ready for bear, as their father liked to say.

He tapped his dashboard screen until music filled the rig. No easy-listening either. Good old classic rock-and-roll with hard beats, long guitar riffs, and plenty of bass. Did a soul good. The Demon King turned up the volume, his palms hitting the steering wheel in time with the music while his voice joined Ozzy Osborne's.

CHAPTER EIGHT

After Aradia dropped the bombshell, she reached over and touched Mercy on the arm. A bolt of electricity raced all the way from her fingertips to her shoulder. "Argh," she exclaimed as she jumped back. That was unexpected.

"What in the world was that?" Mercy rubbed her arm where moments before Aradia's fingers had touched. She looked as shocked as Aradia felt.

She shook her head and stared into Mercy's dark eyes. So pretty. So filled with confusion. "I don't know." Didn't have even a guess for that one.

"That happen a lot when you touch people?" She continued to rub her arm.

"That would be a definite no." She searched Mercy's face, looking for what, she didn't know.

"Anybody want to fill us in?" Tim looked between them while Rufus nodded.

"Yeah. We're kinda out in the cold here," Rufus added.

Aradia tried to process and make sense of it. She couldn't. Might as well admit it. "I touched Mercy, and it was like a bolt of lightning went up my arm. I've never had that happen before. What are you? Besides Wiccan. I've known plenty of Wiccans, and that doesn't happen if I touch them." Her gaze didn't move from Mercy's face. She might declare herself to be simply a practitioner of Wicca and a skilled herbalist, but Aradia now knew she was far more than either of those things. "What can you do? What are you not telling us?"

Besides wanting to understand the electric connection, she wondered if the extra something might help them.

Mercy held out her hands and kept her gaze steady. "What you see is what you get." Clearly, she wanted to hang on to her secrets.

Aradia turned her attention to Rufus. "We already know you have a gift. What about your friend here?" Maybe he'd be more forthcoming.

Rufus gave Mercy a soft look before turning to address Aradia's question. "Sorry. Not my story to tell."

Darn. She'd hoped for more. Still, she couldn't blame him for staying tight-lipped. She'd expect her good friends, the very few of them she had, to do the same for her. Worth a shot anyway, given the urgency of their situation.

"Fair enough." She looked back to Mercy. "Well? As the man said, your story to tell."

Tim spoke up again. "Come on, Mercy. You know me, and you know you can trust me. This isn't the time for secrets, and this is as safe a group as you'll ever be in. Whatever you say here stays here, but we have to know what you're holding back."

Mercy closed her eyes for a few seconds. When she opened them again, Aradia could see a change. A decision had been made. Hopefully, it leaned in their direction. "The truth is, I can see things."

"A psychic?" In a way, Aradia hoped that to be true. They could use all the help they could get at this point, and someone who could see ahead would be priceless. The dogs possessed the ability and the power to keep the demons at bay for as long as the cracks stayed small. If even one made it past Clemons or Tara, it would turn into a full-scale battle, and a race would ensue to seal the portal before it became too large to close. She shuddered slightly at the thought of what would happen if the portal opened all the way. To the best of her knowledge, it had never happened before, and she sure didn't want it to happen on her watch.

"No." Mercy shook her head slightly. "More like a pre-cognitive. Sometimes, and I emphasize, sometimes, I see things that will happen, barring any intervention. I've never considered myself a psychic, just someone who is a little more intuitive than most."

Still a psychic in Aradia's book, and she liked it. That skill could be very useful. "Have you seen the danger out there?" If Mercy could give them any little edge, it could prove to be priceless.

Mercy shook her head again. "Not really. That said, I feel it more than see it. Rufus has a better way with visions. I'm hit and miss, while he comes from a long line of seers, and I really believe he'll be more helpful than me."

Aradia wasn't so sure about that, or why would that *thing* have happened between them? More than attractive, Mercy possessed something special. Took effort not to reach out and touch her to see if they connected at the electric level again. Frightening and exciting all at the same time. "This is all good."

Mercy's eyes narrowed. "How so?" Appeared Aradia's powers of persuasion were still short of a hundred percent.

Aradia squared her shoulders and held Mercy's gaze. "Tim and Clemons are an experienced team, Tara is extraordinary, and you two can see ahead. That might just be the edge we need to stop this breach."

The explanation sounded great, and she meant every word. What she wasn't saying could stay inside her head for the moment.

❖

Mercy didn't have a single thing to base her thoughts on, but she knew deep in her soul that Aradia held back. Something. Could be that Aradia saw more than she let on. Mercy certainly did. That touch blew her away. Aradia wanted to know what Mercy was, and how she wanted to say, "Back at you." Dog breeder, trainer, handler, protector, sure. No issue believing that. The problem? She'd known her fair share of dog people, and not once, not one single time, did touching their hands make her feel like the universe expanded.

That wasn't all of it either. That charge had affected Mercy's heart in a way she'd never experienced. As if perhaps she'd touched her soul mate. She might be running with it now, but that's how it felt, and she'd learned a long time ago to give feelings their proper due. She'd explore that subject later, maybe. Right now, they had bigger issues to deal with.

Mercy looked to Tim and Aradia. No more fighting against what she didn't fully understand. Like Tim told her, Aradia could be trusted. "What do you need us to do? How can we help you?"

Aradia tossed the questions to Tim, which surprised her. Aradia appeared confident and in charge. "Your thoughts?"

Tim didn't hesitate. "I'm leaning toward taking the dogs and camping near the cracks. Give us some time to track down the location of the portal."

"I like that idea." Aradia nodded. "Clemons and Tara can do their work and find the weaknesses."

Rufus had been relatively quiet until now. Not like him but this wasn't exactly a normal situation. "It's not safe out there." He frowned and shoved his hands into his pockets.

"How so?" Mercy spent tons of time out near the mountain, and other than the eruption some forty years ago, it had always been a beautiful place to enjoy nature. Of course, until today, she'd seen it as a peaceful getaway, not a gateway to hell. While she agreed with Rufus that it felt wonky, she wanted more on his assessment about the safety, or lack thereof.

"Mercy, this really is more than plants that can kill a man. This is much deeper." Rufus went to the window and gazed out as if searching for something. "It feels wrong. Evil."

"You've seen something?" Given the way he stared out the window, she wondered what messages the universe sent him. She trusted his instincts, and if he said evil, she believed him.

He shook his head slightly as he continued to stare outside, where the sun was beginning to drop. "No. Not yet, anyway. It's a feeling." He tapped his chest. "A feeling I'm not liking much."

"Clemons and I are going to set up camp and keep guard." Tim stood and started to move toward the door. "I can't stay home and do nothing. This is too big and too dangerous."

Rufus stood up taller and turned away from the window. "I'll help you."

Something in Tim's gaze caught her eye. Well, well, well. That she didn't know. "That's a good idea. Rufus isn't as familiar with the area as you are, Tim, and he could assist you. His instincts are excellent, and there's that vision thing." She leaned in toward the two men getting closer. It felt right. It felt like destiny. Made her wonder if they'd experience that same electricity when their skin touched.

Tim nodded. "Come on. Let's go pick up some gear." He gazed up and down at Rufus, who wore blue jeans and a short-sleeved T-shirt. "You have some warmer clothes you can bring?" At first glance, it looked like a kind of creepy assessment. Second glance, it proved more worry than creepy. Tim appeared to be concerned about Rufus being both comfortable and safe. Interesting, very interesting.

"Give me sec." Rufus turned and sprinted down the hallway, while Tim headed out to his truck, where a waiting Clemons kept guard in the backseat.

"What's your thought?" Mercy turned to Aradia.

"Along the same lines. I'd planned to stay in your rental, but after all this, I think we should be on site. The closer Tara is, the safer we'll all be. Besides, the sooner we find the precise location of the portal, the better."

"Can she stop these demons?" Mercy shuddered, thinking of darkness streaming out of the mountain and destroying the beauty she'd come to love. Hard to wrap her head around the concept of demons stepping out of the underworld. Not hard to believe in the existence of evil, and so she wasn't about to dismiss anything.

"It's less a case of stopping the demons once they've breached the barriers and more about keeping the portals locked down so they don't have the chance to step out. My girl can find it, which will allow us to make sure it doesn't open."

Mercy's mind raced, and she made a quick decision even though it filled her with dread. Not caused by the current company. "I'll go with you."

"Not necessary." Aradia might have said the words, but they lacked force. Mercy got the distinct impression that the offer of her company wasn't unwelcome.

"Too bad. My mountain, I'm coming. Besides, if you don't want law-enforcement intervention in this, and I'm assuming you don't, then you need me. They won't listen to you, but they will listen to me." The truth. The local cops all knew and respected her. She could be an asset in more ways than one.

"Friends in high places?"

She tilted her head. "Something like that."

Aradia studied her face and seemed to reach a decision. "All right. Meet me at my truck in half an hour. We want to set up before it gets dark."

"Set up?" What exactly did she plan to do out there?

"I brought a tent and all the gear we'll need to stake out the area to locate and protect the portal."

Okay. That made sense. The woman did, indeed, show up prepared for battle. "Do you know where the portal is? I mean, I get it has something to do with what happened to that man out there, but is that it?"

Aradia frowned and shook her head. "Not necessarily. Certainly, there's a weakness there, which would account for the fatal ground cover. The portal itself could be miles away. These cracks are like ripples on the water after you've tossed in a big rock. They spread out far and wide from the epicenter." She held her hands out, fingers apart.

Aradia's tone seemed to suggest an obvious situation, and yet, to Mercy, it sounded a lot like looking for a lost wallet in a packed football stadium. The odds were not in their favor. Heading out to the wilderness, where darkness would blanket them thick and dark, didn't work for her. "Then how will we know what to protect?" She could be strong and useful; she just needed more.

Aradia held up two fingers. "I'm banking on two things. The dogs."

Mercy's math was pretty good, and Aradia's wasn't adding up yet. "That's one."

Aradia looked straight into her eyes with an intensity that made her shiver. "And your magic."

❖

By the time August crossed into Washington state, it had grown dark. As much as he wanted to begin scouting the mountain right away, it would be foolish to attempt at night. Particularly considering he wasn't an outdoorsman. More a city guy who occasionally ventured into the wilds.

The vibes in the air whispered that he had time. Strong yet not urgent. Those he would soon release and then rule were waiting for him with the patience born from centuries of practice. A good night's sleep would be a wise choice on his part. Besides, it might take him another day or two to pinpoint the portal. And to dispatch the Guardians sure to be on their way, if not already there. Attention to the details remained important to his success. A lesser man might rush out there and risk failure.

At a big chain hotel in Vancouver, he pulled into the parking lot. Plenty of nice places closer to the scenic beaches were available, and he'd enjoy listening to the ocean and waking up to the sunrise over the water. The problem with those towns was their small size, making strangers stand out. Critical to go unnoticed. If his sister and Ama weren't dogging him, he wouldn't care, and he'd have treated himself to the ocean view. They were big enough pains without making it easier for them to find him. While he couldn't stop them from following, he could make it difficult. He liked difficult.

He grabbed both his suitcase and his bag from the back and walked inside. The quite-helpful clerk behind the desk didn't even pause when August told him he didn't have a reservation. Less than ten minutes later, he walked down the hallway on the seventh floor. Once inside his room with two queen-sized beds, he set the deadbolt and the safety lock. It wouldn't be enough. Before he turned out the lights, he'd be certain to put into place the invisible locks that would allow him to sleep deeply. No way would he take a chance the bitches would show up. He didn't think they would, but he had long subscribed to the better-safe-than-sorry philosophy.

Right now, a little homework dominated his immediate agenda. A bit of sleuthing, magic-style. He did love magic and thanked the gods every day he'd been born into it. If he'd had to live his life as one of the masses, better than average odds he'd have probably knocked himself off out of boredom. All those people out there going through their days doing the same thing over and over without ever realizing how much more existed around them blew his mind. Thrilled him that he knew exactly how much more and exactly how to harness it.

He had an idea of what he was about to face as the main obstacle to his ultimate goal. What he didn't know, yet, was exactly who it would be, and it would be a who rather than a what. Time for a little work. He planned to be locked and loaded when he arrived. Neither May nor Ama knew everything about him. They might believe they did, but they didn't. He remained a mystery to everyone, and that gave him a card to play that he alone possessed.

As a student of the Magic of the Light, he practiced the power of Abramelin and cherished what it would do for him. In the many, many centuries since the mage had written his magic, thousands had tried to harness it and failed. August would be the last to try it, as he would not fail. His father had hoped to be the one, hiding the texts where he believed no one would find them. Fool had missed the signs of greatness in his own son. August had found the texts by the time he turned ten and had been studying them ever since. When good old Dad left the mortal plane, he no longer had to sneak into his father's study. He walked through the door, took those books out of his father's desk, and never looked back. He'd been waiting ever since for the right night and the right portal. His patience would soon pay off.

First, however, it remained critical that the purity ritual be performed. To arrive on-site tomorrow cleansed and pure added to his advantage. In a normal situation, he would take three full days to purify his body through meditation and fasting. Thanks to his studies, he'd learned a faster way to achieve the ultimate end result. It might be risky, but sometimes the risks were worth the prize. Desperate measures and all that. It might be a little more fun too, and he did have a penchant for a good time.

Showered and dressed in the best clothes he'd brought along, he sat in front of his laptop at the room's built-in desk. The search he entered into his browser returned three very good possibilities. A Wednesday night usually offered promising options. Churches loved to have mid-week services, and they weren't disappointing him tonight.

After he settled on the Mid-Town Baptist Church, he pulled up the address in his navigation app. Easy enough to get there while far enough away from the hotel to establish reasonable doubt. Not that he'd need it. Mostly he didn't want Willa or Ama to stumble upon his movements. Not much to worry about when it came to them. Finding him at a church would be the last thing they'd think of. Given his love of craft beer, he suspected they'd start with local breweries. Perfect. The misguided assumption of his movements would keep them out of his way.

The church didn't disappoint. Had to be the largest in the area, if the number of the cars in the massive parking lot were any indication. Made him wonder what Sunday mornings looked like. August shook his head. People were so gullible. To him, these big churches with the bands, the big screens, and the flamboyant preachers were all theater.

In the back of the church or, more accurately, the auditorium, he found an empty seat and sat down. Heads turned, and he returned the brief smiles and nods afforded him as he settled in. While, down the road, they might remember him when asked, he didn't worry too much about it. By the time that happened, his control would be firmly in place. He'd be untouchable.

She made herself apparent to him within a minute of sitting down. He took the hymnal and held it as if it interested him. It didn't. She did. The minister had barely finished his greetings to the assembled worshippers when he caught the light. Long, shiny, black hair and a little overweight. When she turned her face sideways, he could see smooth skin and plump, rosy lips. He could almost smell the wave of innocence that wafted off her. Perfect. Pretty, young, and full of life.

"That was a nice service." As worshippers streamed out of the open church doors, he stepped to the side and stopped. August waited for her to come out, and then he matched her stride as he came up beside her. She smelled as good as she looked, her light perfume wafting through the gentle breeze.

Her smile lit up her face. Even prettier when she smiled. Maybe twenty-five, his raven-haired pick was better up close than when he'd noticed her with rows of pews separating them. "Pastor Wainwright is the best. I always walk away lifted up to God." Her soft voice remained upbeat and friendly. Trusting.

He managed to suppress a triumphant smile as he kept pace with her, moving closer and closer to the full parking lot. "I felt exactly like that as he spoke. Lifted me up. I'm John." He reached out a hand as she turned toward a small blue POS car.

She didn't hesitate to take his offered hand. "Mandy. Are you new here? I don't remember seeing you before." She studied his face, her expression soft.

"Just passing through." He smiled as he reached out and squeezed hard on a spot on at the base of her neck.

"What…" She collapsed, and he caught her before she hit the ground. Worked every stinking time.

Fortunately, with his black Yukon parked a few spaces away and in the shady corner of the parking lot, he had her in the backseat, taped, and tied with record speed, no one the wiser for what had gone down in the few minutes since the church service let out. No one appeared to be paying attention anyway. The worshippers felt safe here in God's house. Or, rather, in God's parking lot. That was on them. Fools to believe they were safe anywhere. Did they miss the part about the devil? If God was present, then so was Satan. Funny how it never seemed to occur to the folks that filled the pews and raised their hands in praise of Jesus.

As he drove away, he waved to several people in the lot, their smiles still warm and welcoming. "Yes, indeed." He turned and peeked into the backseat. "Like the pastor promised, your God will most assuredly lift us both up tonight."

CHAPTER NINE

A radia packed their things back into her rig before hooking Tara's harness into the seat belt in the backseat. In a weird way, she'd actually prefer to leave Mercy out of this. She had some skills that could help. She also had no clue what could come their way. Danger at a level impossible to describe. A feeling of protectiveness swept over Aradia, making her want to ensure her new friend remained safe. Mercy didn't seem inclined to agree with her on any of it. She stood at Aradia's truck watching her reload all the gear she'd taken out only a few hours earlier.

When Mercy said she could see things on occasion, it wasn't a stretch to believe her. Aradia couldn't follow her own destiny if she failed to believe in things that couldn't be seen or touched. Her work with the Guardians would be useless if she didn't embrace a universe bigger than imagination. Point in fact: the Guardians. These were dogs born different, raised different, and living their lives different. Little could harm them, as if they were surrounded by an invisible yet impenetrable armor. No, wrong. Not as *if* they were. They were. She had seen those who came in search of the power the demons of the underworld promised try to kill the Guardians in all ways imaginable. They failed again and again.

"You want this in the back?" Mercy walked around the rear of the truck, a pack slung over her shoulder.

Good. She'd come prepared. She liked that about her. Aradia hadn't needed to tell her what to bring. She'd been bright enough to figure it out for herself. "I do. Toss it in there, and we'll get going." She leaned into the passenger's seat and grabbed her cap. Putting it on, she pulled her hair through the space between the cap and the adjustable strap. She slipped on her sunglasses to counter the glare of the setting sun.

They were rolling down the road toward the mountain five minutes later. For the first few minutes, they were quiet. Mercy broke the silence. "I'm going to refund your card."

"What?" She kept her eyes on the road. She'd been focusing on the task ahead of them and wasn't quite following what Mercy said.

"Your credit card. You know, the rental. I'm not going to charge you." Mercy almost sounded apologetic, which made Aradia like her even more.

"You don't have to do that. I rented it, so I owe you the fees regardless of whether we sleep there or not." And really, the fees for the rental were the least of her worries at the moment. Bigger fish to fry, as the old saying went.

"Under normal circumstances, I'd agree with you. These are not normal circumstances, and what you're trying to do is way more important than me collecting a bit of passive income."

Aradia glanced over at Mercy. She stared straight ahead, clearly serious. "Okay, point taken, but how about we table this topic for now and focus on what's out there. We can revisit the money issue later." If they needed to, she thought. "Tell me the best place to park, and then we'll hike in. Tim is coming in from his side and patrolling the areas that Clemons has been alerting on. He's a good dog, and I trust they'll keep the sites guarded enough to prevent a breach."

"You sound so confident." Mercy looked at her now, her dark eyes narrowed. Confidence didn't roll off her. Maybe Aradia should have insisted she stay back at her farm. Too late now. She could imagine what Mercy would say to her if she suggested she take the truck and return home.

"I am." She was confident, and she hoped Mercy could hear it in her words. Her faith in Clemons and Tara to lead them where they needed to go remained solid. The two dogs would get them to just the right spot so they could proactively protect against the evil that longed to walk into the daylight. She also had confidence in her skills to seal the portal. A lifetime of lessons gave her faith in the level of her abilities, which she hoped wouldn't turn out to be misplaced.

"But it's already killed one person. How do you know the poison did it and it wasn't because a demon escaped again, like you told me earlier? Could a demon be out here now, watching and waiting to hurt us?" Mercy looked around as if expecting one to step out from behind a tree.

She put a hand on Mercy's arm, loving the warmth that spread between them. Still a bit of a charge, though not as shocking as the first time they touched. "I'll be honest. I can't be one hundred percent certain. I think we'd know if it was more than the leaching of darkness. Most important, I'm leaning on history and what the elders taught me." She wanted to reassure Mercy without sounding full of herself.

"You mean this has happened before?"

Good question. Said a lot about Mercy that she had solid questions. She'd had to do some serious recall to come up with the last episode. Her mind raced as she thought through all that she'd learned over the years. "Yes. Those spider cracks leak, and it's far from roses and champagne. What leaches out is a toxin of the lethal kind. For that poor man, a case of wrong place, wrong time." She didn't tell her that while she understood, somewhat, the nature of the toxic leak, she couldn't be sure that a demon hadn't escaped. She almost shuddered at the thought but caught herself. Didn't want to alarm Mercy or make her think she wasn't ready for the battle.

Mercy didn't move away from her touch. "I still would have liked to analyze that vegetation matter."

She was beginning to really like the way Mercy's mind worked. Instead of focusing on the death itself, she concentrated on why it had happened in the first place. Her intelligence and inquisitive nature outweighed any fear this danger presented. She'd make a good warrior. Another time, another place, she'd recruit her as a Guardian handler. Come to think of it, she still might, once this was all said and done. Her earlier reservations about having Mercy here with her disappeared. Right place and right time to team up with this interesting woman.

Aradia glanced over at her and said, "You may get the chance yet. This is the beginning of a cycle, for lack of a better description, and that's why I want to be at ground zero. We need to be proactive rather than reactive. We had no choice with that poor man, and I feel

bad about that. But we can prevent anyone else from being harmed."
She really did hope that wasn't a lie.

"Understood. Now, take a right at the next road." Mercy pointed where she wanted Aradia to turn.

Aradia followed her directions, and in fifteen minutes they pulled into a wide gravel lot. Trailhead signs warned that a current park pass must be displayed in the window, and while she should have been surprised when Mercy produced one out of her pack, somehow, she wasn't. For someone getting dragged into a fight she didn't even know existed twenty-four hours ago, she could make any Eagle Scout proud.

"So, if I understand correctly, Tim, Clemons, and Rufus are on the east side." Mercy pointed east. She clearly had a great sense of direction. More to like about her.

"Yes."

"Then we're going to want to take the west side, closer to the crack where that man died." Now Mercy looked toward the west.

"Yes." Aradia followed her gaze. Beautiful with the majestic mountain, acres of wildflowers, tall grasses, and various species of trees. Without the threat of evil, it would be glorious and soothing.

Mercy opened her door and stepped out. "Let's get our gear and then follow me, and I'll get us where we need to be."

"Okay." Boy, did she sound dull with her string of one-word answers. Mercy probably wondered if she had any grasp of the English language beyond *yes*, *no*, *okay*. Sure to instill a sense of confidence in Mercy.

In the backseat, Tara used body language to tell her she sensed the heightened vibes in the air. As soon as Aradia slipped Tara out of the seatbelt harness, she jumped out of the truck on full alert. The moment her paws touched the ground, her head went up, and she took off running.

Mercy frowned and turned to Aradia with visible concern. "Shouldn't you call her back?"

Aradia shook her head as she pulled out her pack and slipped her arms through the straps. Large and actually quite heavy, it contained everything she and Tara would need for several days. She hoped it wouldn't take that long. In fact, tonight would be a good time to stop evil from leaching anything else into the world, but she knew better. The forces of darkness that always hovered so close, waiting for any opportunity, didn't give up easily. Or ever.

And she hadn't shared something with Mercy yet—the Black Moon. The threat of a breach at the portals always existed, and that was why teams like Tim and Clemons were located in areas where portals were believed to exist. It was why she bred and trained Guardians. Why her family had done it for hundreds of years.

Then there were events that turned everything upside down. They took the threat of danger to frightening levels. One of those events, that would happen again soon, was the appearance of a Black Moon. In the right hands, the power of a Black Moon could make a breach unstoppable. In two nights, it would rise again for the first time in many years. For now, she'd keep that information to herself. She prayed they'd stop all of it before the moon became an issue.

Aradia looked in the direction Tara had run. The girl had speed and determination and had already vanished from sight. "She's working, and we need to let her. She'll come back to take us to any place that needs reinforcement, and if, God forbid, a demon escapes, she'll be able to hold it at bay long enough for us to banish it."

"She can do that?" Mercy looked amazed, which warmed her heart. All her dogs were special. Tara even more so. Something about the beautiful girl set her apart and always would. She supposed after all the years of work, she'd found her heart dog.

"She can." She shifted her pack until it settled against her back as it should, tossed her sunglasses into the truck, and then her gaze met Mercy's. "She will."

Mercy felt like she should be scared. She wasn't. Odd that it seemed like her destiny lay out there where the wild grasses grew tall and thick, the mountain soared, and if she were to believe Aradia and Tim, demons threatened to spill out into the world, bringing chaos, evil, and death. Sort of on the fence about the whole demon thing, but hey. Stranger things between hell and heaven, as Mom used to say. She'd keep an open mind and open eyes. Surprises weren't her thing.

Particularly considering the strange death that had happened out here. Even if she hadn't been able to fully study the vegetation and determine what toxin might have triggered it, Mercy couldn't think of anything native to the area that could cause death through absorption. Dangers existed out in nature in every part of the world. Things like mushrooms, flowers, and plants. How many people had been unintentionally poisoned by eating wild mushrooms? Easy enough to do if a forager wasn't fully schooled on the mushroom varieties. This wasn't the case here. Maybe the guy ate something he shouldn't have, although Frank had texted her that preliminary reports pointed toward the toxin having been absorbed through the skin. When things quieted down later, she planned to make a few more calls. Pick a few very educated brains. Surely the expert herbalists would have come across a similar situation, rare as it might be. They would be able to shed light on what happened, because right now, she sure couldn't figure it out.

It also wasn't that she discounted anything Aradia had told her thus far. She could buy into the cracks, except that didn't make it any less important to understand the biology. At least to her. A few might call her obsessed. All right, perhaps more than a few. She could live with being called obsessive. Obsession was part of what made her successful. A lot of what made it possible for her to not just survive on the farm, but succeed quite well. It had been a hard-won success, and she didn't plan to take things for granted now. Easy come, easy go. She knew better than most how a life could change forever in a matter of minutes.

Mercy pointed toward the distance. "There's an area not far from the scene that would be perfect for a tent. At this time of year, we can build a fire too, and we'll want one now that it's getting dark. It can get chilly around here, and if the rain sets in, it can get downright cold."

"I don't mind cold. Tara and I have camped in the snow."

Mercy didn't doubt Aradia for a moment. Pretty certain she had stories to tell, and someday, she hoped to hear them. "You might be ready for the Iditarod, but I'm not. I prefer dry and comfortable." True enough. Ever since that night in the park, wet, cold, and scared, she'd leaned toward creature comforts.

Aradia laughed lightly. "We've camped in the cold, in the snow, on the side of a mountain. Yup, we did it, but wouldn't like to do it again unless absolutely necessary. I can get down with dry and comfortable. Tara is a lot more flexible."

Mercy laid her hand on Aradia's arm. As with every time they touched, a charge raced through her. This time, more intense. The way her vision dimmed made her fingers tighten on Aradia's arm.

Flames reached toward a sky dotted with millions of stars. Beauty mixed with waves of apprehension. Chills raced down her spine despite the heat rolling off the roaring fire. It wasn't the weather that turned her skin cold. The eyes that stared back at her from the other side of the fire did. Not red. Not wild. Not demonic.

Blue eyes as cold as an Alaskan glacier. Tall and muscular, a face that belonged on a Hollywood billboard, he sent ice through her. Someone that beautiful shouldn't exude the kind of evil that rolled off him.

"Beware, little one." His voice was soft, lyrical, as if he could launch into an aria at any moment.

"Who are you?" Her words echoed the fear tearing through her, taking her back to her childhood and another cold, dark night. Her stomach rolled, and for a moment she thought she'd throw up.

"I am called Beliar, and you may bow to me." His lips curved into a smile that would have lit up anyone else's face. His didn't.

"Why are you here?" How she wanted him to go far away. How she wanted to run as hard and fast as she could. Her feet felt as though they were encased in concrete.

"To kill you." His smile stayed on his face. Brittle. Icy. She screamed.

"How did I end up on the ground?" Rocks bit into her back, and overhead the stars sparkled in the ever-darkening sky. The scene might feel romantic except for her still-rolling stomach and the trill of fear racing through her.

Aradia held out a hand to help her up. Mercy didn't take it. The last time Aradia touched her, something awful had invaded her mind. Instead, she lay staring at the sky, trying to get her bearings.

"You dropped like a hot rock." Aradia kneeled next to her and stared into her eyes, searching for what? Her long hair, freed from the hat she'd had on earlier, framed her face.

Mercy pushed herself up to her feet and took a step away from Aradia, who also stood. "That's a new one."

With her eyes narrowed, Aradia continued to study her. "Are you afraid of me? You have nothing to fear. Not from me anyway." Did she hear a tinge of disappointment in her voice?

Mercy shook her head and then spoke the truth. "Not you exactly." Yes, the touch seemed to have been the catalyst. Not for a second did she believe the darkness that had washed over her had anything to do with Aradia.

"Then what?" A bit of hurt shone from those beautiful blue eyes.

Might as well be honest. Not exactly the time or the place to hold back. "Afraid of what I might see if I touch you again. It sent me to another place, and he was there." Did not want to go there again either. Something about that guy sent a chill straight to her soul, and she shuddered as though an arctic wind had hit her hard. She looked into Aradia's eyes, and it clicked, her belief in demons just solidified. On the fence no longer.

Aradia kept her hands clasped behind her back. "Tell me what you saw. Tell me who you saw." If she was offended by what Mercy said, her words held no hint of it. Instead, her questions were filled with more urgency than offense. The hurt she'd seen in her eyes a moment before vanished.

Mercy took a deep breath and told her everything from the moment they touched and the second she found herself standing in front of the roaring fire. When she finished relating all the details of the disturbing vision, a shadow passed over Aradia's face. Not disbelief. More like fear. "Did he tell you his name?"

She'd remember that word until her last day. "Beliar."

"Damn." Aradia bit her lip, and her eyes grew dark. It clearly wasn't a name she wanted to hear.

"Who is he? He seemed bad, as in very bad." Even now, long after the vision, her nerves still tingled, and not in a pleasant way. His creepy lilt would echo in her head forever.

Aradia nodded, her expression grim. "He is bad, and worse, he's powerful. This is not good on a whole lot of levels. We've got to stop him."

Took Mercy a second to process what Aradia had just said. "Wait a minute. You think he's actually here?"

Aradia blew out a long breath. Their eyes met, and once more a chill slid down Mercy's spine. "If he's not, he's very close. We don't have much time."

❖

Pretty, trusting Mandy would undoubtedly be more than a little surprised by what August wanted to do with her. Quite naive to believe a handsome man wanted only to share a friendly conversation, and that would be it. Hard to feel sorry for someone that oblivious. Seriously, did her parents teach her nothing? Who got close enough to a total stranger to let them take advantage? Even at church. Maybe, especially at church. Had he become a father, his children would have been provided with a much better education as to the ways of the world.

Shortly after he drove out of the city limits, a perfect location revealed itself. The nice thing about this area was the lush vegetation. Complete beauty for the beast to accomplish his mission. Not that he really considered himself a beast. Some might see it that way, after the fact anyway. He preferred to look at his actions as a necessary stepping-stone to greatness. Every great advancement required sacrifice on the part of some of those brought into the fold. He could do the hard work in order to reap the great payoff. Every action had a purpose, and that's what set him apart from a true beast.

The light sedative he'd injected into her arm when he'd had her safely restrained in the back seat acted quickly, and she breathed slow and easy in a matter of minutes. He drove, enjoying the silence, while she had no idea he'd turned away from the church and begun to drive in the opposite direction, the lights of the city growing dimmer. The sedative wouldn't keep her out for long, and that was okay. He only needed it to keep her snoozing just long enough for him to get set up.

He pulled off the road, where a rough, apparently rarely used access road gave him enough space to tuck the SUV out of ready sight of the main road. Its black color helped to shroud it within the shadows. Someone would have to try hard to notice it, and he suspected no one would. His work would proceed without interruption. Opening the rear passenger-side door, he caught her before she tumbled to the ground. Still out, she wouldn't move, and he didn't have a worry about leaving her there for the time being as he scouted the area. He shifted her back into the seat, leaving her looking like nothing more than a young woman taking a nap.

From the back, he grabbed a bag that he slung across his shoulder. Inside, it held everything he'd need for the ritual, except Mandy, of course. She represented the most important element of tonight's activities. Overhead, the sky grew darker, although thankfully due to the passage of time and not the herald of an impending rain storm, which happened often in this part of the country. Not that rain would stop him. Weather wouldn't change the effectiveness of his work. Lack of rain, cold, or other adverse weather conditions did make the whole thing a lot more pleasant. It worked for him.

In the old days, a fire made from olive wood would be the central point of the ceremony. Easier these days to bring forth the fire needed. He didn't have to go scout the surrounding area for dry, dead wood that would easily ignite. Instead, the candles he pulled from the bag were ones he'd made himself with camphor, laurel leaves, salt, and sulfur. They were as powerful, if not more so, than the olive-wood fires of old. Magic, like all things, evolved and grew over the centuries. His had grown more than most, and he leaned into that advantage now. First, he walked off a large circle, stopping every few feet to set down one of the small candles. When he finished that task, he walked it all again to make certain the configuration created a perfect and tight circle. No room for error. Not really his style to make mistakes, and he wouldn't run the risk now.

Confident all was as it should be, he turned and walked back toward the SUV. Time for the centerpiece. "Come on, lovely girl." He laughed as he opened the passenger-side door and caught Mandy before she tumbled out onto the ground. "Umph," he muttered as he strained to hold her. He'd had to estimate the dose for a woman her size, and it could be possible that he took it a little too far. Oops. Her chest still rose and fell, so there was that.

She proved to be a lot more trouble than he'd like. She couldn't walk in her current state, and despite his level of fitness, he couldn't heft her up and over his shoulder. The only option he could see: drag her to the middle of the circle. "Good god, woman. Have you no pride? You're as big as a heifer."

At his berating tone, she blinked and opened her eyes. Surprised him that she'd be able to do that, except she didn't look his way. Her gaze appeared to be locked onto something out in the darkness. If she were to go home tonight, the drugs would do their job, and she'd never remember any of this. A nice little side effect of his substance of choice. Easy enough to get his hands on too. Only needed to know the right people, and oh, did he know the right people. They seemed to come to him, drawn in like worshippers to a messiah. Given that she wouldn't make it home tonight, it didn't really matter if she remembered or not. Her eyes closed again, and he continued to drag her through the underbrush. In the distance an owl hooted. Made him smile as he imagined the forest creatures welcoming him. They could all sense his greatness.

After dropping Mandy in the middle of his circle, he gave himself a minute or so to catch his breath. He'd definitely feel this exercise in his shoulders come morning. It would be worth it. No pain, no gain. He smiled at his own joke.

As his heart rate returned to normal, he took time to slip out of clothes, folding them before setting them outside the circle. From his bag he took a bottle of water and a clean cloth. He used the water to soak the cloth and the cloth to wipe himself down. A light breeze blew across his skin, drying it quickly. He tossed the bottle and the cloth outside the circle. Ready now.

Well, except for the last thing he'd need from inside his bag. As with the candles, he'd forged the knife himself. Tools made by one's own hand always carried far more power, and he would never use anything that might weaken his work. Anything and everything that gave him an edge, he utilized. Mama didn't raise no dummy. Well, Mama didn't have much to do with his upbringing. Too weak, and she didn't fully grasp the potential of her only son. Her loss. His gain.

Ready at last, he straddled Mandy, who moaned softly, her eyes still closed. Her fingers twitched. Were the drugs losing their potency? Not a problem. This would be done in a matter of minutes, and even if the potency began to lose its edge, she'd remain woozy and weak. Holding the knife in both hands, he raised his arms. No time like the present.

His head tipped toward the sky, August began. "Oh, Dark One, come to me now. See that I welcome you with great rejoicing. The underworld stirs with life again, and your children journey toward me for a triumphant return. Cleanse me—mind, body, spirit—that I may rejoice in the return of the chosen ones. That I may reign as their ruler."

He smiled as a warm wind brushed against his skin, a hint of sulfur on the breeze. His words were heard. Overhead, the moon, full and bright, sent down its golden light. Another sign. "Hear me, for now I draw near. Hear me, all who sleep uneasy in an unjust prison. Receive now my gift, and be full of life. Hail to the Dark One. Hail to me, the rightful Demon King."

He plunged the knife into Mandy's chest.

Chapter Ten

The more Aradia thought about it, the more she realized that having both Mercy and Rufus here with their gifts of sight had to give them an added layer of protection. The reality that the majority of the battle would still fall mostly to her, Tim, and the Guardians didn't change a thing. Despite the burden, any bit of extra help would be welcome. What Mercy had just told her sent her pulse racing. Helpful, yes. Bad, also yes.

She sank to the ground and put her head in her hands. "Damn." Had to think quickly about what to do next. She could almost hear Belair's footsteps across the ground coming closer and closer.

"Help me out here. I'll be the first to admit, I'm not up on demon hierarchy. I can tell you about the plants out here, but demons, no. So, who's this Beliar? I'll tell you what. He scared the crap out of me. Weird thing is, he was extremely good-looking. For a man, anyway."

Aradia raised her head and studied Mercy. Wasn't that last comment interesting? She'd felt a draw to her right from the start. Now, it grew even stronger. Definitely glad she'd brought her along. "He's a major demon, and yes, he's been described as incredibly handsome. It's part of his arsenal of weapons. He uses it to suck people in before he destroys them."

"If you go for that." Mercy's gaze didn't leave hers.

"Yes, if you go for that." Her breath almost caught.

"Not my thing." Mercy said it quietly. "You?"

She shook her head. "Nope." First time she'd admitted that truth out loud. Oh, how she'd tried to be what everyone wanted her to be. She'd even married her best friend. He'd been so good to her. Other than Tim, everyone in her life had been straight, and she'd assumed she was too. She'd still been married on the day of her epiphany. Not that she'd admitted to her husband or anyone else why she had to leave the marriage. He'd been hurt, but only a little, and she had to wonder what that meant. Her fingers strayed to the gold band as it lay against her skin. Now, after all the years of solitude and silence, she stared into beautiful eyes and wanted to get lost in them. No more silence. No more solitude. No more denial.

What a messed-up time to decide she wanted to step out into the light. To take the kind of risk she had been avoiding for years. Sort of tracked with the rest of her life. She did things the hard way.

Mercy's words tugged her away from her introspection. "Good." She gave Mercy a tiny nod. "So, what did that whole thing mean? Why did this Beliar come to me?"

The conversation's reversion to demons was probably a good thing. No need to get into personal issues right now. Better to stay focused on world-ending evil. She'd been giving thought to Mercy's vision, and the conclusions she drew didn't bring any comfort. "I think we have more trouble coming than we anticipated. This feels way more dangerous."

Hard to explain the level of darkness that accompanied the demon Beliar or, as some called him, Belial. Handsome and charming, he could appear as the picture of hope and light. The façade hid an evil that would harm any and all who crossed his path. That he appeared in Mercy's vision brought chills deep into her bones, both because of what it represented and because she wanted to ensure her new friend's safety. How she wanted to believe Mercy's vision foretold what might happen and not what had already happened.

Mercy adjusted the strap on her pack and looked up at the sky. Her expression darkened, and she almost sounded scared. "We better get going."

Not wrong. Night was growing deeper and darker the longer they stood here. Not wrong to be a little scared either. "Agreed." The hike might help her think more clearly.

"What about Tara?" Once more Mercy glanced in the direction of the mountain, the same direction Tara had taken off running the moment she'd left the truck. An aura of nervousness came from her, and Aradia couldn't tell if it was concern about Tara or the lingering terror from the vision. She wanted to reassure her about everything, except she'd be lying.

The one thing she could share was her lack of worry about her dog. Tara would locate Aradia, as she always checked in during the course of a search. Never a need to babysit her. She knew her job and did it well. If an issue arose, Tara would let her know. That's how all the Guardians worked. "Don't worry. She'll find us." She hoped her confidence came through in her words.

Mercy looked around, frowning. "Are you sure? She's been gone a long time." Failed on the confidence sharing.

"I'm sure. She can track us with ease, and besides, she'll have been heading toward the cracks. She'll start at the most recent evidence of a potential breach and work her way out from there." A little worry niggled at her, and she opted not to share it with Mercy. Such weirdness was happening out here that she'd be a fool not to be concerned. Even as well as she trained all her dogs, evil had a way of changing the rules.

From the moment Tara had raced away from the truck, Aradia had known where she'd headed, and that did give her comfort. Tara would have the area surveyed by the time they arrived. When they got there, Aradia would be able to tell through her dog's behavior what she'd found. Once they got the information, she'd radio Tim to learn what Clemons had reported. They might be canines, but they had a way of communicating with their handlers that rivaled written reports. Mercy would learn that soon enough, and hopefully, that would give her some comfort too.

"Okay. I believe you." Mercy nodded and started walking without further question. "Let's get going before it gets so dark we can't see anything. I know my way around the mountain, but darkness muddies everything. Twice as easy to trip and fall in the dark." Again, a little shake in her voice. Maybe just the strangeness of the situation. Maybe something else.

Aradia looked up to the west and had to agree. "I marked the location with my GPS earlier when we took a look at the body location." She glanced down at her handheld GPS unit and started walking. "Follow me." Then she looked over at Mercy and smiled faintly. "That was a little dumb. You were actually there before I arrived, so I'm guessing you have the coordinates too."

Mercy smiled back, something Aradia was grateful to see, and held out her own small GPS unit. "True enough, but lead the way. I'll follow you."

Aradia liked the sound of that. She'd like it better if it weren't for the fact they were walking into danger of a magnitude that worried her.

❖

If pressed, Mercy would admit to being somewhat insulted by Aradia's "follow-me" comment, given she'd been there first. That Aradia caught herself and offered an apology of sorts counted for a lot. Made her like her even more than she already did. Something about the self-aware woman, and her beautiful dog, resonated with her. She not only wanted to follow Aradia here. She would follow her anywhere. It had been quite a while since she'd been drawn to anyone like this. To be more accurate, it was the first time she'd been drawn to anyone like this.

Mercy gazed at the darkening sky, and a shiver rippled through her. She blew out a quiet breath as she reminded herself that it was her problem to deal with so she wouldn't become an anchor during this endeavor. No need to air her neuroses to a beautiful woman working to save the world from darkness and evil. A woman she already found fascinating and wanted to know better. She just had to keep her secrets close and remain calm. That way, no one would be the wiser. A couple of sideways glances from Aradia made her think she wasn't hiding her misgivings very well. She'd have to do better. No need to become an anchor out here.

When they closed in on the area where the body had been found earlier in the day, Tara was there waiting for them, just like Aradia predicted. "Wow. You weren't kidding about her, were you?" Easy to see what Aradia meant earlier about Tara working. The tension in the dog's body and the intense look in her eyes told a story.

Aradia nodded toward Tara. "No. I wasn't. If anything, I underplayed her abilities."

"Why is she lying there like that?" Tara held a down about five feet away from where the body had been discovered. She'd watched the two of them hike toward her, not moving. At the very least Mercy would have expected her to come toward Aradia in greeting. That had been her experience with most dogs, although she'd already begun to understand that Tara and Clemons were not most dogs.

"She's telling us to beware."

"How do you know?" Though she didn't move, and Mercy could tell she remained on the job, nothing beyond that seemed special.

"It's the alert and the position of the body. See how she's in a down, but her body's tense?"

Mercy didn't notice the distinction until she pointed it out. Once she did, it became very clear. Tara wasn't just resting and waiting for them. "Beware" seemed to roll off the dog like the sound of a fog horn. "She senses danger." A little chill slid down her spine. It took effort not to shiver.

Aradia nodded. "She does. We'll camp here."

Now that she'd made it to the same page as Tara, Mercy wasn't sure that idea was such a great one. More than her personal issue with the night. "If the danger is concentrated here, shouldn't we give it a wide berth and keep an eye on it from a distance rather than sit on top of it?" Shadows began to crowd in on her, and she shoved her hands into the pockets of her jeans.

Now, Aradia shook her head. "We'll steer clear of the poisonous vegetation, even though I neutralized it earlier. Still, I want to stay near the cracks. If they spread even a millimeter, I want to be ready to act."

"We can stop it from growing?" All beyond her comprehension. Not a stretch, given this would be her first hunt for demons. Last thing she imagined when she got out of bed this morning. Potential killers wandered into her life now and again, but demons not so much.

"I've trained for this my whole life, and yes, barring something unanticipated, Tara and I can stop it. Not only that, we can seal it. That's the biggie."

"Why not seal the cracks and call it good?" That would make more sense to her. Why not stop it beforehand rather than wait until after it actually happened? Mercy was missing something important here.

Aradia dropped her pack and glanced around. "It's more of an infrastructure thing. The cracks are showing outwardly as tiny and unthreatening. Beneath, they're broader and more dangerous. We have to close them all the way down, so we wait. It's critical we target the center. That's how we'll stop them."

Mind blown. Interesting that in a few hours she'd gone from yeah-right-demons to how-do-we-stop-the-demons. "Who knew this all existed out here? Those of us who live around here thought of it as only an active volcano, not a doorway to the underworld."

Aradia knelt and opened her pack, beginning to pull out items. "Kind of the don't-judge-a-book-by-its-cover situation. Things are far too often more complicated than they appear on the surface. Not to mention it's human nature to see what we want to rather than what actually is."

That lesson had already begun to sink in big-time. She'd never look at the mountain the same way again. Also made her wonder all of a sudden if Mom knew more than she'd shared with her. Training as an herbalist had been wonderful, and she loved her career. Learning the craft was equally as wonderful, but had Mom known this day would arrive? Had she wanted Mercy to be prepared and ready to help? Mom could be sneaky like that. Mercy dropped her pack too. "Copy that. Well, let's set up camp before it gets pitch-black." She glanced up at the sky again and willed her hands to stop shaking.

August estimated it would take less than twenty-four hours before someone noticed Mandy missing. No worries about the timeframe. He'd be long gone before they figured out she wasn't coming home, and it wouldn't even be a big deal if someone remembered him. By the time anyone got close to determining his identity, his power grab would be complete. He'd be above mortal justice. Not that he wasn't already. Human accountability had never applied to him. His father's death remained a primary example. He chuckled softly at that particular memory.

At the hotel, he showered, changed into clean clothes, and ordered room service. Amazing how a cleansing ritual triggered his appetite. As anticipated, his muscles were already letting him know that he'd lugged a fair-sized woman hundreds of yards into the wilderness. Worth it. As was the time he'd spent covering up the drag marks made when he pulled her into the circle. When he drove away, the ground leading up the ritual circle looked little different than when he'd arrived. Someone would have to walk all the way in before they'd discover Mandy's body. He figured it would be days, if not weeks, before that happened, given the unused look of the service road. Mandy might be missed soon enough, but her final resting place would remain undetected for a long time.

Room service delivered, August handed the young man a decent tip. Not too low, not too high. The kind that wouldn't make him stand out. He finished the steak and sat back as he brought a glass of the high-end wine to his lips. Some might think it wrong to pollute his body with alcohol after the extreme cleansing ritual. He disagreed. It might be bad if he'd opted for a cheap, rot-gut version. The fine red came with a spendy price tag, and it deserved its cost. It enhanced the sensations that flowed through him, all of them letting him know he walked a path of righteousness. Many had come before him intending to harness the power of the underworld. They failed. He would not.

After taking a healthy drink, no need to sip, he picked up his cell and punched in a number. Maybe the wine made him a little reckless, or maybe it put him in the mood for some fun. He leaned toward the latter. Might as well embrace the joy along the journey. "You ready to die?"

Willa didn't sound surprised by his call, as though perhaps she expected it. "Fuck you, August."

"You wish." She'd been a very skilled and willing partner in bed, about the only place they actually meshed. The thought of sleeping with her now made him throw up in his mouth a little.

"Can't believe I ever saw anything in you." Venom in her words. It would darken her face too. He remembered it well and how ugly it made her.

"I'm as sexy as they get." Not bragging. Truth, and she often didn't appreciate the truth. The ugly face she'd be making would get even uglier.

"In your own head."

"You'll be seeing things differently by this time tomorrow." It might have been better to leave Willa alone, except she made this all so much fun. She started it, after all. He took great delight in winding her up, especially considering her attempts to do the same thing to him. Tit for tat.

"Oh, that's the only thing you're right about, but let me clarify. I'll be seeing you exactly the same, but things will definitely be different." Interesting how calm and assured she sounded all of a sudden. Made him wonder what she had up her sleeve.

"Always so confident." Consistent in her sense of self. The reality, her perception of self-importance exceeded her reality and always had. It had been cute, at first. A little girl with long, shiny hair, hands on hips, defiant and mouthy. It had soon gotten on his nerves. Now, decades later, it made his eyes twitch.

"I learned from the best."

"At least you learned something from me. Problem is, darling, it won't be enough." Regardless of what she'd learned after their years together, she'd never be able to harness it into the kind of power she'd need to defeat him.

"It will." She remained dedicated to her illusion.

"Oh, please enlighten me. Enough for what?" Could be interesting to hear what she thought she'd be able to accomplish. She had a habit of believing her own fiction. Should have been a writer instead of a woman with delusional fantasies of grandeur.

"To kill you."

CHAPTER ELEVEN

A radia worked side by side with Mercy as they set up a small tent and two folding, battery-powered lanterns that were a good size when they were extended to light up their little camp. Together, they worked in silence that was far from uncomfortable. It felt a lot more like they'd been doing this together for decades. From the moment they'd met, she'd enjoyed an ease she hadn't experienced before. Not even with her now-ex-husband.

Not exactly accurate. She worked amazingly well with her sister and with Lizzy. This was different, though, and she didn't have to have earned a doctorate to figure out why. Or, at least, a piece of it. Mercy was one of the most interesting people she'd met in a really long time. Attractive and engaging didn't hurt either. That they were bound to find themselves in a life-and-death battle threw a damper on getting to know each other properly. Or perhaps Aradia should think about it more as a trial by fire. If they survived this, and she held out high hopes that they would, that would be a good sign. Combining that with her out-loud admission of being attracted to women meant something. Right?

Stop. Stop. Stop. She shouldn't be focusing on her draw to Mercy when the world faced a very real threat. What waited beneath their feet screamed danger, and if she had any doubt, all she'd had to do was look at Tara. The nature of the threat showed in the intensity her Guardian displayed. Tara had finally risen from her alert, apparently satisfied Aradia understood her message, and had been out working the area since she and Mercy began to set up their small camp.

The only thing left to do now would be to reassess and secure any additional cracks. Tara showed great interest in the area, although the only true cracks so far appeared to be in the same spot where the man had lost his life. When they'd arrived out here earlier, she'd closed everything visible. She had to take the time to secure any that occurred after they left or risk a widening that could potentially allow an escape. Mercy's vision had her on the lookout for Beliar, who she believed might have already made it through. She hoped to be wrong, and they still had time to stop him from escaping the underworld.

"I have to secure the cracks." She grabbed a small bag from inside her pack and slipped a headlamp onto her head.

"What about the rocks?" Mercy's hand moved the light of her flashlight between the visible cracks and a nearby mound of rocks. "What do we need to do to fix those?" She pointed to the cracks that weren't there earlier.

Aradia held up the bag. "It's surprisingly easy and right up your alley, I think." She unzipped the bag. "Powdered death-cap mushrooms."

Mercy's eyes widened. "You're not serious? That substance is incredibly dangerous. I'm less concerned with wildlife, as they'll avoid it, but it terrifies me for Tara and Clemons. There's no antidote if they ingest it, even if we could get them out of here and to a vet quickly. Just so you know, it would take us a couple of hours to make it to the nearest vet clinic."

Aradia walked toward the disturbed ground, her light tilted down so she could study as she moved. Important not to miss anything. The directed beam of her headlamp helped a lot. "I know it's dangerous, and trust me, it's okay. You have to understand, the Guardians are not your run-of-the-mill dogs. They're trained from day one not to ingest anything other than food provided by their handlers. You could offer Tara a huge New York strip steak, and she'd walk away." It might be hard to believe and yet the truth. So far, she'd been up-front and honest with Mercy, at least when it came to the Guardians and her work with them.

"That's actually pretty amazing." No disbelief in her voice, the shadows hiding any expression on her face.

She had more to share and wanted to. "It's a safety thing for the dogs. The Guardians are special in many ways, including an otherworldly protection."

"I'm not following." Mercy stepped closer and peered down at the ground. Her voice was even, but the vibes coming off her were filled with tension. Could be nothing more than not understanding the Guardians.

She comprehended Mercy's confusion. Without the knowledge Aradia had, who would know, or even believe, the nature of these dogs? "Their ability to detect demons is the first. They're born with what I call the shine, and it tells me they are destined to be a Guardian. The second is more like a reward for the work they do. Conventional methods can't harm them. Bullets will miss them, arrows will fly past them, they can't be drowned, they can't be stopped. The only method of destroying a Guardian is to make it ingest poison. That's why we spend an inordinate amount of time training them to eat only what we give them. It's the one way we can protect against what could potentially incapacitate or even kill them."

"That's incredible."

If she'd told this to Mercy when they first met, no doubt she'd have laughed at her, while topping it off with the expected eye roll and perhaps a suggestion that Aradia suffered from delusions. Funny how in a matter of hours her perception had changed. No laughs. No eye rolls. No suggesting she might be having delusions. She'd made the right call to share with her.

Aradia glanced in the direction of Tara's path. "I have to say I think it's pretty amazing too. I grew up around the Guardians, and it still astonishes me. They are freaking fantastic." It wasn't an exaggeration. The statement came from her heart.

Mercy put a hand on her shoulder, which surprised her, given the earlier fear that contact would induce another terrifying vision. This time only warmth, and she didn't take her hand away. "Has anyone ever been able to poison one of the dogs?"

Good question. Smart woman. With Mercy's training, she'd understand better than most the danger of the powdered mushrooms. "That I'm aware of, only once has a Guardian been successfully poisoned, and that happened a couple of centuries ago in Tibet. We breeders and trainers stepped up our game after that, and since then, those who want to release the demons into the world have tried and failed repeatedly to do it again."

Bothered her that one of the Guardians had been killed, even though it had happened hundreds of years before her time. Very good that those responsible for the Guardians, like her, came up with solutions to make as sure as they could that it wouldn't happen again. She'd do anything to keep the dogs safe, and the knowledge her predecessors had passed down helped her to do just that. Guardians or not, she hated losing a single dog. Unlike humans, herself included, dogs could be counted on to be honest and true.

For a few seconds, Mercy searched her face and then nodded slightly. "All right then, I'm with you. Let's plug this thing up with the powdered mushrooms. There's enough evil in the world already without allowing help to flood in. Finally I understand a use for those mushrooms that actually makes sense."

Relief loosened the tension that had been building in her body. "Helps to keep Tara focused too. If she doesn't have to worry about that." Aradia pointed to the ground. "Easier for her to keep her attention on what else is out here if all the cracks are sealed."

"There's more?" Mercy turned full circle, the beam of her headlamp bouncing on the ground.

Aradia didn't look down. Instead, she stared out into the darkness that continued to fall like the theater curtain. She hated to turn up the tension, but she also didn't want to lie to Mercy. "Oh, yes. There's always more."

❖

The ominous way Aradia said those last few words sent a chill down Mercy's spine. That danger existed out here wasn't in question. That it went far deeper than she imagined changed things. Particularly with blackness starting to wrap around them. At least when she put her hand on Aradia's shoulder she didn't sink into another creepy vision. Small favors and all that. Besides, one demon in her head was one demon too many.

As much as Mercy wanted to help and not just be a bystander, Aradia suggested she move out of the way, and she agreed, if not somewhat reluctantly. There could be more to the cracks that she might not recognize. Bad enough what they saw in the daylight. No need for ugly surprises in the pitch-dark, and she'd be a fool to suggest her level of skill in this arena was anything beyond sorely lacking.

"Are you sure I can't help you?" Before she stepped away, Mercy offered what little she could. At least she could try to be helpful, all the while hoping Aradia didn't notice the way her hands trembled.

Aradia shook her head. "I appreciate your offer. Truth is, it's actually better if you stay back a bit." She pulled out a respirator and disposable gloves, holding them out for Mercy to see.

Mercy's respect for Aradia grew as she watched her slip on the protection. Not only did she have amazing dogs, correction, Guardians, but she also had mad respect for plants. That spoke to her herbalist's heart. "Smart move. I didn't bring any protection with me."

Aradia looked at her, her pretty eyes distorted by the face mask, her voice oddly distorted as she spoke. "You'd most likely be fine, but I don't want to take any chances with the powdered mushrooms going airborne. I have only the one respirator, and inhaling any of the powder isn't a risk I'm willing to let you take. Besides, it will take me only a couple of minutes to close these things."

She smiled and stepped back. "Fair enough." Aradia adjusted the strap on the respirator and slipped on gloves before unsealing the container of powder, Mercy stepped back even farther. Her point was well taken.

While Aradia worked at fortifying the cracks, Mercy moved toward the trees. The wind picked up as she walked, blowing her hair around her face and making the tree boughs sway. The wind carried the scent of the forest, fresh and wonderful. She always wished she could capture and hold the serenity that nature so freely offered. It was right there, just beyond her fingertips, if only she could reach out and grasp it. Pull it close and hold it tight. Mom had tried to help her, to banish the ghosts of her past. Mostly she succeeded. Out here, the ghosts still waited in the darkness. Made her wonder if she'd ever heal completely.

Mercy stepped into the tree cover, her heart pounding. Not going to give in to the fear. So many years had passed, and the time had come to let it go. *Be strong. Be fearless.* Tara raced toward her, head up as if to capture the scents on the wind, her body tense, her paws pounding against the hard earth. "What is it, girl?" She forgot her own terror.

Tara stopped in front of her, which surprised her a touch, as she'd expected her to run past and to Aradia. Instead, she looked up at Mercy and then back in the direction she'd run from. "You want me to go with you?" Sure seemed that way. "Okay. Show me what's bothering you."

The words were barely out of her mouth, and Tara turned back to the woods where the trees crowded closer together. She ran after her. At least Tara seemed to sense that Mercy wasn't a real runner, and the pace she ran stayed right in her wheelhouse. She skidded to a stop a couple of minutes later, her breath coming quickly. Tara hovered at her legs. She put her hand on her head. "Yeah, girl. I see him."

Tara hunched close to the ground, a low quiet growl in her throat. For at least a minute they stayed like that, Tara on the ground and Mercy watching from behind the trunk of a large pine. He looked normal enough. Handsome, actually, though not particularly tall. A face she instantly recognized as he stood staring up at the sky, smiling. Goosebumps broke out on her arms, and she swallowed over and over as she tried not to throw up.

She leaned down to Tara. "You stay, girl. I'm going to bring Aradia." An idea occurred to her. Hoped it would turn out to be a good one. She raced back to the clearing where she'd left Aradia sprinkling the powdered death-cap mushrooms. Once she got close enough to see her, she called out, "Aradia!"

"What?" Aradia knelt next to her pack, stowing her gear back into it. She zipped it closed and looked up only when Mercy didn't respond right away.

"You need to come with me now." She sounded breathless, and her heart pounded. Not necessarily due to the run.

"What's wrong?" Aradia rocked back on her heels, and concern flashed over her face. "Tell me." Her words held an urgency.

Trying to even her breath so she could speak coherently, Mercy gave herself a few seconds to breathe before she blurted out, "Tara found your demon."

❖

Laughing, August ended the call with Willa. He'd anticipated this scenario for so long, and now that it'd finally arrived, it turned out to be way more entertaining and satisfying than anything he'd imagined. Made him think of karma, with a hand on his shoulder telling him: watch this. Yes, that much fun.

He threw back the rest of the wine in his glass and then filled it again. A cause for celebration without any concern for soiling his purified body. With the level of divinity he now possessed, the amount of this most excellent wine that he might consume wouldn't diminish him in any way. Besides, it went down warm and beautiful. Trite as it sounded, he felt like a million bucks. Oh, hey. He smiled. Wouldn't be long before he'd have a million bucks. Owning the world had a way of doing that for the gifted. Money, women, power, and admiration. All of it would be his.

The wine sent warmth throughout him, and when the tremor hit him, it went almost orgasmic. First time he'd combined drink with destiny. If he'd known that it would enhance the sensations like this, he'd have tried it sooner. Then again, he'd never been this close to the ultimate success before. Everything about this adventure happened at a new and much higher level. Or perhaps it would be more accurate to characterize it as a lower level, given where his minions would be coming from. His laughter heightened his most excellent mood.

He walked to the window and stared out into the night. In the distance, a church spire, lit from within, rose into the sky. He never really did buy into the God and Satan mindset. Good and evil, sure. Those forces existed and were far more powerful than the idea of a creator and a fallen angel. His minions were evil, plain and simple. That's all he needed to turn the world into his kingdom. Bring enough evil into it, and all that good would evaporate like rain on a hot day.

It might seem like he bought into religious beliefs, given he'd lured Mandy from a church service. That impression would be wrong. Not a case of his buying into religion as much as about the kind of people who did. The Goody Two-shoes variety could be counted on to show up in the houses of God. Case in point: Mandy. Didn't matter if he believed in her God or not. She did, or rather had, and her belief had kept her pure. That's all he'd needed for the success of his ritual.

Another tremor hit him, and he dropped his almost-empty glass. Red wine splashed on the wall and trickled onto the carpet, leaving a small, dark stain, like blood. He pushed the glass away with his foot. Once more, he turned his attention to the world outside the window. The sensation that had raced through him this time wasn't from a demon stepping out from the underworld. This one warned of danger. Damn. Damn. Damn. "How in the fuck did you find me?" His breath caused a fog to form on the window.

So much for spending a quiet night here. One of the three— Willa, June, or Ama—had used their own particular set of skills to track down his current location. No psychic ability necessary to determine if he read it correctly. He stared outside and pressed his lips together. Right now, the three biggest pains in his ass walked together across the parking lot toward the lobby doors, the bright security lights highlighting their smug faces.

Now, he stomped on the fallen wine goblet. Shards of glass shot out from beneath his shoe. "Fine, *ladies*. You want to play? Let the games begin."

After his shower, he'd tucked the clothes he'd worn earlier into his bag. He hadn't unpacked anything else, making it a quick and easy exit stage left. He took one last swig directly from the wine bottle before leaving his room. Using the stairwell, he hustled down to the main floor, slipping out the doorway at the end of the long, carpeted hall. He threw his bag into the backseat of his SUV and got in behind the wheel. Instead of circling past the front entrance, he followed the parking lot around the back of the building, where he pulled easily into traffic. No need to announce his departure by passing the lobby doors.

He laughed as he put distance between himself and the hotel. "Bye-bye, suckers." His laugher brought tears to his eyes. When would those idiots learn they would never get a leg up on him? "Keep on coming, ladies. I have more rabbits in the hat." Now he really laughed.

CHAPTER TWELVE

Well, crap, Aradia thought. She said, "I had a hunch we'd see him after your vision. Kind of hoped I'd be wrong. Didn't really think I would be." She reached for her bag as her mind raced. As much training as she'd received over the years, this would be the first time she'd actually come face-to-face with a demon. Her hopes of never having to call on the lessons learned went up like the smoke of a campfire. "We've got to go back and stop him before he hurts anyone or, worse, helps others topside."

"Stop him? I'm not sure I'm up for that." Anxiety was clear on Mercy's face. In fact, since the sun dropped, she'd been noticing how tense Mercy seemed to be. The darker it got, the twitchier she got. Like she might be afraid of the dark.

Aradia put a hand on her shoulder. She remained twitchy over the causing-a-vision thing and kept her touch light, going more for reassurance than a strong connection. She almost sighed when nothing happened. Two for two, with no dramatic reaction to the contact. Maybe it had been an anomaly and not an every-time-they-touched event. "You'll need to show me. I'm assuming that Tara stayed to guard him." She'd be shocked if Tara hadn't continued to guard.

"Looked to me like she planned to stay rooted to her guard post. Her eyes never left him while I was there with her." Mercy stared into the darkness in the direction she'd just come from.

That was her girl. If Tara were a human, she'd be a four-star general. Urgency pushed Aradia forward to ensure her general didn't get hurt. "We have to hurry. Tara's big and powerful, but we can be sure of one thing—he'll try to hurt her. They hate the Guardians."

"He better not." At least for the moment, the uneasiness she'd noticed with Mercy appeared to be fading. Maybe focusing on Tara helped her deal with whatever made her uncomfortable out here.

Aradia took her hand off of Mercy's shoulder and then gazed out into the darkness. "With her skill set, she knows how to take care of herself. Still, I'd rather be there to make sure she's not injured. It doesn't pay to just assume. You know what I mean?"

Mercy squared her shoulders. "I do. Follow me, and I'll show you where I left her."

Aradia dropped to one knee and opened her pack. She pulled another smaller bag out. Didn't need everything she'd brought along. Only a few important items. If all went well, she could stop Beliar before he caused any damage. Hopefully, no one else was out here camping for the night. Unsuspecting strangers would be no match for the demon. At least she and Mercy had a fighting chance against him. "All right. Lead the way." She followed Mercy, who moved with the graceful step of an athlete.

About a quarter mile away, she caught sight of Tara, only she wasn't in a down and guarding an escaped demon. Instead, she ran toward them at full speed. Damn. A problem.

"That doesn't look good." Mercy said. "That's not where I left her. Not where I saw *him.*"

"No. It doesn't look good, and I don't see Beliar." Her nerves started to sing. Not a happy tune either.

"He was right there." Mercy pointed to a small clearing in the trees. Even in the darkness, Aradia could see the tremors in her hand.

"Show me." Aradia wasn't talking to Mercy. She commanded Tara, who made eye contact and then turned, racing away. She followed her, with Mercy right behind, at least initially. She was in good shape, but Mercy appeared to be in better shape as she followed Tara, her long strides putting her in front of Aradia.

Mercy skidded to a stop a few seconds later. She pointed down. "Oh, no. Another crack." The fear had returned to her voice.

Aradia didn't pause but kept going. "We'll come back to it." No time to worry about it right now. She needed to follow Tara, who was clearly in scent. As she ran after her, she considered the best way to banish the demon. After a brief pause, the sound of Mercy's footsteps came from behind her. Good. She didn't need something happening to her, and she preferred to have eyes-on.

"Stay close," she said over her shoulder. No time for a search-and-rescue mission should they become separated.

"Copy that." The words were a little breathy.

Tara slowed just as a scream came to them on the wind. A man's scream. At that moment, Clemons appeared out of the trees, a beam of moonlight hitting his tawny coat. At the same time, she saw him. Beliar. Mercy had called that one right. Definitely Beliar.

Clemons jumped over a body, and in the darkness, it became difficult to determine who it might be. As Tim came running from the trees, the light of his headlamp bouncing, she realized that more than likely Mercy's friend, Rufus, lay motionless on the ground. She prayed to the gods he wasn't dead. She hadn't known him long, but she already liked him.

Smiling, Beliar stopped and looked back and forth between them. A red glow surrounded him, as if he brought some of the fires from hell with him as he stepped out of the underworld. His expression was so smug it turned his beautiful face a little ugly. "So glad you could all join me. I do love a party, and it's been way too many years since I had a chance to enjoy one. I hope someone brought the wine." His laughter filled the air and sent chills through her.

"You won't be here long." Aradia kept her voice steady as she motioned for Mercy to stay behind her. It had come to her as they ran how to successfully conclude this encounter. Well, successful for them. Not so much for Beliar.

"Oh, you think your big, bad dogs can take me down?" His laughter sounded brittle. Made his beautiful face a little less beautiful, a façade that hid the darkness behind it. But not from her, and not from either Tara or Clemons.

Clemons stood alert and staring, his big body between Beliar and both Tim and Rufus. Tara did the same for her and Mercy. The Guardians held the line, low growls in their throats whenever Beliar took a step. He didn't push the dogs. As the saying went, not his first rodeo. Even with the dark forces at their back, demons feared the Guardians, and that remained their advantage.

Aradia stood tall and stared into his eyes. They were dark and almost seemed to flow like water in a black river. She kept her words even and hard. "They don't need to take you down. I'll do that just fine." How she hoped she would be right.

"Oh, aren't you scary." He laughed as he waved his arms toward them. "You stupid humans and your stupid dogs have no idea what you're up against. We're here to stay this time. Nothing you can do."

His threats didn't rattle her. No time for hesitation or second-guessing herself. She began to chant, pulling the words from a long-ago lesson that she'd hated at the time and now appreciated. "Beliar, Beliar, demon unwelcome, return to the underworld."

Mercy stepped forward and put her hand on Aradia's shoulder. Power surged through her and made her stand up even taller, her feet grounded, her spirit strong. The charge between them had returned, and gratitude filled her, though she kept her gaze on the demon, not looking away from his black eyes.

Aradia continued, and now Tim joined in, understanding in a flash what she could do with the banishment spell. "Belia, Belia, demon unwelcome, return to the underworld."

The demon's eyes grew hard. "No! Enough. Stop now. I command you." He reached his arm out and pointed toward her. "STOP!"

Their voices grew louder, his so-called command nothing more than hollow words. "Beli, Beli, demon unwelcome return to the underworld."

"Stop!" He screamed again as he tried to advance on her. Tara and Clemons moved closer to him, growling louder, their lips pulled back to show gleaming white teeth. He retreated. He might be willing to take her and Tim on, but he wasn't as eager to test the Guardians.

As his body began to shimmer and grow translucent, Aradia led Tim into the final verses. "Bel, Bel, demon unwelcome, return to the underworld. Be, Be, demon unwelcome, return to the underworld. B, B, demon unwelcome, return to the underworld."

His screams filled the night as his visage began to sink toward the ground. She finished the chant. "Demon unwelcome, return to the underworld."

He dissolved into the earth and disappeared.

❖

"How in the world did you do that?" Mercy couldn't believe what she'd witnessed. The man, correction, the demon, had been standing twenty yards away, solid and as real as any human. Yet, as Mercy and Tim chanted, he'd slowly begun to sort of dissolve until he sank to the ground and disappeared. Like a handful of dust thrown into the wind. Gray and voluminous one moment. Nothing but air the next.

She'd caught on after the second repetition that they were diminishing his name letter by letter. Such a simple change, yet by the time they completed the last one, he'd gone poof. If she didn't believe in magic before, she sure did now. Of course, she did believe magic existed in the world. But this took it to a brand-new level. The trembling in her own body faded as she witnessed the amazing display of magical power.

Aradia either didn't hear her or ignored her. Instead of responding to Mercy, she raced over to Rufus, which spurred her into action as well. Didn't matter how they did it, only that they did. Now, time to see to her friend and make sure he hadn't been harmed.

"What happened?" Aradia knelt next to Rufus, her fingers on his neck.

His eyes were closed, his chest rising and falling evenly like he slept, oblivious to all that had gone on around him. "Did the demon hurt him?" Mercy glanced back to where he had disappeared into the ground. She resisted the urge to run over there and stomp on it. "Motherfu…" No, a potty mouth wouldn't help here and probably wouldn't much impress Aradia.

Tim explained. "We were searching after we set up camp, and Rufus ran into him. Nobody expects a demon to look like a model. I doubt Rufus had any idea how dangerous the demon was."

Mercy noticed he didn't say his name again. Better safe than sorry? "Did the demon hurt him?" she asked again. Rufus still didn't move, and the shaking in her body started to return. This time it wasn't because of her fear of darkness.

Tim shrugged. "Thing is, I don't really know. He runs into a good-looking guy out here, who probably came across as pleasant and all. I suspect Rufus tried to tell him in a nice way he shouldn't be here tonight, and then that demon did whatever it is he did to Rufus. When we got here, we found the same thing you did. I don't know what happened." His voice caught, and Mercy understood. She felt the same way.

"Let me." Mercy usually avoided anything that might trigger visions. In the last few hours, it seemed like all she did was summon them. If somebody had told her a week ago that she'd be tapping into that side of her psyche willingly, she'd have told them they were out of their ever-loving mind.

Thing about it, Rufus had been one of her best friends forever, and if she could figure out how to help him, that's exactly what she planned to do, even if opening the door to another realm over and over scared the daylights out of her. What if that door stayed open after today? She shivered but knelt next to Rufus anyway. Worth the risk.

Putting her hands on his face, she closed her eyes and concentrated. She sent silent pleas to the universe, asking for help. Asking it, for the first time ever, to come to her. Waves rolled through her body—strong, warm. Rufus hadn't left her. Without speaking out loud, she reached out to him. *Come back to me, Rufus. I'm here. Tim is here.*

She'd seen the way Rufus looked at Tim. A little like love at first sight. She hoped maybe that might be the case, even though she wasn't much of a believer in that, or in forever love, for that matter. Regardless of her skepticism when it came to love, they would be stronger together. If what he felt for Tim made Rufus stronger, she was all for it.

His eyelids fluttered and opened. Mercy couldn't help it. She smiled and kissed him right on the lips. "Don't you ever do that to me again." A few tears slid down her cheeks. She didn't bother to wipe them away.

He smiled and kissed her back. "I promise to try not to."

Rufus pushed up and looked over at Tim. Yeah, there it was. That look that spoke so much. If they survived this, she could see a future for those two. Clemons came over and licked Rufus on the face. He laughed and hugged the dog. "Thank you, big man. I might have been out cold, but I could feel that you had my back. I owe you a giant steak."

Tim knelt down too and put one hand on Clemons's head and the other on Rufus's shoulder. "He most certainly did have your back. He wasn't going to let that POS get close to you."

"Good boy." Rufus hugged Clemons again.

"I wasn't going to either." Tim's words were soft, but a tone of steel resonated in them.

Rufus put his hand on top of Tim's. "Thank you." He put his other hand on the ground and started to push up. "All right. I've been down here long enough and gonna have bruises from the rocks." Tim rose with him but didn't let go. He rubbed his lower back once he made it to his feet. He gave Tim a look and then turned to Mercy and Aradia. "We've got bigger things to worry about than me getting suckered by a demon with a pretty face. And, yeah, I realize now he was one of those demons you've been warning me and Mercy about."

Tim stood close to Rufus. "You're right on that one, Rufus. Ladies, we need to talk."

Now that she felt confident Rufus would be okay, Mercy worried more about what she'd seen back in the direction of their camp. No way did she want to encounter another like Beliar. "There's another crack. We didn't have time to seal it."

Tim nodded and pointed to where Clemons and Tara moved in unison. The Guardians, assured that the humans were safe, had returned to work. "We need to follow them. Rufus, can you make it? If you need to wait here, I'll come back for you." His voice remained full of concern. Oh, there was definitely something happening between the two men.

Rufus nodded as he rolled his shoulders. "Bro, I may have taken a pretty hard tumble to the ground, but I'm good. I'll have some bruises for sure. I'll show them off as war wounds and be the talk of the town." Rufus always rolled with a situation, whether good or bad. She'd learned a lot from him over the years.

Mercy hurried back toward the danger spot and beat everyone. Pretty impressive for someone who hated the dark as much as she did. Maybe there was hope for her yet, or maybe all the years of farming had kept her in great shape. She stood near the dogs as they waited for the rest to join them. The crack had turned black, and she suspected it had something to do with the banishing she'd just witnessed. When they'd run by it earlier, it had looked completely different. More natural. It sure didn't look that way now. "Is it closed? Did your spell do this?" She'd figured it would take the power of the death-cap mushrooms to seal it.

Tim and Aradia stared at it. "No. It's not closed." Aradia reached into her bag. "I'm almost out of powder. I wasn't expecting to have to seal so many cracks. What do you have?" She looked at Tim.

"I've got it." He slipped his arms out of the straps of his small pack. "This will do it. Everyone step back."

As Tim sprinkled some kind of powder, he spoke quietly, the words too soft for her to hear. Another spell, she supposed. Funny how easily she fell into believing these two were magic. Seeing a demon in the flesh had a way of doing that, she supposed.

❖

August drove through the night, putting distance between him and the hotel. Let those bitches try to find him now. Not sure what magic they'd used to track him, given he'd made sure none of the more modern methods were enabled. No GPS. No phone tracking. He appreciated the twenty-first-century conveniences. He just didn't quite like the way they could track movements. It hadn't taken all that much effort to disable the tech that could be used to locate him.

Their rash action showed they'd all forgotten who he was. Who he descended from. Foolish on their part. He possessed all the power of his forefather, Dr. John Fian, and so much more. Compared to what August possessed, Dr. John had been an amateur. Infamy became his legacy after his torture and death. The family he left behind learned from it and grew until he alone hit the zenith of power. He studied. He learned. He practiced. He succeeded. He would be the King of Demons because the position rightfully belonged to him, and no matter what his sister did, no matter what Willa or Ama tried to do, it wouldn't be enough to stop him. A lot too late.

Driving north, he pulled into a truck stop in Troutdale for dinner. Nobody paid attention to a lone man eating chicken-fried steak and mashed potatoes at a table in the corner. The food was hearty, and the waitress called him "honey" several times. He hated that trite endearment and would have called her on it, except it wouldn't do well to draw attention to himself. Besides, a few minutes after sitting down, it became clear she addressed everyone she served like that.

Instead of coffee, he opted for Earl Grey tea and stirred in a bit of cream and sugar. Not too much. Wouldn't do to get fat and sloppy. As he sipped, he closed his eyes and blocked out the noises of the busy restaurant. The pull from the north remained strong, though a bit less urgent. He opened his eyes, and the here-and-now crowded back in. Voices, dishes clanging, a chime from the kitchen alerting a server to a pickup. The scent of coffee and fried food wafting through the air.

He sipped his tea. What had changed? What had they done? Never a question the Guardians would be there. A given. They believed they could alter the course of what barreled their way. The only truth, and the one they couldn't escape, was that he would succeed, and a new world order would belong to him alone. The Demon King. The more he said it, the more he liked it. Demon King. Demon King. Demon King. He wanted to shout it aloud and drown out the mundane sounds of the restaurant.

Once he returned to his vehicle, he repeated the title over and over. Parked in the far corner of the truck-stop lot, he leaned his head back and closed his eyes, still whispering to himself. A little too tired to finish the drive tonight. Besides, he'd need daylight to search for the portal. There'd be cracks and fissures, signs that would lead him to the right spot. Then, once and for all, it would be his. Hard to wait and yet he must. A true leader understood the discipline required to succeed.

A tap on his window made him snap his head up. She smiled and gave him a little wave. He lowered the window. "You wanna date?"

He glanced at her. Could be twenty. Maybe. Not too long on the job, as her face still retained some freshness. Her eyes told a different story. Also told him most likely why she stood at his window asking the loaded question. When he didn't answer right away, she frowned.

"You a cop?"

That made him laugh. "Little girl, I'm most definitely not a cop."

"You gotta tell me if I ask." She put her hands on her hips, or maybe her hips, too thin to have much in the way of curves.

He tilted his head and stared into her eyes. Not pretty ones. "I am not a cop."

Her smile returned. "So, about the date. You wanna party? You won't be disappointed."

For a few seconds he considered her offer and thought why not. Then better sense kicked in. He couldn't afford to sully his body after his purity ritual. If he went along with her suggested party, he'd have to find another Mandy before the Black Moon, and he was too close to his target to risk it.

"I'm sorry, darling. Not tonight." Purity won over pleasure.

She frowned, her disappointment clear. "You sure? I'm real good." She crossed her arms over her skimpy shirt. The marks on her arms told him even more about her.

"I'm sure." He gazed at her arms again.

She shifted from foot to foot. "Really? I'm good." She licked her pink-tinted lips.

He dug in his pocket and pulled out a twenty. He offered her the bill. "Not tonight. I just need to sleep for a bit, and then I'm out of here. You go get something to eat."

She smiled once more, and now he thought, eighteen, maybe. A big maybe. "Thanks, mister." She turned and disappeared into the shadows of the parking lot and the rows of big rigs parked behind him. He suspected that twenty wasn't going for a chicken-fried steak.

He put his head back against the headrest and drifted into sleep.

CHAPTER THIRTEEN

Aradia sat next to Mercy and across from Tim and Rufus. Interesting how close the two men sat together. They'd met only a few hours ago, and it appeared that something already brewed between them. Nice for Tim, who'd lost his partner to cancer five years ago. He'd been alone with only Clemons since then. Every time she asked him how he was doing, he said all he needed was Clemons. She didn't believe him.

At the same time, she kind of got him. They shared some similarities, like the fact she'd been alone most of her life. Not like she lacked good friends, had plenty of happy clients, and couldn't ask for a better sister. Even her ex-husband remained a friend. She always told herself it was enough. Deep down she knew it wasn't, and there were nights that reality kept her awake. She'd get out of bed then and head out to the kennels to sit with the dogs just so she didn't feel alone.

"How are you feeling?" Aradia looked at Rufus. His color had changed from the pasty white she'd noticed when he lay on the ground to a healthy hue. He'd bounced back quite well.

He spread his arms, hands up. "Feeling fine overall. A little weirded out by what happened." His resilience impressed her.

"What did happen?" They hadn't really talked in detail about it since sealing the crack and returning to the camp she and Mercy had set up. The four of them had decided to stay together after the incident with Beliar.

"Man," he muttered. "It all happened super-fast. I saw the guy, and it struck me odd that he'd be out there all alone. Even at that, nothing about him screamed dangerous. Nice-looking dude, smiling and waving hello. The thing that did make me stop for a sec—he wore street clothes and carried nothing with him. Out here, whether it's a long hike or a short one, people will have at least a small pack. More strange, most folks aren't hanging out here once it gets dark."

"Makes sense he'd catch your attention, and even more so given why we're out here. Tim, where were you and Clemons?" She hadn't quite connected the dots yet as to why Rufus would be somewhere different. Like her and Mercy, she'd expected them to stay close together. Worried her that they'd been apart.

A shadow crossed Tim's face as he cut his eyes to Rufus. "A fluke that we got separated. Clemons found a couple of cracks, and I was following him to get them closed and make sure a bigger problem wasn't brewing."

Rufus glanced at Tim before returning his gaze to Aradia. "Not his fault we weren't together. I heard noises, which turned out to be that guy walking. I followed the noise without letting Tim know what I was doing. That Beliar dude went directly east of Tim and Clemons. We sure didn't mean to get separated. It just happened." He took Tim's hand.

A picture formed in Aradia's mind, and it all started to make sense. Her worry lessened. A little. "Got it. Go on."

Rufus continued. "He smiled at me all friendly, and for a second, it seemed cool, except for the street clothes and no-pack thing. Then when I got close to him, he reached out and tapped me on the forehead. One finger, that's all, and I'm telling you, I've never felt anything like that before. It wasn't good either, like fire roaring inside my body, and the second he took his hand away from my face, I was out. Total blackness until I woke up to your mugs."

Aradia grew cold. Not good that a single touch took Rufus down. They were lucky he hadn't been killed. Said a great deal about his inner strength. "How do you feel now?" The fire thing concerned her, though he looked well enough.

"By the time I came to, that sensation was gone. I feel pretty normal now." He kept hold of Tim's hand.

She nodded to him and then swept her gaze over all three of them. "We need to stay together. This is evolving fast, and we can't afford for something like that to happen again. Rufus, you were lucky. If we hadn't come along when we did and banished him back to the underworld, you'd most likely be dead."

After what he'd just gone through, it might be cruel to be that honest with him. This wasn't the time to pull punches. Critical that they all be on the same page here. The Guardians could do a lot to warn them and to give them the space they needed to do their work. But the Guardians couldn't do it alone, and neither could she and Tim. It would take their little village to make sure no more demons came through to hurt anyone else or, worse, take over the world. They couldn't allow that to happen, which meant they couldn't afford mistakes.

"The cracks are closed, and the dogs will continue to patrol the mountain tonight." Tim sat on a downed tree next to Rufus. "We should take turns resting. Come morning, we're going to have a lot of work to do. I feel it." He patted his chest.

A gust of wind blew over Aradia, picking up her hair and tossing it around. She brushed it back and took in a deep breath. An astringent smell filled her nostrils, making her shiver. Message received. She looked over at Tim and held his gaze. "Black Moon."

He nodded. "Yeah. Black Moon. We need to be ready."

Aradia agreed. Things could change fast when optimal conditions existed, and the better prepared they were, the faster they could shut this threat down. "You and Rufus can get some sleep first. Mercy and I will keep watch. Okay with you, Mercy?" Her adrenaline had her wired, and sleep would be hours off. She hoped Tim and Rufus might be better able to rest now.

Mercy nodded, her eyes wide and bright in the light of the lantern. "That works for me. Have to say, after all this today, I'm not real tired anyway. I'm a little wired." Good. They were on the same page. Hopefully, the men were too.

Rufus had one hand on his hat as he tipped his head back. "I don't think I'll be able to sleep." He glanced at the tent. "Somehow a demon knocking you out has a way of making you want to stay awake for like the rest of your life."

Before Aradia could respond, Mercy got up and went over to give Rufus a hug. "Try to sleep. For me. Please." She took off his hat and kissed the top of his head.

He returned her hug before he stood. "Okay. For you I'll give it the old college try." Aradia didn't miss the glance he gave Tim. Sure, he'd do it for Mercy. Despite the gravity of the night, she managed not to smile.

❖

For a few minutes, the sound of Rufus and Tim chatting quietly inside the tent floated through the night air. Then everything went quiet. In fact, too quiet. They were out in the middle of the wilderness, yet it felt like they were inside a padded booth. No soft conversation from the men. No birds. No rustling from small animals moving through the underbrush. No wind swaying the branches of the trees. No nothing.

"Anything strike you as odd?" Mercy sat next to Aradia on the ground. Would have been nice to have a couple of chairs, but they'd decided to travel lighter, so they left their chairs in her truck. The ground was hard and cold, without a single vibration. If not for Aradia's comforting nearness enveloping her, Mercy would be trembling once more.

"Beyond how tight those two seem already?" Aradia nodded toward the tent. "It's heartwarming yet fast." No judgment sounded in her words.

Mercy shook her head. "No. That doesn't strike me as odd. Feels a lot more like destiny." She didn't add that she had an equal draw to Aradia. Now that, for her, was odd. She tended to keep her emotions pretty darned close. Then again, casual relationships had their advantages, and maybe...No. She glanced at Aradia out of the side of her eye. It could never be casual.

Aradia's words took her away from her uncomfortable thoughts. "Could be. Could be. Sort of a strange time for it to pop up, but hey. I guess destiny has its own schedule."

Mercy looked out into the night. "What I mean is, do you hear anything? Like anything at all?" More than her discomfort with darkness. The night her father abandoned her, there'd been noises everywhere. Most had been frightening. The one sound that forever gave her comfort had been the thump-thump of Mom's dog coming toward her. She forever associated the sound with a savior. Maybe that was part of what was drawing her toward Aradia—her dog.

Aradia's eyes narrowed, and she too looked around. "Now that you mention it, no."

"That can't be good." If anything, Mercy understated her feelings. The silence creeped her out.

Aradia stood and walked around scanning their surroundings. "It's a sign." More curiosity in her voice than discomfort or fear. Pretty certain no one had dumped her in a park at an impressionable age.

Mercy crossed her arms and pulled up her knees. "A sign something bad is about to happen?" Like what happened to Rufus and the poor man who died out here wasn't enough? Good chance she hadn't fully thought through the ramifications of demons walking the earth.

"In a way. I'm reading it as something bad is coming." Aradia tilted her head as though she listened to something Mercy couldn't hear.

"Damn." She'd had enough for one night. Actually, she'd had enough, period. Right now, it would almost be nice to go back to random people showing up on her doorstep asking for plants that could kill. At least she knew how to handle that scenario. Out here, not so much. She looked around, wondering if another demon waited to step out of the darkness to hurt them. It took a whole lot of effort to sit still.

Aradia took her hand, making her uncross her arms. "Mercy, we've got this. Yes, it's bad, but if we weren't here, it would be catastrophic. We're here and we're strong. In fact, with you and Rufus joining us in spirit, we're even stronger. We can stop them."

"You, Tim, and the dogs are strong. Not sure what Rufus and I bring to the mix." She didn't feel real strong right at the moment, even though Aradia's words helped. Her confidence in Mercy made her want to be tough and ready.

Aradia gazed out into the darkness. "I'll be super honest with you. I wasn't so sure at first either. The last few hours have changed my mind. It's like you said. It's destiny at work. I'm coming to believe you're meant to be here, and so is Rufus. None of this is a coincidence."

Mercy wasn't sure about that. All of this fell outside her experience. True enough that she sometimes had visions and her skill with plants came naturally to her. Not that she didn't work at it too. Natural skill wasn't good enough in any profession or calling. She studied, she learned, she improved. Something inside her drove her to be the best. She was proud of what she achieved and pleased that she'd made Mom proud. Still, in the back of her head she could hear the old warning: pride goeth before a fall.

She looked around, the darkness deep and complete. They were far from trailheads and roads where maybe lights could be found. And, maybe not. Out here, the land once scorched by the lava and ash that had spewed from Mt. St. Helens had been renewed. Reborn, as it were. It should be a place of wonder and grace. Any other time it would be. Tonight, it scared the shit out of her.

"Is it the volcano that makes this a portal location?" Mercy decided that knowledge would be her best weapon against the fear that threatened to immobilize her.

Aradia nodded, still holding her hand. "It does make it prime real estate for entry from the underworld. We keep a very close eye on all active locations. I think something about the lava draws them. Massive heat like the fires of hell is my guess."

"Pretty philosophical."

"Just sort of makes sense in my head."

Mercy relaxed a little. "Tell me about you and what you do." Yeah, diversion. Couldn't hurt for a few minutes to talk about something besides evil, death, and destruction.

Aradia's fingers tightened on her hand, the gesture reassuring. It felt nice. It felt comforting. Her fear of the deepening darkness lessened a little. "Demons have always been with us. Read texts from any of the world religions, active or abandoned, and you'll find story after story. My family has been around forever, fighting them and sending them back to the underworld. The Guardians too. The family business, so to speak."

Mercy liked sitting here holding Aradia's hand. Comforting in a way she'd been missing since Mom died. "The dogs are amazing." The more she was around Tara and Clemons, the more she liked them. She'd always been a fan of dogs anyway. Even more of one now.

Aradia smiled. "They are flat-out magical and have done more to protect mankind than anyone can possibly imagine. Tara and Clemons will guard nonstop until we're certain the portal is protected. They won't sleep, and it will take coaxing to even get them to eat. Their drive and focus is nothing short of incredible."

Wasn't hard to believe. Once the dogs seemed assured that the humans were safe, they ran off. Searching, she intuited. Making certain that if another demon managed to breach, they'd keep it at bay until Aradia or Tim could banish it. "Both are beautiful. Huge, but beautiful just the same."

"That they are. Whether they're born guardians or working dogs that I place in normal situations, they're all stunning. I love the part of my job that lets me breed and train these beauties. It also allows me to meet some wonderful people. Like you."

Mercy tilted her head and studied Aradia's face. The light of the lantern made her dark hair shimmer as though it were made of satin. "I'm nobody special. Just the person who had the closest rental."

Aradia shook her head. "True enough that it was your rental that brought us into the same orbit. It's a lot more than that, and you know it. You can feel it too, can't you?" She turned and stared into Mercy's eyes. The lantern light made her feel as if they were together in a cocoon. Safe, warm, intimate.

Her stomach flipped like she'd just regressed to being a teenager again. After a second to regroup, she found her voice and turned her focus to the danger of the night. "I think it's a case of the circumstances. There's the guy who died out here. Then Rufus dropping like that. And now this." She waved toward the quiet darkness with her free hand, not wanting to break the contact with Aradia. "Circumstances that have brought us here."

"That's not what I'm talking about." Aradia's words were soft yet packed with emotion.

She stared back into Aradia's eyes, and her stomach did it again. Some very not-teenager feelings rolled through her. No sense denying the obvious, no matter how many times she tried to change the subject. "I know." The two words were a whisper.

Aradia didn't break eye contact. "This has never happened to me before. Has it for you?"

"No." Girlfriends, sure. Feelings like marry me this second and spend the rest of your life with me. Never.

"Destiny."

"Maybe."

"Absolutely."

She trembled. "Destiny."

Aradia pressed her lips together before she said, "I want to kiss you."

For a moment Mercy stared into her eyes, her blue eyes even more beautiful in the soft light, and then she smiled. "I want to kiss you too."

Aradia leaned in and kissed her.

❖

"Come. Come now."

August sat up and looked around. "Hello?" How did he get out here? The last thing he remembered, he'd been sitting in his car, his head against the headrest after sending little miss party on her way with the twenty-dollar bill. He'd decided to take a few hours to recharge before finishing the drive up to Washington. Now, he stood in the middle of a grove of trees, a cool breeze blowing, and tall grass tapping against his legs. The scent of honeysuckles drifted to him across the wind.

"They're getting too close. Too powerful. You need to come now and set us free." A man stepped out into the moonlight. Tall, slender, and extraordinarily handsome, he had long blond hair that glittered as the light hit it. He was so handsome it almost took August's breath away, and given he wasn't into guys, that said a lot. August knew him immediately.

"Beliar." He couldn't keep the awe out of his voice.

He nodded slightly to acknowledge the greeting. "We've been waiting for you."

"I will set you free. You have my word." Not that the King of Demons had to give his word to anyone. Even a demon as powerful as this one.

A frown darkened Beliar's handsome face. "They have banished me."

"What? You made it through?" That did shock him. He'd never heard of a single one coming through without human intervention. It took someone with the powers of a king, like August, to facilitate reentry into the world. Without him, they should all be waiting below.

"I am stronger than you think." He stared straight at August as if attempting to intimidate him.

Nice try. A lesser man might tremble. Beliar didn't seem to realize who he faced. Should he point out the obvious? No, no sense in pissing him off, as tempting as that might be. At least not until August had a firm grasp on the power he'd need to rule the old ones like Beliar, as well as the others he intended to call forth. While there were plenty to choose from, he knew exactly who he wanted at his side—the best and most powerful that he would be able to control while harnessing their skills and abilities to mold the world he envisioned. All things were possible when they were in the right hands.

"Good." August opted for false flattery. Make him think the world awaited him. He'd surprise Beliar with the reality later. Surprises could be such fun. "We're going to need strength to defeat those who will come to try to stop us."

"They're already there." Again, darkness flowed over Beliar's face. "They are skilled, and they are dangerous."

He shouldn't be surprised, and really, he wasn't. More irritated than surprised. "I knew they'd move fast, but I thought I'd have more time."

"Time is a luxury of which you have none. Stop wasting it. Come."

He didn't like being told what to do by an inferior, even a preternatural one, and really didn't appreciate Beliar's note of condescension. He reminded himself to be patient and exercise a neutral appearance. The time would come soon enough when Beliar and those like him would know exactly who they dealt with or, more importantly, who controlled them.

He straightened his shoulders and said loudly, "I am on my way."

"Then wake up!"

CHAPTER FOURTEEN

Aradia couldn't believe she'd just said that and, even more, couldn't believe Mercy had said yes. A smile hovered at her lips while her heart pounded. Hard to take a step back when she really wanted to kiss her all night. "Okay. That was pretty nice." Understatement, but it would do for now.

Mercy smiled, and even in the dim light of the lantern, she was beautiful. "Very nice."

Her smile took hold. "So, you feel it too?" No matter what she might tell herself, the draw to Mercy had been immediate and had been growing with each passing hour. Despite the danger they faced, this feeling wasn't about to be ignored. The weight of the gold band was heavy on her skin, as if warning her to be careful.

"I could lie." Mercy tilted her head back and forth.

"I'd prefer you didn't." Confident in her life with the dogs, even with fighting demons, she didn't have the same level of confidence when it came to her heart. She'd failed the first test tossed her way, and she didn't want to hurt anyone else like that ever again. Now she did put her hand against her chest, the band pressing into her palm through the fabric of her shirt. Thing was, she'd rather be alone the rest of her life than to break another's heart. Though, if honest, she'd admit in this moment it might be a bit of a lie. After the kiss, a life alone was the last thing she wanted.

Mercy took her hand and drew it to her chest, no ring beneath her shirt. "Not typically my style, so the short answer is yes, I feel it too and, in the spirit of honesty, have since you showed up. You might not believe it, but I don't usually kiss my renters."

Aradia sat back, still holding Mercy's hand, and laughed. "Thank the gods. It would have been bad if you didn't feel the same way. I'm telling you, the draw to you is strong. And I'd be shocked if you went around kissing your renters. You don't seem the kissing-random-strangers type. Present company excluded."

Mercy chuckled. "Agreed on all points."

She kissed her cheek, happy to feel her soft skin against her lips. "I'm glad you're here."

"I'm scared about what's going to happen out here, but a bit less scared with you next to me." Mercy glanced back at the tent. "And with them around as well."

Aradia followed her gaze. "I'll tell you with all sincerity, Tim's the best, and I have a feeling your Rufus is too. He has a glow about him that I haven't seen in many people. The Guardians, yes. People, not so much. Definitely makes him a special man."

"He is amazing and can see things other people can't. I trust him with my life now and anywhere, anytime."

"That's quite the endorsement. Very glad because I think those two are headed toward the long-term." Aradia didn't hang out all that much with Tim, the distance between them making it impractical. Still, in the years since he'd lost his partner, he'd kept to himself. From what she'd seen, he hadn't let anyone in close. How Rufus leaned near Tim, and how Tim didn't back away said so much. Something special was happening there, and she was all for it.

Mercy nodded. "I'd put a hefty bet on that one. Rufus is smitten, and it sure looks like the feeling is mutual. I hope that's the case. Rufus deserves love. He's done a ton of good for many people and asked for nothing in return. Past time for love to come his way."

Once more Aradia glanced at the tent. "Tim as well. A man cannot live for missions alone, and that's what he's been doing since his partner passed away. He might say that all he needs is Clemons, and he might even convince himself that's true. I don't believe him. A sadness hangs over him, and I think Rufus can make it go away. Can bring the light back into his life."

"Sure looks to me like Clemons has given Rufus his seal of approval. I mean, you know the dog better than I do, but that's my observation."

Aradia liked the way Mercy read the dogs. People either got dogs or they didn't. Mercy looked to be a got-it person. "You're not wrong. I see it in Clemons too. He likes Rufus."

"Let's send up a prayer that it works out for them. All three of them."

"Consider it done." Aradia squeezed her hand, and Mercy squeezed back. Oh, did she like that. "They make a great trio. Two guys and a dog."

"Has all the makings of a match made in heaven. Or would it be a match born of hell's fire?"

"Let's go with heaven." She didn't like to give hell, or the underworld as she thought of it, any credit. Ever. She'd prefer to lean toward divine intervention of the white-magic kind.

"Done." Mercy leaned near and asked, "So, now what?"

Aradia would love nothing more than to be at Mercy's house sitting around the kitchen island sharing a cup of coffee and taking time to really get to know each other. A proper coffeehouse date, of sorts. But that wasn't in the cards for them right now, and if things went sideways, maybe never in the cards for them. Perhaps that's why she'd acted on the urge to kiss Mercy. If she died in the next few hours, at least she'd die having experienced the joy of connecting with her. It wasn't only Tim and Rufus experiencing something special.

Sadly, it would be some time before they could make a coffee date happen, regardless of how much she wanted it now. She sighed and said, "We sit out here and keep watch until the guys take over. Make sure the mountain stays secure and, hopefully, our lanterns don't run out of battery."

"What if there's a breach somewhere else? How will we know? More demons like Beliar could escape, and we won't realize it." The notes of fear crept back into Mercy's voice. Aradia tightened her fingers around her hand, hoping the contact would give her comfort. She wasn't wrong.

"Tara and Clemons will keep us posted on that front." It wasn't something she said just to make Mercy feel better. The Guardians were out there right now doing their jobs, searching the vast acres around them, inhaling the wind, listening for any sounds that didn't belong to the night. They would come back in a minute if they sensed danger or, worse, confronted a demon. She had great faith in their abilities and hoped she could pass that faith along to Mercy.

"It's a big area." She looked out into the darkness, frowning.

Aradia stared into the darkness too. The moonlight cut it a little, the stars sparkled, and yet the dark prevailed, deep and ungiving. Endless. She still had faith. "They're fast, they're smart, and they're exceptionally good at what they do. We've got this." She didn't add the "I hope" part out loud. Holding Mercy's hand, she could feel the slight tremor in her body. She wasn't sure if it happened because of their growing bond, the danger, or something else. It didn't matter. Not really. Just holding her hand made everything better, and that ring lying against her skin lost a bit of its heaviness.

From the outside, Mercy presented a strong, proud façade. Before the light had faded, she'd seen something else in Mercy's eyes that told her underneath she carried more. She ran a successful farm, was clearly well thought of in the community, and even law enforcement came to her for assistance. A successful, confident woman who trembled when the sun went down. Why? What kind of demons did Mercy battle? Would she trust Aradia enough to share them?

She pulled Mercy's hand up to her lips and placed one kiss on her palm. "Tell me."

The pause was long before she answered. "I don't know what you mean?" Mercy kept her face turned away.

With her thumb, she stroked the soft skin on the back of her hand. "Tell me." When Mercy pulled her hand away and continued to stare beyond their makeshift camp, she didn't take offense. She understood self-protection. She understood secrets.

"It's nothing, really. Doesn't have anything to do with what's happening out here." She clasped her hands together in her lap. Could be to keep them from trembling. Or, it could be to wrap herself in an invisible armor.

"I know. I also know that sometimes talking through our demons can banish them as effectively as what Tim and I did to Beliar," Aradia said. Big talk from a woman who didn't even speak her own truth until a couple hours ago. Irony at its best. She could live with it.

"It's embarrassing." Mercy continued to look away, the light of the lantern falling softly on her profile. Her long silver hair shiny, a gentle breeze picking up strands of it to blow it around her face.

"Embarrassing is my middle name," Aradia said. "I am so socially inept that I need a minder anytime I go out in public. I'm great with dogs. I suck with people. Trust me, you can't tell me anything that will make me feel less about you." Another truth bared out here in the middle of the wilderness. Keep it up and she'd be naked, metaphorically speaking, in no time.

"I don't believe it. You're so smooth and competent. Good family and a lifetime of purpose. You've been amazing since the second we met."

"Good families and purpose help. I won't dismiss that," Aradia said. "Who we are and who we become takes years of work. I don't know that I'm any less inept because of where I came from. I've just learned to cover that better. Funny thing is, I've managed to find peace in the in-between. I can't talk about it with everyone, but I know the ones I can." She looked pointedly at Mercy. Instinct drove her to push this subject. "You know I've never admitted out loud that I prefer women. I was actually married to a man." She pulled the gold band out from beneath her shirt and held it up as it dangled on the chain.

Now Mercy turned and stared. "No way. You were?"

"Oh yeah. I'd known him since middle school, and he was my best friend." She could still see him way back when, tall and skinny with a head of curly hair. He'd been cute back then and a handsome man today.

"Why did you marry him?"

The million-dollar question. "He loved me. Everyone expected it. I wanted to fit in."

"But you didn't."

She shook her head. "I so didn't fit in anywhere. I convinced myself it would all be okay if I just rolled with it. One day I knew nothing was okay, and so did he. I walked away, and ninety days later, we were divorced, much to the shock of everyone except us. We're still friends. We just went our separate ways. Thing is, I've kept quiet in all the years since. Didn't want to disappoint anyone."

"Your family doesn't know?"

Aradia thought about her answer for a few seconds. "I think they know, or at least suspect. No one has ever asked me outright, and I've kept the truth to myself."

"I'm really sorry. That has to be hard. Pretending is a lot of work."

"Amen to that." The work wore her down most of the time.

"Can I ask why you wear the ring on a chain?"

Did she want to share that particular secret? She stared into Mercy's eyes, and the answer became clear. A little voice in the back of her head pointed out that if she hadn't wanted to share, she wouldn't have shown her the ring. "It's a constant reminder of how easy it is to hurt people you actually love, and I don't ever want to do that again. Wearing the ring around my neck reminds me to be honest with everyone, including myself."

"Honesty, like being attracted to women."

Aradia nodded. "Like that and having the courage to say it out loud. To stop hiding."

Mercy said, "I've always known, and Mom did too. She didn't love me any less."

"Funny thing is, I don't think anyone in my family will love me less either. I guess it came down to I had to find the right moment to embrace my truth." Strange how that right time turned out to be at the base of a mountain with a woman she'd just met. Life could be so unpredictable and wonderful. One more reason to make certain they kept the world safe.

"Maybe you needed the right person." Mercy smiled.

She smiled back. "And there's that. Now, your turn. I shared mine. You share yours." Turnabout was fair play. Besides, for some unexplainable reason, Aradia sensed she needed to share her truth too.

Mercy blew out a long breath. "I hate the dark."

"Why?" She asked the question softly.

"When I was five years old, my father abandoned me in a park in the middle of the night."

❖

The fear she'd experienced all those years ago washed over Mercy just as strong now as when she'd been a preschooler staring into the scary darkness, alone and confused. Most of the time, she could tuck that painful time in her life away. Who wanted to remember a father, the person most could depend on to love and protect them, running away like a pro athlete? Even after all these years, she didn't want to relive a single moment of the experience. Instead, she preferred to live in the here and now. The past couldn't be changed. Her birth family couldn't be changed. How she dealt with it could, and that's what she'd spent a lifetime trying to accomplish. Mom helped her in that endeavor, and for the most part, it worked. Despite what her father had done to her—or tried to do to her—life had turned out pretty good.

"That's messed up." Arada's voice caught.

Most people would jump right on asking how, why, when, where. Seeking all the dirty little details. Not Aradia. She got to the heart of the matter, and honestly, she appreciated it. The simple act of acceptance without explanation meant more than she would ever be able to express.

She drew in a deep breath and let it out slowly. Hard to dive right into this one. Too many times it turned into pity, and the last thing she wanted to see on Aradia's face was that. "Let's just say he was a messed-up guy."

Not a trace of pity showed in her expression. "I'm sorry that happened to you. No child should ever have to go through something like that."

She'd been sorry too, her whole life. "It could have been worse. I could have died out there. I could have been attacked. I could have ended up a victim of the foster-care system or, worse, trafficked. None of that happened, and I believe some higher power looked out for me."

Aradia squeezed her hand and whispered, "Tell me."

Again, no questions. No digging for gritty details, and it made her want to share them all. She had to take a deep breath before she could get a word out. "My birth mother had died of cancer six months earlier. My father, despite being a patrol officer on the local police force, had always been the weaker of the two. When she was gone and he'd been left with this small girl child, he broke. His solution was to drop me off in the park and leave. No child. No little girl he couldn't relate to. No responsibility. Apparently, it made sense in his alcohol-muddled mind."

"You were five." There was a catch in Aradia's voice, and she got it. Decency couldn't comprehend someone doing that to a child.

"The darkness, the sounds, the isolation were so scary. I sat in a bush to hide, which made me feel a little safer, and I cried for what felt like hours. I wondered what I'd done wrong to make my father run away from me. I wondered that for a long time, even after I was loved and safe."

"It was him, not you." A hard edge entered Aradia's voice.

She nodded. "I know that now, in my heart anyway. But when you're a little kid and you love your parent, you can't see that. You believe he'd only do that to you if you'd done something bad."

"He was an ass." Now anger.

Mercy's anger had faded years ago. Not the hurt though. Not the fear. "Yes, and a flawed man. Thing is, he paid the price in the end. To this day, I'm not sure how he thought it would all go down. I've tried forever to come up with a rational explanation for an irrational act."

"There is no rational explanation."

"No. No, there's really not."

"How did you get out of the park?" Aradia's voice stayed calm and soft.

She closed her eyes and flashed back to that night. Much like this one, it had been dark, with a bit of moonlight and a few stars. Mercy opened her eyes. "A stranger found me. Or, rather, her dog did."

Aradia squeezed her hand. "Thank the gods for small favors."

Mercy smiled now. "I've thanked the gods every day since. The dog's owner became my mom, and really the only mother I've ever known. She's why I ended up here. My father, the respected police officer, went to jail, and he didn't make it there. Cops don't do well in prison, and within a year, he was dead. Hanged himself in his cell. My savior adopted me, and I never had to look back. She gave me my best life, even if she couldn't banish all my personal demons. She did enough, and for that I will be eternally grateful."

"She sounds amazing."

Hard to describe Mom and what she did for Mercy. How she changed her life. An angel who walked the earth. "She was, and through a cruel twist of fate, I ended up losing her to cancer. We had a lot of years together. She taught me everything, and she healed me. Mostly."

"The darkness." Aradia turned out to be a most exceptional listener.

A tiny shudder went through her, and then it was gone as quickly as it appeared. "Yes, the darkness. Sometimes, like now, it creeps into my soul and reminds me I was that little abandoned girl that the dark almost devoured."

"I'd say 'almost' is the operative word here. You did survive, and better than that, you thrived. You have a true gift, and I'm really glad the universe put us together." Aradia hugged her gently.

Mercy leaned into Aradia's hug. "I'm really glad too, and it's weird how the occasional vision thing always kind of bugged me, and Mom always tried to convince me that a reason for it would one day be revealed. Since meeting you, it feels like it's important, and that's a first. I think Mom was right about it."

"I believe we are given what we need. We don't know why until we need to know why. I think that time for you is now."

"I think you're right." It shocked Mercy how light she suddenly felt. The trembling in her body had faded as she'd talked, until now, calmness like a blanket warm and comforting spread over her. Maybe Aradia had been right that the words needed to be said out loud for peace to have a chance to settle in. Or, maybe it had something to do with Aradia herself. Her spirit also wrapped around her like a favorite blanket. She inched a little closer.

They sat together without talking as the moon moved across the sky. The silence, broken only by the occasional check-ins by Tara and Clemons, remained soothing and comfortable. When the dogs ran in, Aradia would get up and make them take a drink of water before they raced back into the night. Once they were out of sight, she'd sit back down. Each time she did, she took Mercy's hand again. No words were necessary. The silence remained the most comfortable thing she'd experienced in years. Maybe ever.

"Time to swap." Tim's voice made her jump, and her heart raced. Maybe she'd gotten a little too comfortable here next to Aradia. She hadn't heard him come out of the tent, and she didn't like surprises, particularly under the cover of darkness.

"We're fine if you want to rest longer." Aradia turned to look at him as he stood in front of the tent, stretching.

"Nope. We're good." Rufus came out of the tent and stood up, stretching his arms over his head. "I don't know about Timmy here, but I feel like I've slept a good eight hours. I'm a new guy and ready for those demons to try to get past us." He took his familiar hat and put it on his head.

"Same here. Rested and ready. You two take a few hours to recharge. We'll yell if anything happens." Tim held open the flap to the tent.

Aradia looked at Mercy. "We probably should." She nodded and pushed to her feet. She didn't feel tired, but that didn't mean she couldn't use some rest.

"The dogs alert on anything?" Tim let the flap fall and walked closer to the lanterns, though he peered out into the darkness.

Aradia shook her head. "Nothing yet. The air and the earth have been quiet too. Maybe a little too quiet. A ploy of bait-and-switch maybe? Lull us into a sense of false security."

Tim still continued to search the night. "I wouldn't put anything past them."

"You see anything?" Rufus looked to Mercy.

She wished she had something to contribute. "No, nothing. I'm not much help here."

Tim turned and looked toward her. "It's early. Save your strength. You'll probably need it before this is all said and done."

"You get anything?" Mercy asked Rufus. Sometimes stillness and quiet could open the gate for information to flow. His intuitive nature had him always receptive to messages from the unseen realms.

He also shook his head. "Nope. A big nothing for me too. At least nothing yet. I'm with Timmy. I have a feeling something's going to pop before too long. Not a thing to base that on except a feeling." He tapped his chest.

His feelings weren't random, and she took what he said to heart. "Then something is coming. Wake us up if anything happens or you see something. Okay? Promise?" She knew he would. She just needed to hear it.

Rufus put an arm around her shoulders and hugged her close. Into her hair he said, "I got you. Now sleep, at least for a little bit. It will help. I feel stronger after a few hours of rest."

She put an arm around his waist and squeezed. This man had become more than a friend, sort of a brother from another mother. No more so than right this minute. "I promise I'll try."

He kissed the side of her head. "Go get some beauty sleep."

Inside the tent, two mats were spread out. She dropped down to one and Aradia to the other. Trying to find comfort, she shifted and turned and pulled at the mat. Aradia whispered, "May I?" She didn't have to explain what.

"Please."

Aradia scooted close, put her arm around Mercy, and pulled her close. Peace flowed in, sweet and comfortable. She closed her eyes and slept.

❖

The sun peeked over the mountains as August continued his drive north. He pulled into a service station, filled the gas tank, and grabbed a very large coffee. For a convenience store, the hot, dark brew wasn't half bad. A long day stretched out before him, and that required starting the day off with something that possessed a good kick. Good or bad didn't really factor in. Caffeine did. His body seemed to sigh with contentment as he sipped.

At the edge of the state land surrounding Mt. St. Helens, he pulled over. Too large an area to simply wander around blindly. He needed more directions pointing toward ground zero. Time to call upon his very special skills and the wisdom of the Great Agrippa, who would reveal the hidden secrets he came here to uncover as well as assist in the subjugation of the demons he would release. He could open the portals if the conditions were right and release the demons into the earth through the same process. The tricky part, the part that only the special one could do, would be to control and rule over the demons. That would come later. First things first. A little assistance of magic to guide his feet.

He set his half-empty coffee in the holder and climbed out. The early morning hour meant he had to park along the side of the road at the entrance to a closed trailhead. Perfect, at least for the moment. A park ranger might get annoyed with his vehicle parked on the shoulder, thereby skirting the requirement for a park pass. He could live with it. In fact, it made him happy to thumb his nose at the park rules in the great state of Washington. He smiled as he hit the remote, the beep sounding to confirm that the doors were all locked. Didn't want to risk anyone disturbing his very special supplies in the back.

August walked toward the trees, across the flowing wild grasses, and then stopped. A buzzing beneath his shoes flowed up his legs and then his arms. As he expected, the point of maximum power had been revealed to him. This would be the precise spot to call for knowledge, to demand guidance due him.

With his eyes closed, he turned his palms toward the sky, tilted his head back, and closed his eyes. "You who are destined to sow the seeds of discord, who infuse hatred and violence into the world, where are you? Hear me now. See me now. Know that I am the alpha and the omega, and I call upon you to show me the way."

Slowly, he turned his palms toward the earth and, for a few moments longer, stood still with his eyes closed. The vibrations beneath his shoes built in intensity. He continued. "You who are destined to sow the seeds of discontent, who infuse fury and bloodshed into the world, where are you? Hear me now. See me now. Know that I am the father and the mother, the rightful ruler whom you shall bow to. I call upon you to show me the way."

A moment later, he smiled and opened his eyes. The wind picked up, and clouds covered the rising sun, casting a shadow over the mountain. Effective communication didn't always require words. Message delivered and received.

His arms spread wide, he smiled. "I hear you and I see you. Thank you all." He liked to be inclusive. True enough that demons tended to present as males throughout history, and many of the elders would have sent thanks to only the males. A wiser man than most, he knew that demons could be male, female, or even gender neutral. He welcomed everyone to his party. They all had their strengths, weaknesses, and their specific uses. Those who excluded them had no idea what they missed out on. Small minds and all that. Good thing he didn't fall into that category.

The sun came out again as he continued his walk, a bit of dew on the ground that wet his sneakers and pantlegs. The mostly cloudless sky promised a nice day to dry out. Besides, who really cared about wet shoes and clothes when glory spread out in front of him? Minor discomforts were easily ignored.

August walked back to where he'd parked, climbed into the driver's seat, and finished his coffee as he watched the sun brighten the morning. The coffee had grown cold. He finished it anyway. Waste not, want not. The driver's door open, he breathed in the clean, fresh air. For an area destroyed by the eruption of the mountain, it had come back perhaps more beautiful in the intervening decades. He thought of the saying: don't judge a book by its cover. Who would guess the secret harbored behind tall pines, flowing grass, and colorful wildflowers? Only those like him with a very special kind of education and knowledge. Oh, wait. There were none like him. He laughed.

August set the empty coffee cup in the holder and leaned his head back. No need to hurry. He'd have plenty of time to find the portal now that he understood the direction of travel. Once he arrived, he'd need darkness to complete the ritual anyway. And the moon. That very, very special moon. He closed his eyes and smiled.

CHAPTER FIFTEEN

Aradia woke up slowly. Warm and comfortable, she kept her eyes closed and enjoyed the sweetness. Made her want to sleep for a week. Then her eyes flew open as reality crashed in. She remembered where she was and why. She also remembered the woman she had her arms wrapped around.

Her heartbeat kicked up, coziness disappearing quickly. Evil and danger loomed outside the tent walls. Inside, peace and contentment—a fantasy, given the darkness that threatened. She liked the fantasy and didn't want to let it go. Who would believe that such beauty could come out of something so dark? She hadn't had even a blip of an idea when she'd gotten in the truck with Tara and begun her drive to the west side. The universe had a way of lobbing surprises at her when she least expected them.

"You awake?" Mercy whispered.

"I am," she whispered back and smiled a little.

"Can't believe I actually got a little sleep."

"Same." She tightened her arms around Mercy. How she didn't want to leave the tent and face reality. She'd always remember this moment of contentment.

"This is nice."

"Nice" didn't exactly describe her feelings. Freaking amazing would be a little more accurate. "It is." She hoped she didn't sound too breathy.

Mercy sighed and shifted away. "We better see what's going on outside."

Cool air dimmed the warmth they'd shared. As much as she'd like to stay right here, Mercy had a valid point. Still, she didn't move. "Five more minutes."

Mercy turned in her arms so that they were face-to-face. "Five more minutes." She kissed Aradia.

Warmth returned as their lips touched, and she put her hand on Mercy's cheek. "What is this? It's like too much and too fast, and it sort of scares me." Honesty came easily, and that scared her too.

Mercy's gaze held hers. "All true, and I don't know what it is exactly. But I'm not sure I care. It just is, and for the first time in my life, I want to let that be enough for me. You push away the darkness. Except for my mom, no one has ever done that for me before."

"Really?"

"Really, and I can't even tell you why. All I know is that it feels right, and who am I to fight the wisdom of the universe? Apparently, it thinks I need you. I don't plan to argue. I don't want to argue. It's like the night Mom found me. A little girl in a park, lost and abandoned. Hiding in the bushes, dirty and crying. In a moment my life changed for the better. I want to believe it's the same now, minus the abandonment, the bushes, the dirt, and the crying."

Aradia wasn't one to give in to emotion, yet tears pooled in her eyes. A few blinks to get back into control. "I feel the same."

Mercy smiled, her eyes soft. "Good. How about we roll with this and see where it goes. What do we have to lose?"

"Not a darn thing." This time, Aradia kissed Mercy. "I wish we could stay right here." She did with all her heart. Inside the tent walls, magic swirled, and she wanted to reach out and grab it. Pull it close and never let it go.

Mercy rolled onto her back and stared at the top of the tent. "If only we could. I'm afraid of what's out there. I'm also afraid not to face it. My mountain. My home. How dare they try to destroy it."

She sighed and rolled onto her back as well. "Right there with you. First, we face the darkness. Then, we stop it. And most important, we send it back where it belongs."

"And then?"

"And then you and I can give ourselves time to see where this thing between us will take us."

"That works for me." Mercy turned to look at her. "It's a date."

Whatever this was, she didn't want it to end. Her mother had talked about the silver lining to storm clouds over and over again. Growing up, she'd thought her mother's quirky personality made her always look on the bright side while brushing off the dark one. Given what they were all trained to do, to Aradia it had seemed more than a little naive. More than anyone, they knew of the very real evil that existed just beyond the sight of normal people. Though she did use the term normal in a quite loose way.

Aradia decided to continue her path of speaking the truth. "This is kind of new to me, and I don't mean relationships. I've had a few, and they were good, at least for a while, even if I kept them on the down-low. But our strong connection and how it occurred like a lightning bolt has never happened to me before. Scares me a little. Maybe a lot."

Mercy rolled to her side and propped her head on her hand. Her eyes were clear and bright. "Back atcha. New one to me too. And scary but in a good way."

Aradia sat up, feeling better that at least she wasn't alone in this situation. Business first, and then they could come back to the magic happening between them. "I guess there's no sense waiting. Regardless of what we'd like to do, we have to take care of whatever's out there first. We need to keep everyone safe."

Mercy sat up too, and Aradia couldn't help but think how great she looked with her sleepy eyes and tousled hair. She could get used to seeing it. Like every single day for the rest of her life. Nope. Nope. Nope. Not going there right now. Other things to do, like her job. She'd been raised to stop evil, and she'd been called here to do just that. Then? Well, she could think a little more about how to wake up gazing at soft eyes and tousled hair after they finished their work out here on the mountain.

Mercy leaned over and kissed her lightly once more. "We'll revisit this later."

"Yes, we will." She touched her lips with the tip of her index finger. Oh yes. A promise she would not break.

When Aradia stepped out of the tent, the early morning sun whispered across her skin. The sensation filled her with resolve, as though the golden light had gifted her with both courage and energy.

The soft wind warned of danger, while the light promised victory, and she chose to lean into the latter. She wouldn't be the first to come up against the relentless quest of demons pushing to take over the world or the humans who wanted to rule them. She didn't know who had come to try this time, only that they did. The demons knocked against the earth as if ringing a doorbell, and someone, somewhere heard the call. They would come here to try to claim the demons as their own, and she, along with Tim and the Guardians, would stop them. Didn't hurt that they could also lean into the skills of Mercy and Rufus. She might have trained to do the job without their skills, but that didn't mean she'd dismiss what they could bring to the fight. Only a fool would do that.

Tara and Clemons were outside, having returned to camp, and Tim was filling two stainless bowls. "Good timing." He handed her one of the filled bowls. He set the one he held down for Clemons, and she set the other in front of Tara.

Side by side, their heads dipped low into stainless bowls, the two Guardians ate. She glanced over at Tim. "Thank you."

Tim looked up at her. "They've been at work all night, though so far so good. They needed food, and I figured you'd be rolling out in time to be able to convince Tara to eat. I think they both really want to get back to work."

"Maybe we can get them to rest for a bit." She wasn't sure if either dog would go for it. They might have to be satisfied with getting them to refuel. They were magical in their ability to work for days on end. Just because they could didn't mean she wanted them to. That kind of nonstop alertness shortened their lives, and the thought of being without Tara didn't sit well with her. She loved all her dogs—those that turned out to be Guardians, even more. Tara stood out from every other Guardian she'd trained. Special in a way she couldn't describe, and she planned to do whatever it took to keep her as long as possible.

"I think we're good." Tim nodded toward the spot where the two dogs stretched out with their eyes closed. "Hopefully they'll take advantage of the daylight and recharge."

"Great." She smiled, happy to see her girl taking some time to sleep. Her relief lasted about a minute.

"You feel that?" Mercy looked at her with wide eyes.

"Damn it." Aradia looked over at Tara. Both dogs jumped up and took off running.

❖

"Rufus?" Mercy swung her gaze from Aradia's face to Rufus. The strong vibrations beneath her feet didn't abate. "Are you feeling that?"

Rufus blew out a long breath, put one hand on the top of his hat, and stared at her. "Damn straight. Shit is starting to get real."

"What was that?" Now Mercy looked back to Aradia. "You guys felt that, right? I know Tara and Clemons did." Both of the Guardians had moved fast, jumping up from what appeared to be deep sleep and running like racehorses in the direction of the mountain. They moved with grace and speed despite their massive size. Impressive under any circumstances. Super impressive given what came their way out here.

Aradia nodded. "Yes. The vibrations are getting stronger. Could be more cracks. The dogs will let us know. Let's all stay alert."

Mercy narrowed her eyes and studied Aradia. Something in her voice alarmed her. "Could be more cracks? What aren't you saying?"

Aradia pressed her lips together, and Mercy had the feeling she didn't want to elaborate. She expected more from her after everything that happened over the last few hours. "As strong as they're becoming, could be another breach nearby."

She'd been afraid of that exact answer. As new as this dilemma might be to her, over the last twenty-four hours, she'd begun to understand it in a strange way. Almost anticipate the course it might take. "What can we do? I feel a little helpless, and I want to do something, anything." Actually, she felt a lot helpless. She just didn't want to let everyone know where she currently stood. She wanted them to believe her confident and able to assist in any way she could.

Aradia looked toward the mountain. "Let's do a bit of hiking. See what we can see. Tim? You have any other thoughts?"

Tim had already picked up his pack and was in the process of putting his arms through the straps. "On the same page here. I want to see with my own eyes what the hell is going on out there."

"Let's do it." Mercy grabbed her small pack, took a drink from her water bottle, and then slipped the pack on. "We have to stop this situation."

Aradia nodded and once more looked to Tim. "Whoever is out there cannot get a jump on us, so let's roll. We'll take the south and east, if you two want to take north and west."

Tim and Rufus stood side by side. "We're on it. Rufus, you in for a hike?"

"As my dad would say, I'm on your six." He followed Tim as he left their campsite, walking in a kind of companionable rhythm that made it appear as though they'd done the same thing a thousand times.

Despite the gravity of the situation and the ominous feelings she got from the vibrations beneath her feet, Mercy smiled. Something about Tim and Rufus warmed her. As if the same sort of connection she felt for Aradia flowed between them as well. She hoped so. She also hoped they both stayed safe.

"They're going to be okay, right?" She looked to Aradia.

Aradia glanced down before she raised her head and looked at Mercy. "You want the truth, or would you prefer I lie?"

Hard to come up with a good answer for that very good question. She thought about it for a second and then answered honestly. "Got it. It's a solid maybe."

Aradia touched her shoulder. "You're a smart woman."

Mercy looked around and shivered. "A smart woman would probably turn and race back to the farm. Pretend all of this came from a really bad dream."

"All of it?" Aradia raised a single eyebrow.

Called her on that one. "Maybe not all of it. Just the demons-trying-to-destroy-the-world part."

Relief showed in Aradia's eyes. "Good."

"Still, it's hard not to want to run away from here." As much as she wanted to help, fear started to creep in, making her question how much she could contribute to the cause. While she might be an exceptionally skilled herbalist, she wasn't sure that translated well to skilled demon hunter. In fact, she was pretty sure it didn't.

Aradia put her hands on the straps of her pack and studied Mercy. "Could you really do that now, knowing what you do?"

Good point. She wanted to say that she could, in fact, go back to her home, and there it would all be business as usual. People coming to her for help with natural healing or, as in the most-recent potential customer, hopes for untraceable tools for death. She almost wanted to return to that scenario and her subsequent calls to law enforcement because they felt normal. As if the world had an order that made sense.

Demons didn't make sense. Yet, they were there just the same. She'd seen one, with her own two eyes, and no amount of denial could ever change that fact. Not at this point. Some moments in life shifted a person's perception. One of those moments had occurred for her when she saw Aradia and Tim banish that demon. No turning back at this point. Denial wouldn't cut it no matter how much she wished it could.

Mercy shook her head. No sense fighting the inevitable. "That would be a big, fat no. I'm not going to be able to look at this place the same from here on out. Everything has changed in the last twenty-four hours."

"Thought so. Welcome to my world. I take nothing at face value. Now, shall we go kick some demon ass?"

Mercy tugged at her pack and tightened the straps against her shoulders. She looked out toward the mountain as she adjusted it until it sat more comfortably against her shoulders. Tall and majestic with the rays of morning sunshine lighting up its peak, it filled her with awe. Beauty surrounded them, evil hiding right behind it. No. She'd never be able to walk away now. "I'm ready, if you are."

A lofty goal that she might not be up to. She didn't plan to say that out loud because she wanted to stay strong for Aradia. Perhaps for herself as well. After sharing with her last night, after sleeping with her arms holding her close, the shadows that had followed Mercy all her life faded. Not all the way, and she was okay with that. Given they'd been a part of her since childhood, anything that drove them back even a little bit felt like a win.

For a good ten minutes they hiked in silence, not catching sight of either Tara or Clemons. While she'd had dogs off and on throughout her life, the Guardians were something quite different. Their independence and dedication to duty amazed her. She'd be nervous if any of her dogs remained out of sight that long. Not Aradia. Confidence rolled off her, and she hoped she could capture a bit of it.

"Oh no." Mercy stopped and stared, her heart dropping. "Do you see that?" She couldn't keep the shake out of her voice.

Aradia had stopped about five feet ahead of her. "Damn it." No trembling in her voice, only disgust

"It's the same, isn't it?" The darkened earth screamed poison. The body on top of it would never scream again.

August picked up the empty coffee cup and stared into it. He could use another one or two to help him prepare for the day. Out of luck on that front, as he didn't want to drive back toward civilization to find more. Today, he'd be running pretty much on sheer energy. Sleep, not so much. Not ideal, though not a hindrance either. He'd have plenty of time to rest once he had everything in place. He could do another twenty-four hours without a serious drop in focus or drive. Given the coming rise of the Black Moon, he didn't believe he'd actually need that much more time.

From the back of his vehicle, he took a good-sized backpack and slipped in a couple of bottles of water, a pack of beef jerky, and, from the cooler, the ziplocked bag of doctored ground beef. He dug around until he found the zippered case with the filled syringes, as well as another smaller bag that held his special tools. All of the items went into the pack. The ancient book, wrapped for safety in black velvet, he slipped in last. He resisted the urge to unwrap it and gaze upon the words written inside, to run his fingers over the parchment pages and feel the power and wisdom of those who came before him. He had to content himself with the knowledge that later he'd not only read those words, but he'd also use them to take his rightful place in history.

The back open, he sat on the bumper and put on a pair of sturdy hiking boots. With them laced up, tied, and ready to go, he slipped on his pack and then closed the back. With the key fob, he clicked the lock twice and, hearing the telltale honk, slipped the fob into his pocket. As he walked away from his vehicle, he whistled softly. The sun promised plenty of light and warmth as it rose in the cloudless blue sky. The ceremony would need to happen once darkness fell.

That gave him many hours to use the welcoming light of day to locate the portal. It would be where his true majesty would manifest.

Every good wilderness guidebook stressed the importance of carrying a compass to avoid getting lost. Of course, in this day and age, who didn't have a compass on their phone? People who got lost now had to work really hard at it. He didn't need a compass of either type. Something better and more accurate than a compass would guide his feet. He just needed to start walking, and he did. The sun warmed his face, the air clear and fresh, the mountain rising majestic in the distance. All the signs pointed to a wonderful day. The buzz throughout his body promised an even more wonderful night.

Off-season, he didn't expect to encounter many, if any, other people hiking. Those who came every year to climb the still-rumbling mountain had already been here, tried and failed, or tried and succeeded. He wasn't much interested in the volcanic activity, or in mountain climbing for that matter. The big eruption decades ago didn't worry him either. The rumblings he felt now did interest him as they had nothing to do with an active volcano.

Well, sort of. Not exactly accurate to say it had nothing to do with the mountain's natural activity. That cauldron of magma resembled a siren's call to the demons he would control. The heat and violence drew them like moths to a flame. It's why August and those like him watched places like Mt. St. Helen's as closely as they did. For each, a mere matter of time before a portal revealed itself.

His SUV faded into the background as he walked on the path that led from the still-closed parking area. He'd had to slip around the pole gate that blocked entrance to the trailhead. Some state plebe would probably grumble when they arrived later in the morning to see his vehicle pulled off on the side of the road. The posted signs were clear that the park wasn't open until later in the morning. True enough for regular tourists. Didn't apply to him, and by the time said plebe arrived, he'd be miles away. Too bad if his SUV sat off the main road leading in. They could drive around it. Not like he'd blocked the road or anything.

For the first mile or two of the hike August stayed on the flat, well-tended path. No sense making the journey harder than it needed to be. Besides, his boots were brand-new, and he liked how clean they were.

Forty-five minutes in, the draw off-trail became an overwhelming sensation. The forces were sending him a strong message on his direction of travel. Not a fool, he followed the guidance coming his way even if his nifty boots were about to get dirty. Not like he'd need them after tonight anyway.

A Guardian appeared twenty minutes after he went off-path. A female, by the looks of her. A hundred pounds, maybe one ten. Not quite as large as the majority of the males he'd seen, which leaned more toward one thirty to one forty. Intense and powerful just the same. A hundred-pound-plus athletic dog wasn't one to challenge. All of these dogs were powerful, skilled, and very well trained. A real challenge for the uninformed.

This one came to a stop, her head high, her eyes intent on him. Her gaze narrowed as if she recognized his spirit of alignment with the demons. These dogs as a breed in general were smart, and the Guardians tended toward smarter than most. He didn't underestimate them for a second. Good thing he came prepared.

Slipping his arms out of the straps of the backpack, he unzipped the main compartment. The burger sat right on top for easy retrieval. He took three chunks out of the bag and tossed them in her direction. After she ate the tainted meat, it would take a few hours for the oleander to do its dirty deed. He'd planned for that contingency by drawing them out in the morning. The poison would have plenty of time to take effect well before darkness, and that's what really mattered. Get her out of the way before the big show, while he took it easy and waited. All he'd have to do was keep an extra watch for the dog's handler. Didn't need a handler getting in his way.

She watched him intently as the meat fell to the ground near her feet, sniffing the air while keeping her eyes locked on him. She didn't look at the offered meat or move toward any of what should be presenting as a high-value treat. What dog wouldn't accept a present of fresh ground beef?

"Come on, *sweetie*. Take one. You'll like it. I promise." He laughed. Oh, she'd like it all right. Gobble it up and enjoy the treat. Double benefit for him. First, with him as the human giving her something yummy, she'd see him as a non-threat. The guy who came bearing gifts. Second, it would put her out of commission, thus out of his way. "Come on, girl. What are you waiting for?" Any other dog would have snatched up and swallowed all three pieces by now. What was her problem?

Her body shifted, and he thought, ah-ha. Here we go. Didn't quite unfold that way. She didn't move toward the doctored treat. Rather, she shifted away from him. A subtle move that didn't pass his notice. He frowned as he studied her. What the hell was her problem? *Take the damn meat.* Given he didn't offer cheap hamburger, it had to smell fabulous. Not a believer in taking chances, he'd brought the good stuff. It should be working. It wasn't. He frowned and took a step in her direction.

In a flash, she turned and raced away. He stopped and stared at her retreating form. She moved as gracefully as a gazelle. A gazelle that sensed the presence of a lion. "Well, fuck you too."

He'd been certain his plan would work. Foolproof in theory. He'd been a very good student in his trade and knew from a young age that traditional weapons were useless against a Guardian. Didn't mean he failed to come prepared for any situation. He carried a small handgun in a holster at his waist, and why not? It wasn't only the Guardians he had to look out for. The bullets would be useless against a Guardian. The handler didn't possess the same kind of protection. Besides, the Guardians were still dogs, even if special dogs, and the promise of tasty red meat should have been enough to entice her. That she ignored his lure made him want to try the gun anyway. If nothing else, pulling the trigger would make him feel better.

He pulled it out of the holster at the same time he heard the sound of her running in his direction. Yes, indeed, he took off the trigger lock. He raised his arms and aimed it in her direction. No reason why he shouldn't just give it the old college try. As she came into range, he smiled. A second later he frowned at the sight of a man following right behind the dog. He didn't hesitate. He pulled the trigger.

CHAPTER SIXTEEN

Bad. Bad. Bad. The one word sounded in Aradia's mind over and over. She'd been on any number of missions throughout her many years of working with the Guardians. This, she'd never encountered before. Her mind raced through a lifetime of lessons trying, without success, to recall a lesson covering a situation like this one.

"It's toxic plants again, isn't it?" She stood staring down at the body of a young woman, her skin void of color, her eyes closed, and her lips tinged with blue. All around her the natural grasses had shriveled and turned black as charcoal. A scent, reminiscent of sulfur, wafted through the air. Not good. Not good at all.

Mercy knelt close, studying the vegetation while keeping a safe distance away. Unlike when they first met, this time, she didn't even attempt to touch the blackened plants. "It appears the same, except I don't understand. Like the man, skin contact with the plants shouldn't have killed her. Only ingestion causes fatal results. I can't think of a situation where absorption would do this."

"This isn't a normal situation. The rules of the order have changed." Scared her to say those words out loud. How could she fight against things she didn't see coming? Nothing in her training prepared her for what they were up against out here. Her mind raced, and she didn't care for the path she seemed to be going down. How she wished Sabina could be here to join their tiny army.

Mercy stood and brushed her hands against her jeans as if trying to rub off something bad, even though she'd touched nothing. "You're saying that the threat of the demons can alter the natural world?"

Mercy was following the direction of Aradia's thoughts. It helped to have someone close who could be that tuned in. "In a sense, yes. They take what they want, and right now it appears they're collecting souls." The only explanation that made sense to her. Perhaps Beliar had taken this soul before they banished him back to the underworld. Or perhaps something worse had happened out here. Someone worse. She shuddered.

"They wanted their souls?" Mercy stared at her, eyes wide but not disbelieving. More like drinking up whatever knowledge she could to help stop evil. "That is wrong on many levels."

To be honest, Aradia couldn't say for sure. Something in the ancient texts popped into her head as she studied the body. Something about the gathering of souls to increase their push into the world. In a weird way, it tracked. It also made her fear factor ratchet up. "I believe so. It helps them breach the portal."

Mercy bit her lip and shook her head. "No, no, no. I don't like it, and it can't be good. We can't let them do this."

They were on the same sheet of music. "It's really bad."

"I've got to call this in." Mercy put her hand in her pocket and pulled out her phone. She looked at the phone display and nodded. "At least we're in service range. I can call the sheriff's office."

Aradia would prefer to hold off, except she understood Mercy's position. Regardless of the impending threat, it wouldn't be right to leave this poor young woman out here unattended. Good people didn't do things like that. She liked to believe she fell into that category, and she absolutely knew that Mercy did.

She put a hand on her arm. "You call your people, and I'll let Tim and Rufus know what we've found. They need to be aware of the uptick in activity. I can check to see if they've found anything yet. Found anybody else taken by the demonic forces, and I'm hoping like hell they haven't. I'm sure they'd have called us by now if they had but will check anyway."

What a start to the day. Everything so far had been pointing to a disaster. This discovery added to the signs. At least Tara hadn't come back with anything yet. That gave her a little comfort. Then again, the evil that threatened liked the cover of darkness to do its primary work. As to the rise of the moon and, in this case, the Black Moon, daylight took some of its power away, and to overcome the protections she, Tim, and the dogs brought required every ounce of energy they could summon.

While Mercy called the body discovery in, she tried Tim. First with her phone, because knowing from the conversation Mercy held on hers, they had coverage here, and she hoped Tim did too. The call went directly to voicemail. He apparently didn't have service wherever he and Rufus had hiked. On to Plan B. She grabbed her radio and pushed the side button. "This is Aradia calling for Tim." She let go of the button and waited.

Within seconds, the radio crackled, and his voice came through loud and clear. So clear, she could hear the tension in his voice. "Aradia, this is Tim. I can't find Rufus, and I heard what sounded like a gunshot. Something's really wrong." The fear in his words set her nerves on edge. She glanced over at the blackened earth and unmoving body. Her heartbeat kicked up. *Too fast.* Things were happening too fast.

"Guns are not allowed out here." Now, that sounded dumb. Rules wouldn't matter to those who would be coming in response to the siren's call undoubtedly on the airwaves. That's how it worked with the demons. The call went out, and century after century, there were those who answered. In centuries past, they'd come with bows, axes, or swords. Given the array of weapons available in this century, it could be anything from a compound bow to a pistol with a suppressor to an AR-15 outfitted with a bump stock. The fact that bump stocks were illegal wouldn't matter to those who responded.

Static came over the radio for a second before Tim spoke again. "Aradia, we need you to come. Something is massively wrong, and I haven't seen Clemons or Tara in a while. Neither one of them has checked in with me. Have you seen them?"

Until this second, she hadn't been worried about the Guardians. They often worked out of sight. Now, uneasiness crept up her spine, and she didn't like it. "No."

"What if they did something to them?" The fear in his words grew deeper. "It's not like Clemons to go this long without checking back with me. If they've hurt him, I swear to God…"

The emotions rolling through her as he talked mirrored what she heard in his voice. Most people didn't understand the bond between a working dog and its handler—far deeper and more personal than could be explained. That's why if someone hurt Tara, Aradia could quickly set aside her aversion to force. She didn't like to consider herself capable of violence. Everyone had that line in the sand, and hurting Tara would be hers. Whoever, whatever, was out here better not have hurt either dog.

"It's almost impossible to harm them." She held on to that fact. She had to and chose to ignore the truth behind the *almost*. Denial would be her coping mechanism of choice at the moment. Tara and Clemons would be okay. They were strong and powerful and smart. They would remain safe. They had to.

"I'm on my way. Give me your coordinates, and I'll locate you. We'll find Rufus and the dogs." She pulled a pen and pad from her pocket. Holding the radio under her chin, she jotted down the coordinates. She read them back to him and, once he confirmed, ended the conversation. She put the radio back into her pocket and didn't turn it off.

Aradia touched Mercy on the shoulder. "I've got to go find Tim. Rufus is missing."

Mercy slipped her phone into her jeans pocket as she spun to face Aradia. Her brows were drawn together, her lips turned down. "Say that again?"

Didn't want to put any more on Mercy's shoulders. She already had to tell law enforcement about the body. She shouldn't have had to do that. Things weren't fair right now. "Rufus is missing," she repeated. Mercy deserved the truth, even if she did wish to spare her. Not her fault she'd been drawn into this, and now her friend could have been hurt or, worse, killed. Not going to say that out loud.

Mercy paled. "What if he got into something like this?" She pointed to the ground where the body of the woman lay. "Oh my god. What if?" Tears pooled in her eyes.

Putting a hand on Mercy's cheek, she shook her head slowly. She didn't know why she felt so confident in her answer, but she didn't hesitate. "He didn't."

"How can you be so certain?" A few tears spilled down her pale cheeks.

"Tim would have told me." She also wanted to believe she'd feel it if something had happened to one of their group. She might have just met Rufus, but they were all a team now, their connection solid.

Mercy's eyes narrowed as she stared into Aradia's eyes. Felt like she could look into her soul. "What are you not telling me?" The tears stopped falling.

They were already in tune with each other, and they'd known each other only a really short amount of time. Destiny seemed to be throwing hardballs when it came to the two of them. She just wished they weren't in the middle of a battle over good and evil. For the first time since they'd met, Aradia lied. "Nothing."

This time Mercy put a hand on her cheek and tilted her head as she searched Aradia's face. "I'm calling bull on that. I'm stuck here until Frank, Deputy Sheriff Frank Long, shows up. He told me to stay, and I can't leave. I'm sure you think you have a good reason to lie. You don't, and you don't have to protect me. I'm a mature, capable woman. Tell me what's happened with Rufus."

Aradia drew in a deep breath and then let it out slowly. No use trying to sugarcoat anything with Mercy. They were beyond that, and she was right. She didn't need to protect her. She'd been doing that for herself since that POS of a father abandoned her. Aradia took a breath and told her the truth. "Tim heard a gunshot."

❖

For a few seconds, Mercy saw stars, and her knees started to give out. Her breath caught, and she had to remind herself to breathe. "I got him into this." She'd been able to accept and handle every weird thing thrown at her so far. Until now. No way could she reconcile with Rufus being hurt. He was out here only because of her. The responsibility for his well-being rested with her.

"He's a strong, smart man." Aradia put both hands on her shoulders. "And at this point, we don't know that anything's happened to him."

"Gunshot." She said the one word and almost threw up. Maybe she should have taken the rifle out of the locked cabinet before they came out. Not that it would have made a difference. The rifle had been Mom's and untouched since her passing. With an aversion to firearms, Mercy preferred them to be unloaded and locked away. A good psychologist would most likely trace that aversion back to her early years with her father. A big cop, gun at hip, he should have been a beacon for safety. Not quite the way it worked out for her.

Aradia continued to try to explain. "Yes. Tim heard a shot, but that doesn't automatically mean Rufus was the target or, even if he was, that he's been hit."

Fair argument. Not all of it though. "Doesn't mean he wasn't. Rufus wouldn't just ignore Tim." The stone that settled right in the middle of her chest told her Rufus had gone down. They were close enough and shared that little something extra that allowed her to tune into him. They'd been that way with each other since day one. The one good thing about that bond, she knew instinctively that Rufus remained alive. For now.

"You're correct. It doesn't mean he wasn't shot, though I'm going to hang onto positive thoughts, and Tim is out searching now to make sure he's okay. If he's been hurt, we'll get him whatever help he needs right away. If it helps you, both Tim and I are also trained in wilderness first aid. Let's just say, it's a handy skill to have in our line of business."

"He's not dead." Saying the words out loud didn't alleviate her fear very much. Alive for now is all she knew for a certainty. Still, it helped to know he hadn't left them.

"How…" Aradia shook her head and then stopped, staring into Mercy's eyes. A look of understanding came into them. "Never mind. Can you tell how hurt he is?"

How she wished she had that kind of power of sight. "No, only that's he still with us. I don't know if he was shot or it's something else." Mercy's body buzzed as though she'd downed a dozen espressos.

Aradia frowned, and a shadow crossed over her face. "It's that something else that spooks me."

"Me as well," Mercy wanted to cry. She sucked it up instead. "I've got to wait for Frank." Every fiber of her body screamed at her to run and find her friend. It took every ounce of effort she had not to. She dropped her gaze to the ground. Someone would be missing this poor girl, and leaving her alone out here wasn't an option.

"I'd offer to stay but…" Aradia looked pained.

Mercy waved a hand and called on her inner warrior. "I get it. Demons and all."

"Demons and all."

"Go. Find them all, and make sure my buddy is safe. He's my best friend and kind of special, so please." She stopped before she started to cry all over again. Her inner warrior better not let her down. She squared her shoulders. "I'll be all right until Frank gets here, and I can't leave this poor dead girl here alone. I know she's gone and everything, but it doesn't feel right to leave."

"You don't want to abandon her." Aradia's words were whisper soft.

Tears pooled in Mercy's eyes again and she blinked hard. "No. I don't." Meant a lot to her that Aradia understood.

Despite her grasp of Mercy's reasons for not wanting to leave, Aradia seemed to hesitate, then blew out a breath. "I'll come update you as soon as I can."

"Thank you. Now go." She needed for Aradia to leave before she changed her mind and begged her to stay. Though it was broad daylight, the old uneasiness that swept over her made her feel like that little girl hiding in the bushes. The quick kiss Aradia placed on her cheek almost destroyed her no-crying resolve.

As she watched Aradia sprint away, Mercy began to second-guess encouraging her to go find the others. The air felt heavier all of a sudden, the day a little darker. Could be her imagination due to the presence of a body nearby, combined with the uncertainty about what had happened to Rufus. Could be more than imagination, given the very real evil she'd already witnessed. Hard to separate fact from emotion right at the moment.

The wait for Frank almost did her in. She'd known when she called him it would take at least an hour, if not more, for him to hike into her location. The wait proved to be agonizing. Rather than sit and grow more agitated, she opted for a more proactive approach.

Dead bodies were not her thing, and Mercy averted her gaze from where the woman lay. She'd been trained to heal people, and much to Mom's delight, she'd turned out to be a natural. Mom had praised her over and over for her skill. Her adoptive mother had been a middle-school teacher and a Wiccan. She remembered watching her practice her beliefs in a most loving and beautiful way. Mom had never pushed her spiritual beliefs on Mercy, yet in a natural manner, she'd found her way to them. It had been one more thing they shared.

Her natural skills with plants, along with what Mom had taught her, combined to make her an extraordinary herbalist. How she loved her job, loved what she'd become, even if it had been born of tragedy. Darkness fell into every life at some point or another. For her, very early, and if the only residual effect came with her uneasiness at night, she could sure as heck live with that. Tragedy didn't have to define her. Often, if she started to lean towards despair, she stopped and counted her blessings. She had many.

Time to take control. Why not lean into her strengths as she waited? Doing that would force her to concentrate and pull her focus away from all the questions about Rufus and the what-ifs of what was to come.

Right now, she knelt and studied the ground a bit of a distance away. Hard to see with all the blackened vegetation, but one of the thin cracks snaked out from beneath the woman's body like the leg of a spider. It bothered her that two people had died from apparent poisoning, yet not through ingestion. Very few substances of any kind could kill through dermal contact. Ingesting the leaves, stems, or berries could kill someone a lot more easily. Hold something poisonous in the hand, rub against it with bare skin, or step in it, not likely to be fatal. Irritation, maybe. Death, no.

As much as Mercy wanted to take a sample back to the farm to study and identify, she resisted. Wouldn't be a wise decision, given she couldn't tell what had caused this or how high the level of toxicity might be. Under normal circumstances she'd know how to handle the plants properly. But these were far from normal circumstances, and if this could kill that easily, no telling what else it might do.

She stood and this time stepped close enough to study the body and the ground immediately surrounding it. Her mind whirled as she searched for a species that could have this effect. Might be jumping to conclusions to assume an organic component had caused this death. Entirely possible the woman had a pre-existing condition that caused her to die out here. Could have been a heart attack or an aneurysm, or even a catastrophic asthma attack. The more she pondered that one, the more sense it made. A medical issue caused this. She could almost convince herself of that precise scenario except for the one thing she couldn't explain. The blackened vegetation wouldn't let go of her herbalist's heart.

Instead of touching either the body or the ground, she walked three hundred sixty degrees around the area to study the ground, the plants, and the trees. Much of it remained very familiar and comfortable. Easy to name each of the plants and wildflowers, and the species of the trees. During all but those first few years of life, she'd grown up with this type of vegetation in her backyard. From Mom, who would take her to natural areas throughout the Pacific Northwest, she'd learned everything she could, soaking it up and making it her life's work. Numerous times she'd been invited to teach, and she'd accepted each invitation, enjoying the chance to share her knowledge with eager students. Traveling throughout the country was such a gift.

At the sound of footsteps, she spun. The sight of Frank and several others from the sheriff's office released the tension in her body. Sort of. Kind of hard to completely relax out here when a war was being waged that nobody except a very few knew about.

"I hope you didn't touch anything." Frank came close, breathing heavily, a sign he'd hauled it here. She appreciated his urgency. Two deaths here in a short period of time warranted that kind of effort, and she hadn't even mentioned the potential shooting yet. In a county not known for unexplained deaths or murder, the two out here had to have their local law enforcement stretched thin.

"You know me better than that." She couldn't believe he'd even said it.

He patted her shoulder. "I do. You're a good kid." His breathing evened out.

Frank wasn't much older than Mercy, and she hadn't been a kid for a very long time. He was maybe five years older than she was. She didn't bother to correct him on the kid comment. "I need to go."

His gaze shifted from the dead woman to her, and he frowned. "We just got here. You and I need to talk before you even think about leaving." He turned to several officers who'd reached her shortly after he had. "Set up the perimeter."

Mercy spoke fast, hoping that with his attention on other details, she could get on her way to find Rufus and the others. "We found her like this. That's all I know."

Frank seemed to be able to focus equally on her and his people. "We? We who? Names. I need to know who else potentially contaminated the scene."

"Aradia." She hated that she had to drag her into this. No time for Aradia to be sidelined by the sheriff's office. She couldn't tell Frank that. He'd want to know why, and no way he'd believe the truth. He'd think Mercy had lost it.

He shook his head. "Aradia?"

She had to think back to the booking information to draw out more. Funny that as close as they'd gotten, last names were a bit hazy. "Aradia Burke. She's from the east side."

"And she is?"

Why would he care about that? She didn't have time to stand around explaining every little thing that had nothing to do with this situation. "A friend."

His eyes narrowed. "A friend?"

She started to say he'd met her yesterday, and then she remembered. Frank hadn't been out here when she came to study the first site. He and his staff had already cleared out. After she'd met Tim and Aradia out here, everything had been going at Indy 500 speed.

"Frank, I have friends, and they're out there." She pointed in the distance. "It's important that I catch up with them. Let me do that while you do what you do here. Call me when you're back at the station, and then I'll come to your office to answer any questions you have for me. Right now, I have to leave." His people were setting up the requested secure perimeter, warning tape being stretched around trees and bushes. "Anyway, I'm in the way of your folks doing their jobs." That fact, he couldn't contest.

One of the nice things about a community their size, everyone did know everyone. What that meant in the current standoff was that Frank understood her well enough to be sure she'd come in when he called. If she didn't, he knew exactly where she lived. He also had a whole lot to do out here without taking time to stop and interview her. "Fine. Fine. Take off, but call me later today. We have to talk."

"I'll give you a call. You have my word." Best not to add that it wouldn't be later today. Both Aradia and Tim had mentioned a special moon. That's what made her believe she'd be spending another night in the company of the mountain. And a woman who made her pulse roar.

Mercy took off running in the direction that Aradia had gone earlier. Her heart pounded, though her spirit continued to whisper that Rufus hadn't left this world, which made her feel happy and scared. After what she'd seen last night, she worried that even if they didn't take his body, they'd still find a way to grab his soul. She ran faster.

August laughed. Scared the crap out of that guy. The shot had sent him running like a frightened rabbit, and he didn't look like someone who did a lot of running. Made him wonder how far he'd traveled before he figured out he hadn't been hit. The best part about it was that his shot had hit his intended target. Clearly, Ama hadn't thought he'd seen her to the left of both the Guardian and the man. With the noise the man and dog made, along with the speed they raced, she'd have believed them solely in his line of sight. She'd have thought herself hidden and safe. More than see her, he'd felt her coming.

After the shot, the Guardian had stopped, stared, and then turned to follow the man as he disappeared into the trees. August had only gotten a quick look at the man's face. Not the Guardian's partner. He had excellent recall, and before he'd headed north, he'd studied the faces of the known teams in this area. That man wasn't one of them, yet, interestingly, the Guardian had appeared to be guiding him in August's direction. A new twist on an old game. Things were getting more interesting by the minute. More fun too.

With the man and the Guardian now far out of sight, he walked to where Ama lay, blood flowing from her chest, nice bright and red. That sight made him very happy. All those hours at the range and out in the wild target-shooting had paid off. It was like she'd had a giant target on her chest. "You should have just stayed in the rest stop like a good girl."

"Fuck you, August. Fuck you." Her words were whisper soft while her skin seemed to grow paler as the minutes ticked past.

"Big words from someone bleeding out in the middle of a remote wilderness area. Probably would have been wiser for you to stay on the path." He laughed as he turned a full circle. "Too bad for you. No road for an ambulance, and that wound looks nasty. I'd help you, but you know how I don't like getting dirty." Not that he'd help anyway. She deserved this.

"They'll come for me." They both knew she wasn't talking about the EMTs.

Now he laughed large. "You seriously think either one of those bitches actually cares whether you make it? Hate to break it to you, but they're in this for themselves. They used you. Oh, hell, I used you. You made it so easy."

"They'll come." Her words didn't sound as confident this time.

He shrugged. "Maybe. Maybe not." If he were to place a bet, he'd make it heavy on maybe not.

"They will." Tears started to slide down her face, down her cheeks, dripping to the ground as it mixed with blood. Messy, messy, and he didn't like messy.

As intriguing as it might be to sit here and watch Ama's blood return to the earth, he needed to keep going. In one respect, she was right. Willa and June would come, though not necessarily riding in for her rescue. In fact, it dismayed him a little how close behind him they'd been. He'd counted on having more time and a lot more help before they finally found their way to him. Oh, well. He'd make do just as he'd always done. It would be fine. The Demon King would wear his crown soon enough. A couple of women with ideas of grandeur wouldn't derail his best-laid plans. They simply weren't good enough.

He looked down at her and shrugged" "Gotta go, my dear. You know, circles to set up, rituals to prepare for, and demons to release."

"You won't win." Her words were garbled and liquidy, bubbles of pink seeping from the corners of her lips. The clock wasn't far from striking midnight for Ama and no pumpkin coach arriving to whisk her away to safety. She should have stayed at the rest area where he left her.

"Oh, my dear. I will. I always do." He touched the toe of his boot to the bleeding wound and pressed down. Her scream made him laugh again. Didn't think she had that much left in her. "Enjoy the journey to the other side." He took his boot away from her and wiped off the blood in the wild grass. It made a glistening wet slash against the yellows and pale greens. Later, he'd have his boots polished to make certain they were pristine.

An invisible force continued to tug at him, and once more he followed his feet as they guided him away from the dying Ama. He didn't look back. Places to go. Things to do. Demons to summon. A new world order to lord over.

He half expected to pass the dog and the man again, as they'd both raced away in the same general direction. That he didn't made him wonder about the supposed supernatural skills of this particular Guardian. August headed directly toward the portal, at least he trusted that the forces of the underworld guided him that way, and according to the legends, the Guardian should be there too. Their great claim to fame throughout the ages had been their ability to detect and protect portals. Now, it didn't appear the Guardian he'd seen was anywhere near him. Another sign this would be his night. The universe offering yet another gift to the King of Demons.

By the time the scream drifted across the wind to reach his ears, he'd put an impressive amount of distance between Ama and himself. That scream told him a little more distance would be good because someone had found her. Or her body. No telling how long she'd survive that wound. Looked pretty dicey before he left.

That she'd been found wasn't a problem as such. He reasoned the discovery of Ama would keep whoever was out here busy while he prepared for the Black Moon. No room for failure or it would be another three years before he'd be able to try again. The portal could be an issue too. Ready at this moment, it might or might not be in three years. Everything had to align. Timing meant the difference between success and failure.

He glanced around and thought he'd probably put some decent distance between himself and the Guardian too. The dog, smart and sneaky, worried him more than anything else. It would be wise on his part to keep an ear open for the sound of paws against hard ground. Their sheer size hindered their ability for stealth.

He kept going, the elevation rising with each step. He also kept listening. If Ama had been out there, June and Willa would be too.

Possible they were both now with Ama, or Ama's body, by the looks of her when he took off. As far as giving them credit for empathy and kindness, he didn't. Odds were, if they had found her already, they'd assessed the fatality of the shot and left her there. That scream he heard, wouldn't have been from either of them. Sure, animals could get her, but did it really matter in the big picture? Why not let nature do what nature did? Ashes to ashes, dust to dust. He could almost hear Willa's voice.

Given those assumptions, situational awareness became paramount. Bad enough he needed to keep high alert for the Guardian team. He also had to be looking for the two women who represented a giant pain in his ass. Would have been better to be an only child and to have skipped the whole marriage thing. One would think that with a divorce, at least he'd have been rid of Willa. She couldn't do divorce like everyone else. Like a bad rash, she kept coming back. He planned to get rid of that rash once and for all tonight. It wouldn't be returning ever again. What a glorious thing to look forward to.

So far, so good. Nothing nearby that caused him alarm. He kept hiking upward. Got him breathing a little heavier than he liked, or his ego cared for. Maybe he'd think about taking on a fitness program, except after tonight, he wouldn't need to. Kings didn't have to work out. People worked out for the king.

All of a sudden, the wind picked up and blew hard into his face. Time to stop, it seemed to say. He stopped. So did the wind. "Yes," he whispered. "Yes." This was it. Destiny would happen right here. He tipped his head to the sky and took in a full, deep breath. He'd swear he could smell victory on the air. Then he heard the pounding of feet and, a few seconds later, a dog, bigger than the first one, burst out of the underbrush.

CHAPTER SEVENTEEN

When Aradia heard the sound of running feet pounding against the hard ground, she didn't need to look up to know who approached. She stood and turned, moving away from Rufus to catch Mercy as she ran in and then stumbled over fallen branches. She put her arms around her and held her for a few seconds. She could feel her heart pounding in her chest. "I got..." she said into her ear.

"Is he?" Mercy's voice caught as she cut off the rest of Aradia's words.

"No." One of only two easy answers she had for her. Rufus was alive and breathing. "He wasn't shot." Easy answer number two. Now came the hard part with the inevitable question number three.

"Why is he down?" Mercy stepped out of Aradia's embrace and stared down at her unmoving friend, Tim on the ground beside him, holding his hand.

The confusing scene threw Aradia when she first got here and saw him there. Rufus lay on his back, his eyes closed, his hands clasped over his stomach. No clothing out of place and his hair as tidy as ever, although his hat had been knocked from his head. He remained so still, it was as if he were dead. Except he wasn't. His breathing remained even and constant, his chest rising and falling. A little like before. No obvious signs of injury yet unresponsive.

Aradia looked into Mercy's eyes. She had told her one lie, and she didn't plan to do it again, ever. "We don't know. Perhaps he tripped and hit his head when he fell. Perhaps he has a condition of some sort that's caused him to pass out? Neither of these scenarios would play out unusual here."

"No. He's as healthy as any decent athlete." Rufus had great respect for his body and remained super healthy. Not a traditional athlete, he still worked out enough to stay in good physical shape. It wasn't a fall, and it wasn't some medical condition.

Tim looked up at them. "I don't think he hit his head either. No lumps on his skull or anywhere else that I can feel. And no blood that I can see. I found him like this, and it's as if he's taken a double dose of prescription sleeping pills. No waking up for hours. I can't even shake him awake." Tim stayed on the ground next to Rufus, a worried expression on his face.

"Tara brought me to him," Aradia explained, though she omitted the fact that Tara, still in a down a few feet away, concerned her. It meant something had happened beneath them. That the ground Rufus lay on remained natural and unspoiled told her the toxins of the demons hadn't leaked through the earth. That Tara hadn't moved also told her it could still happen. Good and bad. Yin and yang.

"Where's Clemons?" Mercy glanced away from Rufus to gaze around. "Tim? Where is Clemons? Is he okay?" Her voice rose.

Aradia shared the emotion she heard in Mercy's voice. She didn't like the way any of this was going down. They had to get control and now.

He shook his head. "I don't know. He checked in once and then took off again at full speed. He's out there searching, and he's worried. I could see it in his body language. Something bad is getting ready to happen, and he's trying to find out exactly where. The portal isn't safe, and neither are we."

"What about Rufus?" Mercy knelt next to him, her hand over his. "We can't leave him here. Look what happened to those two other people. And if he didn't get shot, what was the gunshot about? Where is the person with the gun? What if he or she is out there getting ready to shoot us all?" Mercy's voice remained full of emotion.

Aradia looked at Tim. He nodded and said, "She has a right to know."

"I have a right to know what?" Fear shone in Mercy's face.

He wasn't wrong. Not fair to have Mercy out here and arm her with only half the information. She had more than a right to know.

While she'd stayed back with the body of the young woman, Aradia and Tim had made a grisly discovery. They had to share with Mercy. "We found another body." She sure hated to have to say that out loud. Too many deaths.

Mercy jumped to her feet. "What? Another one? What in the actual hell is going on out here? This kind of bloodbath can't be happening here. This is my home."

"I would like to say it's not true, except it is. We found another body, only it's different." She hated how things had been spiraling since the sun came up. While it was early in the day, she nonetheless felt the pressure of the coming moon. Time wasn't their friend right now.

"Oh, for heaven's sake, spit it out. I'm not a child, and I can handle whatever you don't want to share with me. I've earned the right to be part of the inner circle." Fear had been replaced by frustration, and it sounded loud and clear in Mercy's words.

"You have." Tim agreed. "Tell her, Aradia."

Mercy put her hands on her hips. "Tell me, Aradia. You owe me that much."

She did owe her. Mercy had come out here to help and had done more than that. She'd captured Aradia's heart. She'd love to take her back to the farm and make sure she stayed safe, except that wouldn't be fair. In their short amount of time together, they'd become equal partners, and as such, she'd earned the truth. "It's another demon hunter."

"Looking for the portal." An expression of near relief crossed Mercy's face. Aradia didn't share the sentiment for a very good reason. The truth had to keep coming so that Mercy walked forward fully armed. The best weapon they had was communication.

Aradia nodded and grimaced. "Absolutely searching for the portal. That's the problem."

Mercy looked from Tim to Aradia, clearly confused. "If he's dead, what's the problem?"

"She is most definitely dead." Aradia thought the shot had been aimed at the right spot for maximum damage. Not immediate death. Rather certain and painful death. Goal achieved. A shooter with better than average skills, and the woman had to have bled out fast.

"A woman?" Not surprise in her voice, more like seeking clarification. "You're sure she is, was, a demon hunter?"

Given the two innocent victims that were taken out here, a legitimate question. "Yes. A woman with a very particular tattoo." Every hunter she'd encountered had that same tattoo. She often wondered if it was an initiation-into-the-club kind of thing. She continued. "That job is and always has been an equal-opportunity one. Evil doesn't care about gender. But she's dead, and for us that means another hunter took her down. Rufus might have witnessed it and is now possibly under the influence of a spell. Don't get me wrong, I'm still not ruling out something more mundane like a trip and fall. Either way, he's not coming to, and that's a problem, given how fast everything is happening."

Mercy walked all around Rufus. "I want to care about the demon hunter, but I don't like him, or her, much at the moment. I'm much more worried about Rufus. Could a crack happen beneath him? Release poisons like what killed the other two. I feel like he's in potential danger the longer he lies on the ground. We don't know how long those others lay out there. I want to get him up and away before something worse happens."

Aradia nodded. Unease made her shoulders tighten. Unease and the truth inherent in Mercy's reasoning. "It's a very real possibility, and you're right. We didn't see any of what happened with the other two, so how do we know?"

"We've got to wake him up." Mercy remained distraught, and who could blame her? If that were Lizzy or Sabina or Mona on the ground, she'd be beside herself. Mercy's deep concern for her friend made Aradia like her even more, not to mention she was holding up amazingly well, given the circumstances. Her good feelings toward her ratcheted up even more.

How she wished Rufus would sit up and say hi. He didn't move and didn't look like he would anytime soon. The consistent rise and fall of his chest gave her a whisper of hope. He'd recovered once before with no ill effects, and Aradia hoped he'd do it again now. Perhaps he was once again in the throes of a helpful vision. She'd go with that. A vision. A vision that would lead them forward to defeat the evil that pushed their way.

Tim looked at her with clear concern and a catch in his voice. "I've been trying to get through to him, and he's not responding. Not sure if he even hears me. I hope so, but honestly, guys, I don't know what else to do. No amount of training prepared us for this. I'm no psychic. I'm just a plain old dog handler."

She got it because she had wracked her brain too for something even close to this. Some little kernel of wisdom that might guide them toward helping their friend back to them. Nothing came to her. "I've tried too, and I've got zip. Mercy? You two share an affinity for visions. Maybe you can get through to him?"

Aradia hated, hated, hated feeling at a loss. At the same time, it doubly frightened her that as the day grew shorter, the danger grew greater. She felt like she was treading water, and not very well, sinking deeper and deeper with each passing minute. Like trying to help Rufus. She didn't want to see anything happen to him. Even though they'd just met, she liked him. From their first moment together, she'd known without question that he was a good soul. A bright light followed him, enveloping those who came near him. The demons had no right to extinguish that light. The world needed more people like Rufus, and she'd be damned if she'd let anything happen to him. All fine and good, if only she knew how to bring him back. She could blabber all she wanted, and it would do zero good if she couldn't figure out a way to revive him.

Mercy knelt next to Rufus once more. "Let me try. We've been super close since the day we met. Maybe I can get through." She put her hands on his face and screamed.

Aradia jumped and put her hands out to touch Mercy. She had to help her. Mercy was in pain.

Tim yelled, "No!"

Jumping back, Aradia pulled her hands away and, for the first time in years, cried.

❖

Pain soared through Mercy, hot and pointed like a devil's pitchfork dipped in magma. She wanted to run away, her screams echoing through the forest. Then, everything around her went black and silent.

Rufus sat up and ran his hands over his face. "Whoa, sister. Welcome to my nightmare. Gotta tell you, it's bad."

"You're hurt." Mercy pulled him into a hug, raindrops hard and fast plastering her hair to her head and soaking her clothes. A wind blew cold and strong enough to almost topple her. She shivered as goosebumps rose on her arms and ice formed on her eyelashes.

"No. It's worse than that. They're trying to grab my soul." Rufus hugged her tight enough that she thought her ribs might break. She hugged him back just as hard. Their hearts beat as one, their shared heat pushing away the relentless cold.

After a few moments, she pushed him away, wiped away the moisture on his face, and stared into his eyes. In them she glimpsed fear that she wanted to take away. "How do I stop them? Tell me how, and I'll do it for you."

"The man." He pointed into the darkness and pouring rain. "The one with the gun. He's wrong in so many ways. He's dangerous."

What he said didn't make a whole lot of sense. She got what he said about the man. They all knew someone roamed out in the wilderness. She also got dangerous. But she didn't understand what she meant about him being wrong. "Where he is? What is he wrong about?" If she could see the man he talked about, maybe it would make more sense. As far as she could tell, they were alone here. Wherever here actually was.

Rufus shook his head vehemently. "I don't know where he is. I ran when I saw him raise the gun and aim. I thought he was going to shoot me. I thought he did shoot me when I heard it go off, except the bullet never came. It didn't hit me, and I didn't hear it go by. He shot someone else, and I felt a spirit leave this world, though I don't know whose spirit. Not someone good. It felt dark. Bad." He put his hand to his chest, and she covered it with hers. Touching him always calmed her. Easier to think that way.

"He shot a woman. Another demon hunter." At least she knew that much about what happened beyond the trees. It's all she had to offer.

He made a face. Obviously, he didn't think much of either of them—the one who killed or the one who died. He'd always been too kind to say anything like she had it coming. He nodded as he frowned. "That makes sense. I had a feeling Tara and I weren't alone in the trees. I didn't see her, which isn't surprising, given how many trees were around us. Some of them big enough for someone to hide behind. Knew she was there just the same. Could feel the darkness she brought with her, black and ugly."

"If you weren't hit with a bullet, why aren't you waking up? Did you fall while you were running? Hit your head? What? Why are you out? You have to come back. We need you." It didn't make sense. He hadn't been shot so, unless he fell, he should be with them.

He looked confused. "We're talking. I'm awake. I don't get the problem."

She felt the difference. The rain fell in steady torrents. The wind whipped around them. Blackness blurred everything else. Wherever they were, it wasn't the grounds surrounding the beautiful mountain that hid a dark secret. "In this realm, yes. Everyone else is waiting for us on the other side. How can I bring you back to the real world? We need you. I need you. I can't do this without you." Truth. She didn't even want to think about life without Rufus. Everyone made friends. Everyone had one or two that were like other halves of themselves. Rufus was that friend for her.

His face cleared, and he ran a hand over his drenched hair. "Ah. It makes sense now. Everything does feel a little, how do I put it? Off. Thing is, that guy cursed me or, probably more precise, said a spell and promptly tried to take my soul. I wouldn't let him, not in any realm. I guess this was his Plan B. Make me drop like a hot rock into some other place and hold me there until I give him what he wants. He's probably happy too that he's scared the bejesus out of my best friend." He touched her face, his fingers warm against her cold cheek.

Mercy could track with all this, the events of the day opening her already open mind even more. "How do we get you back? How do we make sure he doesn't take your soul? I won't let him do that to you." Anything else she could deal with later. All she wanted to do right now was to get Rufus back to the three of them waiting on the other side. Had a hunch Tim wanted it as badly as she did.

For a second Rufus said nothing. He pulled in a long breath and let it out slowly. "He's powerful, and he's going to summon the worst of the worst from the underworld. That much I got from this place, *wherever it is. I've pulled in every favor from the old ones to protect my soul, but if he opens that portal and commands the demons, we're all lost. You need to bring me back. It's going to take all of us to stop him."*

She had to believe he had more to share. He had to because she still remained lost. *"Tell me what to do. We're running short on time."*

"You have to save my soul." He put his hand on his chest.

She put her hand over his. *"How? How do I do that? Rufus, think. I can't lose you. Tim and Clemons don't want to lose you."*

He looked at the sky and then returned his gaze to her. His dark face revealed nothing. *"She'll know. All you have to do is trust her."*

"Her? Who? Rufus, I don't understand. I can't help if I don't know what to do. You have to give me more details. You have to tell me what to do." Her frustration spilled into her words, and a sob escaped from her throat.

His eyes closed, and he lay back down on the ground, his hands once more clasped across his midsection. She shook him. *"Rufus! Rufus! Don't you dare leave me. I don't understand yet. I don't know what to do!"* His eyes remained closed.

Aradia's arms were around Mercy as she blinked and focused on the here and now. Sunlight replaced the rain, her hair dry, her clothes dry, and the ground dusty. No trace of the icy, torrential rain that had soaked her and Rufus. At her side, Rufus continued to lie on the ground, silent and unmoving. Tears flowed down her cheeks, and she didn't try to stop them. Aradia's hug, even tighter now, gave her comfort, though it didn't stop the tears. She'd so hoped that Rufus would open his eyes and sit up.

"I've got you. You're safe. Are you all right? You screamed and screamed. Scared me to death."

She took a couple of full, shaky breaths, only now noticing how Aradia trembled. She had scared her. "Physically, yes, I'm fine. Emotionally, I'm a train wreck. Rufus is in some kind of suspended hell. He said that a man, a demon hunter, shot the woman, who, like you said was another demon hunter too. After he shot her, he tried to grab Rufus's soul." She laid a hand on his chest and then looked into Aradia's eyes. "Why would he do that to Rufus?"

Aradia rocked back on her heels, looking first at Rufus and then back at Mercy. "Did he tell you anything else? Could you see or sense anything else?"

Mercy thought hard for a few seconds and then shook her head. "Nothing helpful. Rufus told me we have to save his soul and that she'll know. I don't understand what that means. He didn't tell me who she is." Frustration colored her words, and she couldn't help it. She wanted to sound more composed, and she hated feeling like she was letting everyone down. The same level of fright that had gripped her all those years ago in the park descended upon her once again.

Now Aradia stood, her gaze drifting to Tim. "Damn."

Tim touched Rufus on the cheek before he stood as well. "We have a real problem. More than this, I mean." He nodded toward Rufus.

Mercy looked from Tim to Aradia and back again. "You guys know something? Tell me. Please."

"Let's get him safe first." Aradia nodded toward Rufus. "Like you mentioned earlier, I'm not comfortable with him on the ground, especially with that." She pointed to the crack.

"Safe? Nothing seems safe right now." Mercy almost cried again as she stayed next to Rufus. Her fault for all of this. She should have made him go home. Hell, she should have gone home. So far, all she'd managed to do was make things worse.

As if she could read her mind, Aradia squeezed her shoulder softly. Comforting and reassuring. "It's not your fault, and we won't let anything happen to your friend. You have my promise."

Much appreciated promise aside, it didn't help a whole lot. "Something has already happened." She wiped away the tears that stained her face. Why hadn't she just stayed home? Fighting demons wasn't in her DNA.

"We'll keep him safe." Aradia held out a hand to Mercy. She hesitated, almost afraid to move away from Rufus. "Come on." Aradia took her hand and helped her to her feet.

Standing close, she stared into Aradia's eyes. Honesty wasn't going to be a problem. "I'm scared."

Aradia nodded and squeezed her hands as she pulled them close to her chest. "Good. If you weren't scared, I'd be sending you away from here. Fear will keep you sharp."

Mercy wasn't so sure about the logic. Besides, she'd probably understated her emotions. More terror than fear. Before Aradia had stepped into her world, she'd thought her otherworldly gifts somewhat scary. Compared to everything happening out here, they seemed downright mundane. "What next?" She took a deep breath and blew it out slowly. Might as well move forward. Crying would get them nowhere in a hurry. Besides, she didn't care to look weak, and all the crying wasn't making her appear strong or confident.

Aradia turned to Tara at the same time she squeezed Mercy's hand. "Show me."

Show me? Show me what? That command didn't make a lot of sense to Mercy. She didn't say anything. Instead, after giving herself a few minutes to think it through, she chose to believe that when Rufus told her to trust, he meant for her to trust Aradia. She sure hoped so anyway. It felt right, and she decided to go with it. At this point what more could she lose?

Tara got up and, head low, began to pace the ground nearby. After a minute, maybe two, Tara barked as she went to a down next to a tree. Mercy decided the exercise meant that Tara believed the spot by the tree would be a good place for Rufus.

"Good girl. Come on, Tim. Let's get him safe." Aradia appeared to confirm her own thoughts. How she hoped it to be true.

Together, the three of them picked him up and carried him to the tree, propping him in a sitting position with his back against the trunk and his legs stretched out. He did look a little better sitting up. A lot better actually. Still not moving, eyes remaining shut. Better nonetheless, and she took it as a good sign. Normal color in his skin, his chest rising and falling easy and even.

"I wish he'd wake up." Mercy kissed the top of his head, breathing in the scent of him. She stood up and shoved her hands into the pockets of her jeans.

"Give me a sec." Aradia knelt next to Rufus and held his hands in hers.

Overhead a bird screeched, sending ice through her, head to toe. Why did everything have to have an ominous undertone right now? She'd lived in this area most of her life and had never heard that sound before. Or, if she did, she'd never had this dark reaction before. What a paradigm shift in a matter of a few days.

Mercy gazed up at the sky, and a shiver shook her. "I don't think we have a lot of time left." No reason for it, just a feeling.

"Oh, hell, no," Aradia muttered, her face dark and drawn as she kneeled close to Rufus. She didn't let go of his hands.

"That bad?" Mercy wanted to hug her and banish the darkness. She might not be able to drag Rufus back to their realm yet, but maybe she could help Aradia.

Aradia rocked back on her heels. She looked up at both Mercy and Tim. Shadows passed over her face. "It's bad. I can feel the tug of the magic that's trying to grab his soul. Rufus is strong and powerful, exactly what the demons like to eat for breakfast."

Mercy's heart almost stopped. "No. Just no." She wouldn't let that happen. They couldn't have her friend. Not today. Not ever.

"My sentiments exactly. No time to waste. Both of you come and put your hands on Rufus. We're going to grab every ounce of energy we can and pour it into him. Power in numbers, my friends." Aradia took a crystal from her pocket and, with a rock from the ground, tapped the two together three times. "Be ready."

Ready for what? The bird overhead screeched again, louder and, to Mercy's ears, angrier. Did it sense what they were attempting to do? Maybe it did, but so what? Fly away to its dark master and tattle on the little cadre of friends working to save Rufus? No way would she let her friend go. No freaking way.

"On three." Aradia looked to them both. "Do not let go of Rufus. One. Two. Three." She touched the crystal to his forehead, and for the third time, Mercy screamed.

Interesting that August didn't need to hike very far up the mountain to arrive at the necessary spot. The portal, with his assistance, would spread wide here in a few hours. Easy enough to open it, as long as he dispatched the Guardians and their handlers. The male that had run in a few minutes ago had alerted him to the fact he'd need to be on the watch for at least two teams. He doubted there'd be more than the two. Not all that normal to have more than one team working a location, though two wasn't unheard of. He couldn't recall ever hearing of there being more than two at an impending breach. Apparently, they thought that a couple of dogs and their handlers were all it would take to defeat those who came before him. True, actually, as they'd done just that. He planned to change their string of luck. They wouldn't defeat him, double-teamed or not.

Now that he understood the nature of the opposition, he felt better prepared for what lay ahead of him. Unfortunately, that also meant preparing for opposition from his own *team*. Willa and June were out there somewhere, undoubtedly coming up with ways to keep him from his destiny. The need to take down his own people would be a bit unusual. They tended to be a tight-knit group working toward the same end goal—changing the power dynamic of the world. It had been goody-goody for too long. Way past time to turn the tide in their direction. Their turn to mold the world in their own image. In that respect, he, June, and Willa shared the same goal. About the only thing they shared.

Time to turn all avenues squarely in his direction. From that standpoint, goal one would be to take down both June and Willa. Didn't faze him in the least that he planned to end his sister's life. They'd never been close, and the chance they ever would be fell right into the never category. Nothing in common beyond the same parents. He didn't see that ever changing. Blood made them related, but it didn't equate to love or loyalty. June remained a straight-up bitch, and he had no use for her in the world he intended to mold to his wants and needs.

As for Willa? The only right thing about their relationship: the divorce. She'd been a pain in his ass longer than any rational man should have to endure. He rarely made mistakes. He'd sure made a biggie with her the day they'd gotten married. Too enamored with her prowess in the sack to realize she could have cared less about him and his ambitions. She married him strictly for the family he came from. Well, mistakes could be corrected, and that's exactly what he'd done once he got over the embarrassment of a mistake of such magnitude.

No doubt Willa and June would be showing their bright, shiny faces before long, which meant he had to decide how he'd handle them when they were face-to-face. What he'd do today when they did show up? Not a clue as yet, although he had what he considered the germ of a good idea. Patting the pack, he thought about the case with the filled syringes. Easy and effective. The poison inside the syringes wouldn't be hard to trace, not that it bothered him. It would take days, if not weeks, to narrow down the toxin, and by then, the world would be bowing before him. Yes, the syringes stood out as his answer to the June and Willa annoyance.

In his march toward supremacy, local law enforcement was the only unknown and a potential stumbling block. Depended on how long before someone with legal authority came upon Ama's body. The hole in the middle of her chest would be the quick giveaway that her demise wasn't natural or accidental. Couldn't be helped. He only hoped it would be hours before Ama was found by law enforcement. Like hours after the portal opened and he rallied his army.

An invisible bolt of energy crashed through him. Damn, damn, damn. He dropped to his knees and drew in long, ragged breaths. For at least a minute, he let his head hang as he breathed in slow and even, trying to steady himself. Once he felt centered again, he rose back to his feet.

Damn it. He'd lost the guy, and he felt the loss as surely as he'd felt the win the second he'd shot Ama. The spell he'd sent the running man's way dropped him somewhere in the woods. If he'd had time, he'd have tracked him and stayed next to the guy long enough to make sure his soul remained under his control. It hadn't been in the cards and definitely not worth the risk. A sad but necessary sacrifice in this instance. August hated to lose him. For the sake of his own safety, they could have him. For now. Things would turn back his way in a few hours, regardless of whatever happened in the interim.

He dropped his bag and looked around. No time to pout. He had things to do, and in a flash, a protruding rock on the ascending side of the mountain caught his attention. No time to waste, he cleared away the vegetation and dirt, then put both palms on the bare rock, closed his eyes, and waited. Vibrations rolled up from his palms and into his shoulders. Deep, hot, promising. Exactly what he'd been hoping for. Even better than he'd imagined.

"Thank you." He tipped his head to the sky, where the sun headed toward the west. Liked what he saw. A few more hours and it would be showtime. He pulled his hands away. At the moment, he needed to focus on preparations for the coming ceremony. Everything else would take care of itself.

For another ten minutes or so he cleared away moss, dirt, and leaves until a section of the stone at least four feet wide and six feet high had been revealed. To the casual observer it would be nothing unusual. Rock formations were common all over the Pacific Northwest. Only those possessed with his special kind of knowledge, of which there were few, if any, would be able to see beyond the obvious. The portal. He didn't have to climb the mountain to find the gateway. It existed here where no one would suspect.

Glad he'd taken the time to purify himself, he felt energy now flow through him unimpeded. The longer he worked, the greater the force. The portal ready, the ritual circle became his next focus. Everything had to be perfect and in its proper place. Nothing happened by accident, and once the Black Moon rose, he wanted to be ready to move fast.

His thoughts turned to the Guardians. If they didn't take the bait he'd left for them, and judging by what he'd seen earlier it seemed unlikely, then they'd find the portal and bring the handlers with them. He must be ready and ensure he had the most powerful demons under his control when they showed up. He might not be able to kill the Guardians through traditional methods, and his alternate plans might also fall short, but the demons would be able to do what he couldn't.

He glanced down the mountain and smiled. At least he'd slowed the male Guardian. Not a perfect solution, and it wouldn't kill the dog. It would give him time, though, and, if all went as he believed it would, enough time to rally his troops. Strategy would play a big role in his success tonight. Unstoppable should have been his middle name.

August would first call Flauros, for the best reason possible. Flauros could destroy and burn the Guardians, along with their handlers. Quick and effective, and that solution would provide him massive breathing room to accomplish his ultimate goal. A close second needed to be Glasyalbolas. His unmatched skill with violence and bloodshed would clear a path for August to ascend to greatness. Critical to first call forth the demons who possessed the power to ensure his swift ascension. After that, others would fall in behind his generals, and they too would bring their individual powers to glorify his new kingdom. All would bow to him and then do his bidding. His plan screamed foolproof.

Close to the cleared portal location, he created a ritual circle with stones he gathered from the nearby area and his special candles. He pulled out the dagger he'd slipped into his bag and laid it in the center. Sunlight glistened on its blade, and he could swear it winked at him. His special weapon captured the building magic too.

Usually, he'd perform all parts of the ceremony in a linear fashion. With Guardian teams roaming the mountain and Willa and June searching for him, better to prep as much as possible. He preferred not to risk an interruption that might lessen the power of his beautiful dagger as he stood over it, his palms turned to the sky.

"I conjure thee, instrument of my power, by virtue of darkness and the dominion of the Black Moon. Harness the four elements, through the stars that rule, all the stones, the plants, the animals of the kingdom, and receive such virtue herein that I may obtain all that I desire. So shall it be."

The wind picked up fallen leaves, pine needles, and dried wildflower petals, swirling them through the air around him. He stood in the center of a beautiful tornado, his smile large. Not a single leaf or pine needle or speck of dirt breached the circle. *So shall it be.*

CHAPTER EIGHTEEN

Aradia landed on her behind and stared up at Mercy and Tim. "Well, that worked better than I thought." Something she'd read about but never had an occasion to even attempt. A payoff from one of those childhood lessons she and Sabina had sat through with their mother. She glanced around. Everyone seemed okay, and Mercy had stopped screaming. Rufus opened his eyes.

He blinked as though trying to focus his vision. In a raspy voice he said, "That was messed up." Rufus sat up, looked around for a few seconds, and then stood shakily, his hands on the tree to steady himself. "That guy is a freak with scary magic. I didn't even see him behind me. I was running and following the dog, then boom. Nothing until you came to me." He looked at Mercy.

Mercy hugged him. "I'm so glad you're all right. You weren't a lot of help though. I couldn't figure out what you were trying to tell me."

Rufus looked at Aradia and the crystal she'd picked back up from where it had fallen to the ground. He nodded toward her hand and then cut his eyes to Mercy. "Looks to me like you figured it out. I told you to trust her, and you did." He winked.

Aradia held out the clear quartz crystal she'd carried with her since the day Mom gave it to her. Sabina had one just like it and also carried it with her everywhere. "You mean this?" It caught the sunlight and sparkled. On the face of it, a pretty stone like those found in specialty shops all over. Underneath, magic and power, if used correctly.

He shook his head as he leaned down, picked up his hat, and placed it on his head. Then, he looked into her eyes. Knowledge shone from them. "No. I meant you."

His words warmed her, and she couldn't explain why. She didn't even know what exactly he'd said to Mercy when they connected in the other realm. "Thank you."

"We have trouble." Rufus now looked at Tim. "I have a pretty good skill set when it comes to other worlds, but I'm telling you guys, this isn't good. He took me down in a matter of seconds. I didn't hear him. I didn't see him. I don't even know if he was close to me. Nobody has ever been able to do that before. I've always felt as though my ancestors protected me, but this guy, it was like he rolled right over them."

Aradia glanced up at the sky and then at Tim. The day had gotten away from them, and she didn't feel like they were anywhere near ready for what would be coming. "We don't have a whole lot of time left, and we still don't know exactly where the portal is."

"Your Black Moon?" Mercy stood close to Rufus, as if ready to catch him should he once more crumble toward the earth. He looked pretty steady to Aradia. Especially for a guy that a couple minutes before had been out cold.

She nodded. "Tara and Clemons need to find the portal before the moon hits mid-sky." She couldn't fault either of the Guardians. They'd been working nonstop and, under normal circumstances, would have pinpointed the portal by now. Demon hunters, spider cracks, and dead bodies made this far from normal circumstances. All the rule books were out the window, so to speak, and all of them had to make it up as they went along. Not ideal, not that they had a lot of choice at this point.

Mercy frowned. "What if we're late?"

This time she took Mercy's hand. The electricity that flowed between them remained strong and comforting. Regardless of anything else, it let her know they were together in this. Maybe together forever. She'd never felt anything like this before with either a man or a woman. It had to mean something important. Mom always taught her to pay attention to the signs wherever they came from. "Feel that?"

Mercy glanced down at their clasped hands and nodded. "I do. It's getting stronger but without the knock-you-out thing."

She squeezed lightly. "It is, and that's got to be important. Rufus, take Tim's hand."

Rufus looked at her for a second as if trying to discern her meaning, then shrugged and reached out to clasp Tim's hand. Aradia didn't know what they could feel flowing between them, but the second they touched palm to palm, energy roared around them all, so thick she'd swear she could almost see it. Exactly what she'd been hoping for.

"Get it?" She looked at the three of them as they continued to connect. The pieces had already dropped in place.

Tim nodded. "You're right." She hadn't needed to explain it further to him. Wasn't his first day on the job and he got it.

Mercy squeezed her hand and said with a healthy dose of wonderment, "We're more powerful together."

Rufus gazed at Tim as though not quite sure about the energy that had to be racing between them. "How? Why? Don't get me wrong, this is cool, but again, how? Why?"

"There's something special and unique about the four of us together. We were evidently meant to be here. The universe in its infinite wisdom brought two Guardian teams together with two naturally powerful seers. Not a happy coincidence. It was intentional. It's how we retrieved you from the realm the hunter banished you to while he tried to steal your soul." It all made so much sense to Aradia.

"It's pretty cool." Rufus kept holding Tim's hand and not looking away from him. That didn't much surprise her. She suspected Rufus wouldn't stop holding Tim's hand or looking at him with an expression of awe even after this was all done. Out of darkness, a little light shall fall. She glanced at Mercy. Maybe a lot of light.

"Hi." A woman's voice made her drop Mercy's hand and spin toward the sound. "Do you need some assistance?"

Two women walked toward them. One tall and dark-haired, wearing jeans, boots, and a pale-blue jacket. One shorter and with light hair, who must not have considered what hiking was about because she wore sneakers with her jeans and black hoodie. Neither appeared threatening, yet an urgent whisper inside Aradia warned, beware.

She stepped toward them, her back straight, her head high. It usually paid off to listen to warnings from the universe. "We're fine. Thank you." Polite enough to not offend. Aloof enough not to encourage.

"Saw your guy there down on the ground and thought maybe you could use some help. Looked like maybe he hurt himself, and I've got a real good first-aid kit in my pack." The tall woman smiled, her green eyes intense. Aradia stared back, no smile, sweeping her gaze over the pair, searching for clues to who or what they were. She didn't take anyone at face value. Especially today.

"Appreciate your concern, but we're fine." Out of the corner of her eye, she saw Tara coming toward her, head up, eyes intense. At work and on guard. That was her girl.

"Nice dog." The shorter woman looked toward Tara, her eyes narrowing. "An Anatolian, right?"

Aradia studied her more closely. "You know your dogs." Could be innocent, a case of a dog lover familiar with Anatolians. Experienced shepherd owners typically knew the various breeds. Love one, love all, or at least that had been her experience.

"Not good with the ankle-biter varieties, but I know my big dogs. She's a beauty." She smiled, but it didn't really move into her eyes.

"Yes, she is." Aradia stepped back toward Tim, Mercy, and Rufus. As they neared her, she had the urge to step back and away. Nope, not a good sign at all. These women were not casual hikers or dog lovers.

Both of them stared at Tara too long, further solidifying her belief about them. "Pretty," the tall one commented. The way she narrowed her eyes said something different.

"We have to be on our way." Aradia glanced at her friends and hoped they understood. They had to get away from these two, quickly. Even Tara's body language had shifted. More on guard than she had been a few seconds ago.

"If you'd like company, we could hike with you for a bit. Make sure your friend is okay." Tall and dark-haired took a few more steps in their direction.

Aradia moved in the opposite direction. Tara's head came up, a low sound coming from her throat. "We're good." Did that sound as snippy to them as it did to her own ears? Did she actually care if it did? So much for not offending.

The shorter one shrugged, frowning as though she'd been mightily insulted. Another thing that told her they weren't what they appeared. Out here, people went their own way and left other hikers to themselves. Polite and friendly. Not all pissy because strangers didn't want to join them.

"All right then. We'll get going. Have a good afternoon." Both of them glanced once more at Tara before heading toward the mountain. No hurry. No backward glances at them.

"I don't think I like those two." Rufus leaned against the tree, watching them as they walked away.

Aradia put a hand on his shoulder. "Right there with you, and so is Tara. They're hiding something, and I doubt it's a good something."

"I'm betting it's a unanimous opinion." Mercy said. "Tim?"

"True enough, and did you see how they looked at Tara? Makes me think they know what she is and were sizing her up."

Aradia agreed. "We better keep an eye out. Way more company out here than we anticipated. First, the guy with a gun and now these two. How can a place this big feel so crowded?"

❖

Mercy stared after the women as they walked away. "You're right, Aradia. Those two are not what they seem." Chills had raced up her arms the moment they got close. They looked normal enough, but they weren't, and it almost rolled off them like ocean waves. Though they were now out of sight, her nerves still twitched as though someone had tapped her with a lightning rod.

Aradia took her hand. "Couldn't agree with you more. They were working really hard to come off as day hikers, and I'm calling BS on that. If they're day hikers, I'm a rocket scientist. The only thing that gave me a moment of pause was that Tara didn't alert. She definitely kept her eyes on them, and that sound she made was clear proof she didn't trust them, but if they were demons, her response would have been definitive. Not demons. Whatever they are, they're allies of darkness."

Mercy hadn't gotten the demon vibe either, not that she'd even seen one before Beliar popped up. She supposed they could appear looking like anyone, including hikers. Still, her intuition didn't lean toward escaped demons. "More like they're up to something, and not a good something. They were way too interested in us."

Rufus nodded. "Definitely up to no good. Got a whiff of something on the air. Wasn't as clear as my visions but letting me know to beware just the same. Glad you sent them on their way. We're gonna want to make sure they're not out there lying in wait. You know, follow us to the portal. I get the sense they're either demon hunters or they're scouts for one. That's my two cents."

Aradia patted Rufus on the shoulder. "Right there with you. I had the same thought. Among all of us, we'll be able to do a three-sixty scan as we go. We don't want any unpleasant surprises from those two."

"I wish we could do more." Tim continued to stare in the direction the women had walked.

Mercy pondered silently if it might be time to try something Mom had taught her years ago. She'd always thought it a bit of nonsense, but all of a sudden, she wasn't quite so sure. It might actually help. Like Mom had known all along that she'd be in this place, at this moment, and with these people needing what the lesson had imparted to her.

She stopped and said to their backs, "I have an idea."

They all halted, turned, and looked at her, even Tara, who'd been leading them closer to the mountain. Aradia put a hand on her shoulder, the touch once more electric. "Tell us. We're open to ideas. Tim and I have a pretty well-stocked tool kit, but honestly, this is different from any mission I've ever been on, and I'm betting it's the same for you, Tim."

He glanced again in the direction the women had taken. "No argument there. This is dangerous. Something new and awful is about to happen out here. I'm open to anything that can help. So, if you've got something, let's hear it."

Mercy shivered. "I hate to say it, since I'm a newbie to all this, but I completely agree. Whatever bit of magic I have is not happy with the vibes. They're not good ones."

"I get that same sense," Tim said. "And I'm worried about Clemons. I haven't seen him for hours. He usually checks in more often. Something's seriously off here."

"Oh, Tim. I'm sorry. We can delay my big idea and look for Clemons. You're right. We need to find him." Mercy's concern for Clemons outweighed leaning into an old lesson that might or might not help.

"Everybody hold up. Mercy, we'll get back to your idea in a few minutes." Rufus took Tim's hands in his and closed his eyes. "Give me a sec, and let me do my thing first. Not as impressive as what you guys do, but it could help. Anything is worth a shot, right?"

Mercy thought she understood. Just as she'd already built a bond with Aradia, Tim and Rufus were clearly linked. If anyone could reach out for Clemons, through Tim, it would be Rufus. His head tipped back for a moment, his lips pressed together, his hair reaching to his waist while his hat stayed firmly in place. Tim watched him intently. Then Rufus opened his eyes, and in them she saw pain. She knew Rufus well enough to realize that what he saw bothered him. How she hoped the news delivered didn't include death.

"What?" Tim's voice wavered, and the emotion she heard in it broke her heart.

Rufus got right to it. They didn't have time to soften anything. "He's hurt, though not bad, and I think he's stuck. That's why we haven't seen him. He wants to come back. He wants to keep working. He just can't."

Tim shook his head, his eyes narrowed. "I don't know that I understand. What could possibly prevent him from coming to me if he's not hurt bad? The Guardians, for the most part, can't be stopped. Traditional weapons can't kill them."

Mercy had a thought. "Could he have fallen somewhere and be unable to climb back out?" They were in mountainous terrain after all.

Rufus lifted a shoulder. "It's possible. It didn't come through clear enough for me to see exactly what held him back. Only that he remained in one place, unable to continue his work."

Tim looked over to Aradia. "There are demon hunters out here, and if they find him…" He didn't finish the thought. He didn't need to. They all had to be thinking the same thing, and Mercy's stomach dropped.

"He'll make it," Aradia said in a confident voice. "He's a Guardian, and if he's stuck somewhere, he'll be okay. I believe it." Mercy wasn't sure if her confidence was real or put on for Tim's benefit.

Tim nodded. "Right. They can't hurt him. Block him maybe, but not hurt him." It sounded to her more like he was working to convince himself. "Still, demon hunters."

"Like those women?" Mercy felt their blackness all the way to her soul. While she wanted to embrace Aradia's faith in the dogs, those women worried her.

Aradia nodded. "Pretty sure that's a yes. They were not hikers."

"The guy I saw is one too. The aura coming off him wasn't good, if you know what I mean. And we all know what he did to me without getting very close. From the way you describe these hunters, he fits the mold," Rufus added.

Mercy believed him. Rufus had an excellent, and quick, grasp of people's true nature. He'd been that way as long as she'd known him, and she trusted him with her life. "So, three of them. Three demon hunters."

Aradia nodded. "Four of us."

Mercy wasn't all that convinced they weren't still outnumbered. So far, they counted three hunters and three bodies. Felt an awful lot like the storm might just be getting started.

No more time to waste. She had to step up. "I think we can tap into more." Mercy held up a hand. It had come to her in a flash, one of those moments of clarity when she finally understood why Mom had taught her a particular ritual. Had Mom known she would one day need this very unique bit of knowledge? Maybe not. But Mom had always seemed to know and understand things that made no sense to her. Even so far as finding a little girl alone and abandoned in the park that night. Why had Mom even been there that night many, many miles from home? She'd never given Mercy a clear answer to that question and always said the dog had been the hero, sniffing her out in her hiding place. Mercy knew it had been more than the dog. Bottom line, she couldn't define Mom's magic, and she couldn't ignore it. Now she fully understood how she'd prepared her adopted daughter for this moment in time. *Thank you, Mom.*

"You have friends you can bring in? Not sure we can get them up to speed with what we're really dealing with here." Aradia looked skeptical.

"I'm with Aradia." Tim weighed in. "You two accepted the possibility that demons might escape from the underworld more easily than most, due to the nature of your own special gifts. That's not true of most people. They'll think we've lost our collective minds."

Mercy swept her gaze across their tiny, unlikely army as they prepared to stand against whoever wanted to release demons into the world. "Not those kinds of friends." Besides, she glanced down at her phone. No service. No one to call even if she wanted to. Well, that wasn't an issue because Mercy didn't intend to use modern technology for this request.

Aradia shook her head as she shifted from foot to foot. The urgency rolling off Aradia screamed go, go, go. "Not following your meaning, and we've got to get moving. We've wasted enough time." A frown on her face, she looked toward the mountain.

"Understood and no reason you should follow this. It's about a ritual my mom taught me. I never understood why because it was so different from our work as healers. Though Mom practiced Wicca and taught it to me, this was older and more intense. At the time, I couldn't figure it out. Now it makes perfect sense."

"She knew something." Rufus nodded. "Your mom! She always was a sneaky one."

The comment had her smiling. "From the moment she found me in that park, she saved me over and over again, in ways I either didn't see or didn't understand. Never realized she'd be doing it even after she left this world." Her heart swelled with love for the woman she'd never be able to hug again.

"She was a gem. Our mothers were good friends, our grandmothers too," Rufus explained. "Which is why we've known each other for eons. We're the kind of family not related by blood."

She took both of his hands. "Chosen family. And now we call on them. You understand?"

Rufus nodded and held her gaze. "Now we call on them."

Aradia studied them both through narrowed eyes. "Somebody want to loop us in? I'm sure as heck not following."

Mercy let go of Rufus and now took both of Aradia's hands. "You know how to close the portal, right?"

"When Tara and Clemons lead us to it, yes. We have the magic to close it. I'd rather it not even reach the point of opening. If we can get to it first, we can reinforce the magic holding it closed. Lock it up and throw away the key, if you know what I mean."

"I get it. You recognized what Rufus and I possess and asked us out here to join power with you and Tim for extra strength in sealing it again. That's the gist of it as I understand it all."

Aradia nodded. "Again, yes. That's how I hoped we could all work together. Power in numbers from four people who've already brought power into the mix."

"What if we can add a few more to said mix?"

Now Aradia shook her head. "Like Tim said a few minutes ago, it's not that simple to get people to buy in to what's happening out here. Most everyone wants to trust in the world they can see and touch. Theoretically they might accept that demons exist. To encounter them in the flesh? The folks with minds open enough to believe that are few and far between. We don't have time to find those few."

Mercy gave Aradia the moment to vent. What she said made sense but didn't apply right now. "Not talking about people per se."

Aradia stood up taller and focused on Mercy's face. "Explain." Had her interested now. Good.

"I can bring back our elders. Our ancestors." She nodded toward Rufus.

"No way." Aradia breathed out the words, her eyes wide. Did she see a flicker of hope in them?

She nodded. "Way."

❖

The hurry-up-and-wait phase had arrived. August got everything prepared and in position. The last piece to reach perfection remained the rise of the Black Moon. The air had grown thicker as the afternoon wore on, foretelling the moon's appearance.

Rather than sit out in the opening waiting for darkness, he moved away from the readied circle and the blessed dagger to tuck away and relax under the cover of the trees. With an unobstructed view of the cleared-away mountainside and his ritual circle, he settled in to wait. Hard to be patient while the anticipation inside him built like a bonfire. He forced himself to remain calm and focused despite the tingling in his fingers.

At the same time, he swept his gaze around the surrounding area over and over. He expected to see the female Guardian and her handler come racing in at any minute. No illusions that she'd fail to track down the portal and make this easy for him. When she did come close, he wanted to be ready. It would be easy enough to dispatch both her and the handler. He patted the grip of the gun still at his waist. Handlers were all too human, and the gun could do a fine job of readying them for their dirt nap. If he had to use a bit of magic, as he'd done on the man, that would work too. Lots in his tool kit for the human part of the team.

The female Guardian, he'd have to disable, as he'd been successful in doing with the male a few hours ago. Saddened him that his oleander-laced treats failed to entice the massive canines. It would have been so much simpler if they'd taken the bait and died somewhere out in the tall grass. The trainers and handlers were most likely responsible for that tactical fail. His educated guess, they trained them not to accept food from anyone except the handler. Smart on their part. Pain in the ass for him.

Not a showstopper. He had other ways to achieve success that didn't involve using traditional weapons to stop a Guardian, pleasant as that might be for him. Getting them out of his way for the time it took to gather his demon forces would work as well. He might not be able to kill them. He could stop them, and that's exactly what he planned to do. One down. One to go. Once the portal opened, once he called his generals to task, the need for the Guardians would be moot. He smiled.

Then he frowned. Still looking and listening, he wondered where Willa and June were at the moment. If Ama had made it out here, then the other two were around as well. A female pack of wannabes. They'd probably put their heads together to plan usurping him the moment they all concluded this portal had the potential to bring forth a new world. All three of them had always been sneaky bitches. Each of them wanted a level of power and importance they didn't deserve. The truth none of them had ever been able to accept was they didn't, individually or collectively, have the backbone to handle it. It took a special person, and that had always been him.

August studied his circle and his frown deepened. What weighed on him was the bitches would know what to do with his circle and how to harness control of the demons who walked through the portal. He couldn't allow them to step inside or touch his tools. He carried his advantage at his waist. Unlike with the Guardians, traditional methods of stopping them would work well. Thing about his sister and ex-wife: they were crafty. He didn't trust that they weren't already close by and waiting, like him, for the moon to hit center sky before they made a move to stop him and steal his glory.

More work than he'd anticipated when he came here. A Guardian team had been a given. Those stupid monitoring teams were always in the way, and he'd convinced himself that getting rid of a dog and handler would be a breeze. The surprise came when he found himself confronted by two teams. That he hadn't expected. Twice the work, and he had other things he'd rather be doing.

Actually, the more he thought about it, the more he hoped Willa and June did show up. He could use them. Sort of like a couple of spare batteries. Or, even better, offerings to the demons who would follow him. Training treats in a sense. He laughed out loud and then quickly slapped a hand over his mouth. No sense giving himself away before he was ready. Not that he hid exactly. Still, no sense in advertising his position.

August hadn't been certain why he'd done it when he loaded the case with the four syringes filled with potassium chloride into his bag. Unlike with his favorite oleander, he hadn't grown this toxin himself. Rather, he'd purchased it off the good old internet. Loved how accessible just about everything had become these days. Sometimes it required the dark web to get what he wanted, and that didn't pose a problem for him. At the time he'd placed the order, he hadn't been thinking about the women in his life. He sure did now. The right tool for every job, and the little black zippered case held exactly the right tools. All he had to do was separate them and boom, jab, jab. The rapid-acting poison would do the rest of the work. From his pack, he took out two syringes and slipped them into his pocket, confident the small plastic caps protected him from the poke of the needles.

Settling back into the shadows with a solid plan in mind for all who would come for him, dogs included, he waited. He touched the syringes and hoped June and Willa would come first. He wanted his gifts to the demons in place before he had to deal with the interlopers.

As if the universe were in tune with him, he heard them long before he saw them. Quiet entry wasn't a skill either possessed. Sounded more like a couple of water buffalos clomping through the woods. The sound of the footsteps stopped, and no one stepped out into the open just yet. No doubt staying in the shadows and studying his preparations. The ritual circle was clearly visible.

While he couldn't hear their whispers, from his spot against the tree, he could see where they stood, their heads together. When they did exactly what he'd been hoping they'd opt for, he smiled. Willa moved toward the left, June went right. Divide and conquer. Could they make it any easier for him?

It made perfect sense to go for June first. He'd spent their childhood years sneaking up on her and terrorizing her. At least a dozen times, he'd hidden beneath her bed and grabbed her ankles when she came into her room. Her screams could have woken up the whole neighborhood. Their mother always scolded him. Their father kept quiet at the same time he gave August a wink. Cheap entertainment. Who knew those years would turn out to be the training ground for today? He took one of the syringes from his pocket and slid the protective cap off the needle, dropping it to the ground. He didn't subscribe to the carry-in carry-out program.

Focused on sneaking about, June clearly didn't hear him until the last second. Kind of like their childhood. No matter how many times he scared her, she never saw or heard him coming. Today, by the time she realized he'd sneaked up behind her, he'd buried the needle in her neck. He pushed the plunger down in one quick move, picturing the poison pouring into her, and then tossed the empty syringe aside. A job expertly done. "You should have stayed home, sister," he whispered into her ear. Always thought she was smarter and faster than him. What she'd never realized? He'd let her think that. All along he'd known that her mistaken belief would be to his advantage one day. Today turned out to be that day.

"You won't win." Her words were muffled because he held one hand over her mouth and used the other to pull her close to him. As much as he'd like the effects to be instantaneous, fast-acting didn't equate to immediate. It took a few, and he held her tight against his body until she went limp. Only then did he release his hold on her. She dropped to the ground with a thud. He glanced around to see if Willa had heard. Not seeing or hearing her, he decided she had continued on her own path blissfully unaware of what would be heading her way. He couldn't leave June here. Too easy to see her. Grabbing her feet, he dragged her into the underbrush and threw a couple of fallen pine boughs on top of her. For a few seconds he studied her before deciding it would take a bit before anyone noticed her. Good. One down. One to go.

The first syringe discarded, he pulled the second, still full, from his pocket and readied it for round two. Once more, he slid the protective cap from the needle and threw it aside. He squatted low to the ground and listened. Willa had gone in the opposite direction of June, surely believing they would be able to overpower him by coming at him from two sides. In reality, their strategy had proved fatal for them while perfect for his needs. Their separation gave him time and opportunity to utilize his own unique set of skills. Stealth had been one of his superpowers as long as he could remember.

Took a few minutes before he heard her light footsteps. Unlike June, Willa tended to be a lot more in tune with her environment. Her propensity toward bad behavior had a big hand in it. She'd never have been able to pull off all the affairs without some talent for deception. It hadn't taken him long to see the real Willa, even with her better-than-average skills.

He continued to listen until he felt like he had a solid understanding of her movements and direction. In silence, he walked toward the sound of her steps. He kept to the shadows and moved as softly as a ballet dancer. She wasn't the only one skilled in deception. As she drew close, he stopped and ducked back into the shadows. She would come the rest of the way to him. A bee to the hive. That was his girl.

"Come on, baby." His whisper was audible only to him.

She moved into his line of sight, clearly unaware of his presence. As he'd done with June, at the right moment he came out of the darkness, moving fast, the needle piercing the soft flesh of her neck before she had a chance to react. How he loved a good surprise. How he loved a fatal surprise even more. Way better than a divorce.

"Miss me?" he said against her ear and laughed, not caring now if the sound carried. "I didn't miss you, and, news flash, I won't miss you." As he'd done with June, he held her against himself. Surprisingly, it brought back memories of a time when he actually liked holding her close. A long-ago feeling. Too bad how it had ended. For about a New York minute it had been a perfect relationship. After that minute passed, it had been ugly.

Now, she tried to kick him, a good effort that failed. He held her up higher until only her toes swept over the pine-needle-strewn ground. Again and again, she tried to kick, the effort growing weaker with each successive try. Gave her props for the effort. When the drug completed its job, which took a little longer with Willa than June, he dropped her to the ground next to a fallen tree. She'd be hidden from immediate view here so no need to drag her anywhere else. August stepped over her twitching body. It was just like Willa to fight the poison all the way to the end like she could change the inevitable result. Delusions were a favorite of hers and, with impending death, still a favorite.

"No antidote," he said to her, not that she'd hear him at this point. At least June had accepted her fate with grace and died like a proper lady. That had never been Willa's way. Grace wasn't a word he'd associate with her. He didn't look back as he walked away.

Overhead, the sun moved steadily toward the west, where it slid slowly beyond the mountains. Soon enough the moon would begin its rise and, as his friends would say, party time! Now that Willa and June were out of his hair, he no longer cared if anyone could see him. He didn't care if the Guardians came. He stepped inside the circle and pulled one last item out of the bag, having saved the best for last. He took the container of salt and poured it around the edge. Better than a concrete wall. He sat in the center of the circle, his hands folded, and waited to hear the sound of paws.

CHAPTER NINETEEN

O h no, no, no." Aradia ran as fast as she could, Tim passing her in a heartbeat. The second she'd noticed Clemons, she'd also recognized why they hadn't seen him for a while. Her pulse raced.

"I'll kill them." Tim's voice rang with raw emotion, and she totally understood. If Tara had her paw trapped in a snare, she'd be scared, frantic, and pissed off. A wild-hog snare, if she wasn't mistaken. Who the hell brought a wild-hog snare to western Washington? Only one answer made sense. Someone who knew a Guardian would be here. Someone who knew they couldn't kill a Guardian.

"How is he?" She knelt next to Tim and Clemons. The dog remained calm and trusting as Tim worked on the snare in order to free his paw. It took careful work to make sure the snare didn't tighten. Tim freed his paw as blood oozed into the white fur on his leg. He threw the disabled snare aside.

"How is he?" Aradia couldn't keep the emotion from her voice.

Tim touched Clemon's leg gently. The big dog stood still while Tim checked him out. "Nothing broken."

Relief flooded through Aradia. "Thank goodness."

"Is that a snare?" Mercy looked down at the pieces of the device used to disable Clemons. Hands in her pockets, her long hair swung down over her shoulders, she had a confused expression.

"Yeah, and when I find the asshole who did this…" Aradia didn't finish. She couldn't recall ever being this angry.

Clemons licked Tim's face. "It's okay, boy. We've got you." He dropped his pack onto the ground and pulled out a canine first-aid kit.

All the handlers carried them for instances like this. The Guardians might have an aura of protection around them, but they weren't immune to occasional injuries. Tim quickly wrapped the bleeding leg, first with gauze and then with vet wrap in bright orange. Clemons licked him again as if saying thank you.

Aradia glanced around. Nothing nearby that screamed of danger, but she worried they were losing critical time and advantage. As much as it pained her, she made the hard call. She rested a hand on Tim's shoulder as he put his first-aid kit back into his pack. "You're going to need to stay here with him. He shouldn't walk on that leg until a vet can look at it." Clemons would try if they let him. The Guardians were wired that way. Nothing stopped them. Not fatigue, not hunger, and definitely not an injured leg. Aradia didn't want the damage to be permanent, and it sure could end up that way if they let him run through the wilderness on it.

"No," Tim said. He didn't look up at her.

She had to insist. "Not up for discussion. Clemons's health is more important. There's still three of us, along with Tara. We can handle whatever we have to out here, and you can keep him safe." Clemons could heal from the wound and continue his career if they prevented further injury. Tim would know that if he were thinking without the rush of emotion the snare had caused. The demon hunter probably counted on both the injury to the dog and the emotion it would stir up in a handler to slow them way down.

Tim shook his head again. "You don't understand. I've got a sling in my pack. We can continue to hike in with you, and Clemons will be safe." Tim dug into his pack again and pulled out what looked like a thick square of canvas. He laid it out flat on the ground, revealing the four openings at the areas necessary for a dog the size of Clemons. No one could accuse Tim of heading into a battle unprepared.

The sling would work to get him up and off the injured leg. She had a similar one in her pack. A little smaller for Tara. Any handler worth their salt carried one for injury-causing events like what had happened to Clemons. Still, he was a big boy, and packing him out would require tons of strength and energy. "He's too big." She didn't say how it would slow them all down. Didn't want to make Tim feel any worse than he already did. Wasn't his fault that Clemons had been hurt. That fact wouldn't make him feel any better. They all took the safety of their dogs to heart.

He paused and looked at her. "Maybe you haven't noticed, Aradia. I'm a big guy too. I'm not leaving him, and I'm not leaving you. Too much at stake, and time is running short. We shouldn't spend any of it arguing. Can you deny you'd do the same thing if it were Tara in that snare?"

He had here there, and he knew it. She didn't look away as she answered. "I can't."

He nodded. "All right then. Let's put him in the sling and get going. I have a feeling Tara is on track to lead us to the portal."

She'd picked up on the same thing. Tara had become extremely focused despite displaying patience for the emergency they were handling. "Let's do this."

"Can we help?" Rufus asked as he and Mercy stepped close.

Tim nodded. "Give me a sec to put his legs in, and then it would make it a lot easier if you lifted him up while I slip the straps on. I'll carry him on my back, and Rufus, I'd appreciate it if you'd carry my pack."

Rufus nodded. "Done and done."

Mercy studied the sling contraption. "He'll let you do that?"

Tim didn't pause. "Absolutely."

Aradia trained all her dogs to use a sling before she deployed them out in the field. That was true for those who had the shine that marked them as Guardians and the dogs that went to working homes. Even those whose personalities made them suitable as pets rather than working dogs. It was important that her dogs be comfortable in all situations, and that included if they got hurt. Clemons had received that training, and she'd be surprised if Tim didn't actually practice it with him. He knew what to do and allowed Tim to pick up each leg and slide it into the holes in the sling. When all four were in, they lifted Clemons into the sling, which allowed Tim to easily slide his arms into the straps. They were already adjusted to accommodate Clemons. Tim shrugged slightly and then nodded. "We're good. Let's go."

Aradia still wasn't sure. She'd feel better if he took Clemons away from the mountain and to a local vet to have his leg attended to. From Tim's determined expression, it would be a heated argument that she'd lose. He gazed intently at the mountain ahead of them as he leaned forward a little to compensate for the large dog on his back. He'd been teamed with Clemons for a reason. Never give up. Never give in. Either of them.

Tara had been pacing back and forth, her eyes on the mountain as they'd worked to free Clemons from the snare, then give him the necessary first aid, and settle him into the sling. Now, she sensed the time had arrived to continue the work. She surged forward and took off running. Out of sight in seconds.

"We weren't wrong about her. Something's up." While Tara worked all the time, her movements and focus were different now. More urgent. She wasn't sensing spider cracks releasing poison any longer. Another breach had either happened already or would soon enough. Aradia believed Tara wasn't just sensing the approaching dance but had narrowed down the location of the portal.

"You saw that, right?" Tim asked her.

"I saw it." She walked slightly ahead of Tim, Mercy in step with her.

Mercy looked around. "What? What did you see?"

"Tara's got it." Overhead the moon neared center sky.

"It? As in the portal and the demons and the evil?" Her voice wavered a little.

"As in all of that." Aradia hoped they didn't get there too late. She glanced at Mercy. "You ready with that spell of yours? Pretty sure we're going to need it."

Mercy stayed at her side as Aradia walked faster. "I'm as ready as I'll ever be."

"Good."

"We better hurry." Tim glanced up at the moon and then back at Rufus. "Stay close."

"Not letting you out of my sight." Rufus did as Tim asked.

Aradia glanced up at the sky and then back at Tim. "Can you run?"

❖

Mercy would be lying to say she didn't feel the pull of forces unseen. The air almost screamed danger. She'd lived in the area since childhood, yet she'd never felt anything like this before. Made her wonder how such evil could have waited beneath the ground she'd walked over year in and year out without her knowing. Could be she'd convinced herself she'd already seen the worst the world had to offer when her father abandoned her and had ignored anything that might disabuse her of that belief.

Also made her wonder about the visions she'd experienced throughout her life. How could she rely on those, as she'd done so many times, when the ability had failed her here? Shouldn't something come to her now that would help them? A big fat nothing made her feel useless and, worse, a drain on the energy Aradia and Tim needed to stop the portal from opening.

Did Rufus feel the same way? They'd both embraced a bit of pride in their extraordinary abilities. Made them feel unique and as if they belonged to a very special club. For a couple of kids who had never really fit in, that feeling of being unique had given them pride. The events unfolding out here gave new meaning to the old saying: pride goeth before a fall. Had a hunch she might be about to fall.

"You getting anything?" She directed her question to Rufus, who jogged behind her and close to Tim.

"I'm feeling a lot, and it's freaking me out. Not seeing anything, and that's freaking me out too." He sounded breathy as they ran.

She wasn't much better, but she kept talking anyway. "Right there with you. I don't get why nothing is coming to either one of us. It's obvious there's activity out here, and it's the kind you and I should be able to tap into."

"The dog is taking us in. I've never seen one move with that kind of speed before. I'm not in shape for this kind of trail running."

"No trail," she spit out at the same time she caught a toe on a rock and almost went down. Rufus grabbed her arm, and she righted herself. They kept jogging along, jumping over fallen trees and protruding rocks, Tara ahead of them occasionally disappearing from sight and then returning to make sure they followed.

"My point exactly. I'm not built for this."

"I disagree. Have you noticed you're keeping up?"

"I'm keeping up with a guy carrying a hundred-pound-plus dog on his back. Not sure that counts." Rufus sounded a little breathless.

"It counts, and I'm amazed at what we've seen, what we might see, and I'm scared at the same time. I hope the ritual Mom taught me works. My gut tells me we're going to need all the help we can get." Her heart pounded and her legs burned. She didn't slow down.

"It'll work." This time Rufus stumbled, and she caught his arm. "I don't think either one of us is going to make it as Olympic runners."

Even in the darkest hours, she could count on her friend to find a moment of humor.

"No. Pretty sure we don't want to give up the day jobs. And if the ritual doesn't work, I may have to rethink my life's calling." Maybe she shouldn't have said anything about the ritual spell. Healing with her plants was one thing. Trying to perform white magic was something much different. They were counting on her, and what if it failed?

"It is going to work." As if he could hear her thoughts, Rufus repeated the phrase with more emphasis.

She wished she had his level of confidence. "You sound so certain."

"It has to work. If those things get loose in the world, we're all doomed." Maybe not confidence as much as a last-ditch effort.

In the deepening darkness, Mercy stumbled again and this time crashed to her knees. Rocks bit through her jeans hard enough that if they didn't draw blood, she'd be sporting lovely shades of black and blue. Before she could push herself back to her feet, Aradia was at her side.

"Are you hurt?" She'd been way ahead of Mercy, Rufus, and Tim, which made Mercy wonder how she'd even known she'd fallen.

"My pride mostly." She let Aradia help her to her feet. "I'm sorry I slowed you down." The touch of her hand steadied her a lot. In fact, each time Aradia touched her, Mercy felt stronger, happier. Even here in the darkness with the fate of the world hanging in the balance, just her touch made a difference. She didn't want to let go.

Aradia put a hand on her hair. "Don't be sorry. We're going to need you. We're all in this together now. All of us." She kissed Mercy on the cheek. "That means you too, Rufus. Stay strong. I'm with you."

A rumbling beneath her feet almost sent her back down to her throbbing knees. "Oh, hell. Did you feel that, or is it just me?" So many weird things going on around them, hard to know.

Aradia squeezed her hand. "I did, and I don't like it. We better hurry. Can you keep going?" She visually searched Mercy's face. Any other night it might be too dark to even see each other. With the light of the moon and stars overhead, not the case tonight.

Tara barked as if she too wanted them to hurry the heck up. A low growl started in Clemons's throat as he bounced against Tim's back. Wounded but still on the job. She'd always thought him smart and gorgeous. Now she realized he was flat-out an extraordinary dog. She glanced at Aradia and didn't wonder why Clemons was special.

"We got it, buddy." Tim reached back and patted Clemons on the head. His legs started to move as if he wanted to run. "Easy, boy, easy." Tim stumbled a little as he tried to calm the dog.

Mercy swung her gaze between Tim and Aradia. "Is this normal? Is this something you've dealt with before? You know what to do, don't you?" Earlier, when she'd offered the only kind of help she could think of, it seemed like it could, in fact, help. The closer they got to the mountain, the more her confidence wavered. As good an herbalist as she might be, as much as she appreciated the visions that came to her now and again, no question of being out of her league here.

"Ah." Tim grimaced, and she wasn't sure if his expression was caused by the strain of the big dog he carried in the sling on his back or because he didn't want to answer her question.

"More intense than what we normally come up against." Now Aradia put her arm around Mercy's shoulders and pulled her close for a quick hug. Much appreciated and gave her confidence a little bump. Might not be enough, but she'd take it. "We'll shut them down. Don't worry."

"How can you be sure?" She wanted to have rock-solid assurance that their combined goodness would push back the evil that marched toward them. Most of her life, she'd believed that good triumphed over evil. Mom seeded that belief the night she saved her. From that moment on, goodness had been a big part of her life. Everything she'd seen out here, everything she'd felt, made her question whether she'd been living in a fantasy world.

Tim stood up taller and patted Rufus on the shoulder. A look passed between them. "Come on. The moon-rise isn't slowing down, and neither should we. Both dogs are telling us in their way to hurry the hell up. I say we listen." Tim charged forward, or charged as much as he could with Clemons on his back. Continued to impress her.

"Show us." Aradia directed the command to Tara, who once more started running into the distance. Unlike before, this time she didn't run far enough ahead that they'd lose sight of her in the darkness. Her hurried intent remained the same and seemed to telegraph a no-time-to-spare message. Now, however, Tara also seemed to be careful that her distance didn't leave them behind. A scary shift had occurred.

"Hey." Mercy stopped and stared at the racing Tara. "She's glowing." She wasn't having a vision, and she wasn't imagining it. The dog glowed like a beacon.

Aradia put a hand on her shoulder. "She sure as hell is. That's how I know she and others like her are Guardians, and usually I'm the only one who can see it. See, another sign of how special you are. Now come on." She nodded in Tara's direction. "Moonlight is burning, and we have demons to send back to the underworld."

"Anybody else see that?" She glanced at Rufus.

"See what?" He jogged beside Tim and Clemons.

"Never mind." She shifted her gaze to Aradia as they closed the distance to the mountain.

Aradia gave her a little nod. "Looks like you might have a new profession in your future. Not everyone can see the glow."

Another change. Like enough weirdness hadn't entered her life in the last couple of days. "I'm scared." More than her fear of the dark, her body buzzed, and her heart pounded. Could be attributed to running, but she knew it to be more than physical exertion. The air had grown heavy, and her eyes weren't failing her. That dog had been glowing. Glowing! Not to mention she'd earlier seen a demon. A line from Shakespeare's *The Tempest* popped into her head: hell is empty, and all the devils are here.

❖

August watched the Black Moon as it rose higher and higher. Though he'd been out here alone for some time, given June and Willa slept the forever sleep, he knew better than to believe the solitude and peace would last. And, his belief proved to be correct. He heard movement behind him. The Guardian he'd been expecting, and if the Guardian approached, then the handler would be right along behind her. This late in the game, they'd be hanging close.

No worries. The moon would be center-sky in a matter of minutes, and he remained safe and untouchable inside the ritual circle. The Guardian wouldn't stand a chance. Maybe if two Guardians barreled in, they might get lucky and be able to breach the circle. But that wouldn't happen, thanks to his always-prepared work ethic.

Speaking of not standing a chance. Neither would the pesky humans coming along for the ride. Behind him plenty of noise. They didn't appear to care if their arrival was announced. Because he could hear the sounds of multiple voices, the Guardian teams clearly came with help. Too bad for them. Too little, too late.

He picked up the wand he'd created while he waited for the moon to complete its path across the night sky. Turned out quite nice, if he did say so. One last tweak and it too would be an incredibly powerful tool. Ideally, he'd use the blood of an innocent, but that wasn't an option out here. Instead, he'd had to make a small cut on his palm in order to cover the wand with the necessary blood offering. His knife, smeared with his blood as he worked, had easily sliced through the branch he'd found nearby. The wand, about twenty inches long, captured the energy of the rising Black Moon as he carved and prayed at the same time. His blood infused it with even more might. By the time he heard his visitors, he had completed the wand. He held it in one hand and the knife, which he didn't bother to clean off, in the other. Both pulsed against his palms.

"That's him." A man yelled, his voice almost shrill. Not very manly, in his opinion. Real men don't shrill. "That's the asshole who tried to shoot me and Tara."

August glanced back, the moonlight like a floodlight over the forest. The Native American man he'd seen following the Guardian earlier pointed at him. Two women and another man stopped beside him. He'd almost been able to capture that one's soul, and it angered him they'd disrupted his earlier plan. No worries. He could revisit after the portal opened, and he'd save him for himself. Later. August didn't like losing.

"Wrong," he said, not caring if any of them heard him. "I wanted Ama out of the way. I could have cared less about you. Your bad luck for being in the wrong place at the wrong time" He didn't admit to caring about the man's soul. Better to let him think he'd escaped August's reach. The truth of it would hit him later.

He turned back around to face the portal. The gun still sat at his waist, and it would be easy enough to dispatch his visitors if and when they became a problem. Rather than drop either the knife or the wand, he continued to hold them as he tipped his head up, his gaze on the moon. At the precise moment it moved to center sky, he smiled and stood. Without bothering to further acknowledge the presence of the incoming guests, he raised his arms, holding the knife and wand aloft. All of his nerves buzzed, and the earth trembled beneath his feet. The time for the Demon King to claim his glory and marshal his troops had arrived. Glory came his way.

"Oh, Dark Father, I fly to your power. Behold me, the new King of Demons, father to darkness, bringer of chaos, rightful heir to all riches above and below. That which is working in me becomes the winds of change and wraps the darkness around me like the royal cloak of kings."

Bolts of energy roared down his arms and into his body. His prayer had been heard and acknowledged. Time to take it to the ultimate conclusion. He filtered out the frantic sounds around him—the dog and the humans who all sought to stop him. Wouldn't happen. They couldn't stop him even if they could breach his circle.

"Behold me, the Lion of Victory, for I will command the power of the Black Moon and release the seven seals. Behold a bolt falling from the sky and granting me the power to crush righteous warriors and the creatures they command. All shall bow to my power. All shall bend to my will. Nothing shall harm me as I call forth my army. Come to me now: Asmodeus, Beliar, Baal, Ashroth, Glasyalbolas. Come to me. Come to me. Come to me and bow."

The mountain screamed as the stone split apart and demons began to step out.

CHAPTER TWENTY

Oh, hell, no." The sound alone sent tremors through Aradia. The sight of the mountain splitting open almost had her heading toward a full-on panic attack. Flames rose in the opening, massive heat pouring out and causing sweat to bead on her brow, the gold band beneath her shirt growing hot. Tara raced toward the chanting man and then skidded to a stop. Only then did Aradia notice the magic circle. Damn it. She should have thought of that. Of course, he'd protect himself.

Tara did a reboot and left the man, going instead toward the demons that stepped from the gaping portal. Not a bark. Her legs spread wide, her head high, Tara let out a scream that had the demons stepping back. Not a bark—a scream. Aradia had never heard that sound from her before, or any of her dogs, and it sent chills through her despite the intense heat coming from the open portal. In the sling, Clemons struggled and kicked. Tim appeared to be losing his footing as he fought to stay upright. Clemons threw back his head and, like Tara, screamed.

Sparks kicked from the open portal, tiny fires popping up in the grass and underbrush around the entrance. Aradia prayed for rain with the strength of a hurricane. Not likely, given the beautiful cloudless sky earlier. Even now, the sky filled with stars and the special moon with zero cloud cover. It gave her a little comfort to see that the fires burned for only a few moments before they went out. Made her think the mountain rebuffed the demons and the fire they brought with them, and that goodness still held the advantage.

"Quick." Mercy reached out. "Let me try. Please, let me try." Her voice rose.

Aradia wasn't sure anything would be enough at this point. One thing to banish a single demon—the same one that came toward them once more—another to banish an army of them. How the man in the circle had been able to do this astonished her. Nothing she'd learned to date had prepared her for a breach of this magnitude or for the speed at which it happened. She'd also never actually witnessed a portal opening. Prior missions had been successful enough to seal a breach before it had the chance to occur. What she saw now sent terror into her soul.

Aradia appreciated Mercy's wish to help. She just worried she didn't have the chops for this. Hell, she'd been trained for this her whole life, and she wasn't sure she had the chops. She looked to Tim. "We've got to do something."

Mercy didn't give Tim a chance to respond. "You asked me to come out here, to help you. I'm saying, let me help you. Now." Mercy put her hands on her hips and stared into Aradia's eyes as sparks flew in the air around them. One dropped on Mercy's shoulder, and Aradia brushed it away.

"It's worse than I imagined." Her mind kept repeating failure, failure, failure. Another spark fell on Mercy. She brushed it away again. Little fires burned at their feet, flaming up and then burning out. The stench of charred grass filled the air.

"Let her try, Aradia. Trust me. I know her better than anyone." Rufus stepped up and took Mercy's hand. "She's got skills she hasn't even used yet, and we don't have a lot of options or a lot of time. We need more help, and I think she can get it for us."

"A little help here, please." Tim struggled to get the straps of the sling off his shoulders. Aradia hurried over to him. She calmed Clemons as Tim squatted down and slipped his arms out of the sling. As soon as he did, Clemons shook himself free in a matter of seconds. Then he ran toward the mountain, the injury to his leg seemingly forgotten. He ran as well as if he had never been caught in a trap. Her heart swelled with pride and ached as well. She wasn't certain he'd survive the demons. She wasn't certain any of them would survive the demons. Fear tapped at the back of her mind, whispering that she'd be the one, after all the centuries, who failed.

Opting to ignore the little voice in her head, she said, "All right. Let's try, but make it fast." It had to work or they'd be in a world of hurt. Time wasn't their friend. Neither were those who spilled out of the breach. She took Mercy's hands and almost stepped back at the force of energy that surged through her when they touched. Okay. That had to be a good sign, right? She squeezed her hand lightly to let her know they were in this together. With everything going sideways fast, it comforted her as much as she hoped it comforted Mercy. She stomped out yet another little fire.

Tim hesitated, his gaze following his injured partner. Then he blew out a breath. "We better be fast. I don't know how long Clemons and Tara can hold them back, and they're picking up speed. The way the fire is sending sparks out the portal, we're going to have a full-fledged forest fire soon if we don't close that thing."

She didn't disagree. The light of the moon flowed down on the faces that emerged from the portal. Beliar caught her gaze and smiled. Bastard. The look on his face made her want to stop and banish him again. Except that gaping hole in the side of the mountain made her realize they were on uncharted ground. Maybe on losing ground. Her stomach rolled.

Tim joined hands with Rufus, and Mercy turned her face to the moon. Aradia held on tighter, their circle complete and pulsing with energy. "I hope this works."

Mercy's heart beat so hard it would be a Christmas miracle if she didn't suffer a heart attack, and nobody would have time for CPR anyway, given what was happening around them. The man inside the ritual circle continued to chant, though she couldn't make out the words. Not that she really needed to. The result of the spell he cast was on full display. If she weren't seeing it in the flesh, she'd have never believed it. The mountain opened like a massive yawn, and the not-quite-human stalked out. Flames roared inside the gaping mouth, and sparks flew around them like a fiery snowstorm. The demons walked out through the flames, not in a hurry and not with any urgency. No, they moved as if they had nothing to fear. She worried that might be true.

Her eyes closed, Mercy called on her memory to be true and righteous. To bring her the words Mom had patiently taught her, correcting her over and over when she got them wrong, forgot the order, or forgot them altogether. The power that flowed through her from Aradia, Tim, and Rufus left her feeling super-charged, like together they could make it work. It *had* to work. The thought of what might happen if it didn't chilled her to the depths of her bones. No time to waste. She looked from side to side, making sure they all held hands. Important that they maintain contact.

"Are you all ready?"

"Go for it." Aradia answered for everyone, urgency underneath the three words.

She drew in a long breath and closed her eyes as she turned her face to the night sky. "Oh, great Goddess of the Moon. I am the daughter of the sun and the moon, and I have been born into this world to give offerings to She who is the Mother. We come together in her name to seek help of the Spirits of Old. We come on this sacred night when the veil between the worlds is being drawn aside and ask to join in spirit with those who have gone before."

Rufus screamed, and she kept her eyes closed, though tears fell down her cheeks. That he'd gone down wasn't a question. The thread of his power faded as she continued her prayer. She held on tighter to Aradia and Tim. "Protect us from the coming powers, and give us the keys to close the gates to the underworld. Hear me now, great Goddess of the Moon. Let your glory shine about us now. Blessed be." She opened her eyes and looked toward the portal. So far nothing.

Then the ground shook, and pine needles began to fly everywhere. A sound to her left had her turning her head, only to see her friend being pulled away. A demon held Rufus by the arm and dragged him across the scorched earth. "Let him go!" She didn't know where the roar came from, but she let it fly.

The man in the circle now turned and stared at her, his face hard. "Nice try." His laughter sounded as hard as his expression. "You lose." He turned back to watch the exodus from the underworld. He raised his arms and cried, "Welcome, my children. Welcome. Come bow before your king."

At first, she thought he was right about losing. Rufus had gone down at the hands of a demon. Another headed for Tim, with others behind staring in their direction. They came for all of them. She could sense the energy that surged in Aradia as she prepared for battle. The dogs, the Guardians, bless their souls, were doing a credible job of slowing the flow. The demons backed up whenever one of them charged. But there were too many demons and not enough dogs. Tears pooled in her eyes. She'd remembered the chant word for word, and it hadn't worked. Mom had been wrong. "I'm sorry," she cried. "I'm sorry."

And then, they appeared.

❖

What in the actual fuck had just happened? August stood empty-handed, all of his weapons flying through the air and out of the circle, landing on the ground with a dull thud. A gust of heat whooshed by him, and in the next second, his sacred circle blew apart. The salt burned away, the rocks rolling into the night here and there. All that had protected him disappeared in a matter of seconds. Everything had been going according to plan until this moment. Nobody should possess the kind of skills it would take to destroy the magic of either his circle or his spells.

He had to think fast, or this would all go sideways. After all the time, the effort, and the murders he'd put into this, he would not fail. He'd been waiting for this moment too long. Now and into eternity, he remained the rightful Demon King. All would bow to him this night and forever. No one would take it away from him.

It had both shocked and pissed him off to see the large male Guardian race to the portal. That big bastard should still be bound tight in his snare, not running toward and holding back his warriors. Together, the two dogs stood side by side at the mouth of the portal, pushing back against his emerging soldiers. They were not giving up, and demon after demon backed away. Behind the Guardians stood four adults, two women and two men. The one he'd wanted to keep for himself went down when one of August's soldiers grabbed his long hair and slammed him to the ground. His screams of pain told him everything he needed to know. One human down and three more to go. He could deal with three, especially when two of them were mere women. Willa and June could attest to that. Oh, wait. No, they couldn't. They were dead.

He spun to face the three remaining humans, ready to take them all on. Except somehow the dynamic had shifted. As he'd been able to open the portal and release the demons he called into his army, these humans had managed to do something similar, and without the aid of a magic circle. Like they'd opened a portal of their own and, instead of three, five stood hand-in-hand staring at him. Irritating, yes. A problem, no. Calling upon the spirits of a couple of dead women wouldn't cut it. They were going to have to do better than that.

Behind him a chorus of voices rang out: "Hear us, oh Dark ones. The ladies of the light come near. Hear us all who emerge from fire's embrace. You who seek to infuse hatred. You who seek to destroy and kill. Step back. Step back. Return to your embers, and leave this world as you found it. Behold the power of the Old Ones. We are the power in all things. We are the earth. We are the sky. We are beyond. Step back. Step back. Return to your embers, and leave this world as you found it." The strength of the voices grew in volume and numbers, and as he stared, more women began to appear. Old and young they stood as one, shoulder to shoulder.

The sound of retreating feet made him turn. The demons were fading away, the portal appearing to grow narrower as each one stepped back through. He screamed and ran toward it. "NO! I command you to stay. I am your king. I am your ruler. You must obey."

The demons acted as though they couldn't hear him, as if the continuing chant of the humans and the spirits they summoned were the only voices they could now comprehend. More than heard them. Obeyed them. All his work. All his sacrifices were disappearing before his eyes, as overhead the Black Moon he'd waited so long for began its descent. Power faded as the orb moved slowly across the sky.

The dogs' barking grew louder as he watched them herd demons to the portal. None pushed back against the Guardians, instead stepping through and disappearing into the flames that dimmed each time one entered. He wasn't imagining it. The portal shrank every time one stepped back into the gaping hole. August turned toward what remained of his ritual circle. The dagger, about three feet away from the spot where he'd created the circle, caught the moonlight. It appeared to wink at him, reaching out toward him as if to say, I'm here. Use me.

Desperation propelled him forward. He raced to the knife, leaned down, and picked it up. Warm and comfortable in his hand, it felt right. He ran toward the line of women holding hands and chanting their prayer over and over. Now that he faced them, he could swear at least twelve were standing side by side. Thankfully the men had been taken out of the mix before his soldiers abandoned him. Both of them lay on the ground, neither one moving. Good. Served both of them right for having the audacity to try to stop him.

Time to take care of the women. "Bitches," he screamed and ran straight for the two in the center, one with dark hair, one with silver. They would pay for their interference. The dagger held high, he readied himself to take those two first and as many of the others as he could. Blood would run this night.

"I don't think so, fucker." The voice came deep and menacing from out of the darkness.

So intent on his charge, he vaguely registered the sound of a man's voice, followed by the distinct boom of a gunshot right before pain exploded in his chest. His fall to the ground was as big a shock as the pain. Hadn't he been the only one carrying a gun out here? A gun he lost to the power of the spirits. Somewhere in the darkness it lay loaded and utterly useless to him. He blinked at the dark sky, the winking canopy of stars, and the magnificent Black Moon before his eyes closed.

CHAPTER TWENTY-ONE

Aradia let go of Mercy's hand. The moment the portal slammed shut, the Old Ones vanished. The chorus of voices disappeared, and the night grew quiet. She had yet to process what had happened. Nothing she'd imagined when they'd begun this journey what seemed like weeks ago and was, in fact, a couple of days ago. She held tight to Mercy's hand.

"Somebody want to tell me what the hell is going on out here? And why was that guy trying to kill you?" A man in uniform put his gun back into the holster at his waist. A big guy who looked even bigger in a bullet-proof vest.

Mercy shook her head. "Frank, thank you for stopping him."

"Wasn't going to let him hurt my favorite resident. Who's your friend?" He nodded in Aradia's direction.

"This is Aradia. You know Tim, and you've met my friend Rufus. Everyone, if I haven't introduced you before, this is Deputy Sheriff Frank Long. Good friend. Great cop."

Both Rufus and Tim were sitting up, blinking. Whatever the demons had done to them thankfully wasn't fatal. Likely they'd be black and blue, given how hard they went down. If that were the worst of it, she doubted either would complain. Not loudly anyway. "You guys okay?" She ran to Tim and helped him up. He in turn extended a hand to Rufus and, as soon as he stood, pulled him into an embrace.

When Tim stepped back, he looked at Aradia. "Bastard caught me off guard. I wasn't expecting that punch of magic. I couldn't move."

Rufus rolled his head. "That was as weird as the shot of magic I took earlier. That guy and his buddies had some serious chops. Hope we don't have to face them again anytime soon."

"Did you see anything?" Mercy took his hand and stared into his eyes.

Rufus frowned and nodded. "What I saw was straight from the apocalypse, and I'll tell you what, little sister. It's a good thing your mom taught you that ritual. Those sons of bitches would have destroyed everything. There wasn't a decent soul in the bunch. Calling on the Old Ones saved us all." Rufus turned and stared at the cleared spot in the mountain, now looking like a barren patch of mountainside and not a fiery, gaping portal to the underworld.

"Again, anybody want to explain?" Frank continued to look around, clearly confused. "I only caught the tail end of whatever was happening out here, and it looked pretty freaky to me."

She turned to Mercy. "You want to explain it to your friend?"

Mercy shook her head. "Frank, you wouldn't believe me if I told you."

"Well, I've got three more bodies out there besides the one you called in earlier." He pointed down the mountain. "This is part of those, isn't it?"

Mercy looked taken aback, which pretty much echoed what Aradia felt at that news. "You found three more bodies?"

"Yeah. All women. One shot. Two, we're not even sure yet. Given the darkness and how late it is, it's going to be hours before we piece together what happened to them."

Aradia pointed to the man on the ground. "Your killer is right there." Given the toxins escaping from the cracks, he may not have technically killed the two innocent hikers. The others, absolutely, and if he got tagged for all of the deaths, even better. She planned to do her part to ensure he got the blame for all the murders.

"How do you know?" Deputy Frank studied her face.

Aradia just did. "It's him. Your forensics will be able to prove it." Again, nothing to back up the bold statement except her gut.

"He dead?" Tim leaned in to look closer.

"Don't touch anything." Frank slipped on a pair of blue latex gloves before he walked over and put two fingers on the man's neck. "He's alive."

"He's dangerous." Aradia didn't trust that he wouldn't pull some magic out, and no way did she want that portal to open again.

Frank spoke quietly into a radio and, after kicking the knife away, checked for any additional weapons. He then handcuffed the still-unconscious man. He looked up at Aradia. "Just in case."

"Good plan." Better that he couldn't use his hands or touch anything inside his disrupted circle. Safety first a good rule for a reason. "You might want to gag him too." She'd feel better if he couldn't talk. Whatever came out of his mouth earlier was at least partially responsible for the breach.

"That's a little outside standard protocol. I'm going to ask again if you want to fill me in on all of this." He waved his arms to encompass the circle, the mountainside, and the sky. "I know what I saw, and I know what I'm seeing now. Either I'm going crazy or you guys have some serious explaining to do. Thing is, I'm pretty certain I'm not going crazy."

Aradia looked at Mercy, who shrugged. "You want the truth or a really good lie?"

For a long moment, Frank stared into her eyes, his thumbs hooked into his equipment belt. "We'll go with the truth, and could be we land on the lie. Let's start with the dogs. Tell me why they're both staring at the side of the mountain like it's a giant marrow bone."

Mercy kept standing, although her knees grew weak. When Mom had taught her that prayer all those years ago, she'd learned it not because she believed in it or thought she'd ever have to use it. No. She'd learned it word-for-word to please Mom. She'd have done anything for the woman who rescued her from a life inside the child-welfare system. Mom had saved her life, flat out, in so many ways, and for that, Mercy had given her utter devotion.

Her devotion had been rewarded with unmatched skills as an herbalist, with a solid sense of self, great confidence, and a head full of appreciation for the legions of skilled, unappreciated women who had gone before them. Those same women who came to her in a moment of ultimate crisis when she'd asked for their help. Her eyes had filled with tears the moment she'd felt Mom's spirit. She, too, had appeared to help her adopted daughter. To see her face once more, even if it had only been for a few minutes, filled Mercy's heart. That she whispered in her ear before she left made the tears fall. *She's the one.* Her gaze now moved to Aradia, and another tear escaped.

"Mercy? Anything you want to share?" Frank had his hands on his hips as he took in the totality of their surroundings.

"Like Aradia said, truth or lie?" Frank would surely think them all ready for professional help if they gave him the whole truth.

"Just spill. We'll sort it out before the rest of the crew gets here, and that means you have about ten minutes. I've already called the coordinates in to them, so start talking. I want the down-and-dirty version for now."

She glanced at Aradia once more, who nodded. "Okay, if you want the truth, here it is."

When she finished, the response she expected to receive from Frank didn't happen. No big sighs, no eye-rolling, nothing except rapt attention and an expression of contemplation. As she wound down after five full minutes of fast talk, he pressed his lips together and nodded. "All right. I might think you all need to get some serious therapy if I hadn't seen what I did."

"You believe me?" Shocked didn't even touch it, and something akin to relief flooded through her.

His subtle nod told her a lot. "Here's the thing. I'm a guy who believes in God, and if I believe in God, I also believe in Satan. What I saw when I got here took the battle of heaven and hell to a level I never expected to see, but there it was right in my face."

"Others won't believe it." She wasn't naive enough to think people in general would accept the truth of what happened out here. She had a pretty open mind, and it still shocked her.

"Naw, they won't." He shook his head as he looked around. "Definitely won't."

"So?" How he planned to spin this she didn't have a clue.

He shrugged and pressed his lips together. "So, we lie."

Mercy blinked a couple times, wondering if she'd heard that right. "We lie."

"Yup. Lie. Spin. However you want to phrase it. We come up with an explanation people will actually believe. If we all stick with it, nobody will be the wiser."

Aradia put a hand on his shoulder. "I could kiss you."

He gave her a little nod. "Another time maybe."

"I don't think so." Mercy looked into Aradia's eyes. "You're mine."

"Oh, so it's like that." Something flickered in Aradia's eyes that made her heart race.

"It is so like that." Her heart pounded, only now it wasn't because the world teetered on the brink of disaster. Overhead, a shooting star crossed the sky. Her first thought at the spectacular sight: *Thanks, Mom.*

Frank threw up his arms. "How about we clean up this mess, and you two can work out whatever that is later?"

Mercy turned and hugged him. "Deal."

Frank cocked his head as he plopped on his hat while he stared at the dogs. "Is it just me, or do those dogs glow?"

EPILOGUE

Eleven Months Later

Aradia stood on the deck drinking her coffee. A couple of the dogs were barking in the kennels. Funny how life changed in the blink of an eye. Or perhaps the opening of a portal. Here she'd trained both herself and her dogs for years, knowing that one day they'd all be called upon to put their skills to work. That had happened on a moonlit night on Mt. St. Helens. No eruption this time, just a madman with otherworldly skills who almost succeeded in doing the unthinkable. No one knew, except for the five of them on the mountain that night, how close they came to losing everything.

She sipped the dark brew, warm and full-bodied. Just the way she liked it, especially when prepared by the hands of a very special herbalist. Turned out her skills extended to roasting coffee beans as well as working with plants. One surprise after another. There'd been more than one over the months. Surreal to think it had been almost a year ago. Across the yard, Lizzy waved as she ran with several of the young dogs in training. Lizzy playing with and working the dogs was, and always would be, a joy to watch.

"You want to talk about it?" Mercy came outside with a mug in her hand. She sat in one of the padded chairs, stretched her legs out, and stared up at Aradia. "The boys will be here in an hour."

"You know they're not boys." Aradia tilted her head as she studied Mercy's face. The breeze picked up her hair and blew it around her face. She loved when it did that.

Mercy shrugged. "Rufus has been like a brother, so he'll always be a boy to me, and Tim gets it by association. The price he pays for loving my brother from another mother." She smiled and took another drink. "If I do say so, I think this is one of my better roasts."

She ignored the attempt to change the subject. "Still not politically correct."

"I can live with it, and you're avoiding the real question here, missy." She smiled, and it took the edge off her words.

It had been eleven months since the showdown on Mt. St. Helens, and they had learned a lot after the proverbial smoke cleared. The man in the circle, August Fian, certainly hadn't been a slouch. He and one of the women victims, June Fian, were descendants of the North Berwick witches. Power had run in their blood for generations. Both lusted after more. His killing didn't stop with his sister either. He had killed his ex-wife, Willa, and another woman named Ama. They never did figure out exactly how Ama factored into the whole thing, and August wasn't talking. Like a spoiled child, he currently sat in a cell refusing to talk to anyone. Frank had developed a rock-solid case against the killer, and August would never have a chance to practice his black magic again.

It wasn't just power that ran in their blood. A desire to rule did too. His plan to release the demons and bring them under his control came way too close to working. For their part, they all benefitted from a big lesson: don't disregard the power of the Old Ones.

She looked out at the kennels and said, "Mona and her hubby are heading to Sabina's for a few weeks. They're going to help with some of Sabina's pups." Her cousin had done a fantastic job with the dogs while they'd been out stopping demons on the mountain, and her hubby remained one of the best vets in any country.

"Your cousin is a peach. I like her a lot. Can't wait to meet your sister."

Aradia thought the same. Mercy and her sister would be fast friends. "Sabina said she'll make a trip here soon." Small talk was good. Not that she was avoiding a more serious conversation. No, not her.

"Stop stalling." Mercy turned her mug around and around between her hands.

Her words were softened by her smile, but she wasn't wrong. Aradia had been stalling for weeks, and this morning was no different. Or maybe, to be more accurate, not stalling as much as processing. It wasn't just a reassessment of how to approach future breaches. More like a whole new paradigm, professionally and personally.

She finally admitted, "I don't know where to start."

"How about something along the lines of how this thing between us is pretty cool, and you'd like to see where it goes. You know, like taking the next step." Now she smiled and sipped from her mug.

"Yeah, that." Aradia leaned back against the railing and tipped her face up to the morning sun. Warm, as though the forces of the universe smiled on her.

"Can you say it?"

Her nerves buzzed, her fingers tingled. She wanted to hold onto the feeling of warmth. She took a deep breath and blew it out slowly. "I—"

Mercy interrupted. "What did you tell me when we first met? That you didn't want to label yourself. That you married a man you loved, your best friend." No bitterness in her words. They were soft and encouraging. No pressure, only a simple request for the truth.

She brought her gaze back to Mercy. "I did, and I dated a few men as well."

"But?" She raised her eyebrows.

Aradia smiled. "But I reserve the right to love whomever I want to. No labels and no expectations. Love whomever I want to love."

Mercy put her mug down on the small table beside her chair and rested her arms on her knees as she leaned toward Aradia. "And where does that leave you now? I know where I stand."

"You don't have much choice. Your mother's spirit pointed toward me."

Mercy shook her head. "Nope."

"Nope?" That denial surprised her. Mercy had told her what her mother's spirit had said to her out there on the mountain.

"She didn't point me toward you. She confirmed what I already knew."

"You believe that she meant I'm the one."

Mercy smiled and nodded. "Without a shred of doubt. You are so the one. You pushed away the darkness, you know. You pushed it away and filled my heart with joy. You. Just you." Mercy pointed her index finger in her direction.

A gentle breeze wafted across her face, and in the distance hung the sweet sound of a songbird. Or maybe, the Old Ones once more coming to help. This time not to drive back demons but to guide her. Aradia chose to believe in the latter and let it all go. The fear. The doubt. "I do love you." Tears pooled in her eyes. The words had actually crossed her lips.

"I know." Mercy picked up her mug again and tilted it toward her in a sort of toast. "You know." She stood up and looked out over the acres that stretched out all around them. "This would be a good place for an herb farm. A couple of greenhouses right there." She pointed to the south. "A workshop over by the birch trees."

Aradia threw back her head and laughed. "And what about your farm on the west side? You really think you can leave it?"

Mercy laughed along with her. "Oh, it's easy to walk away from, given it's a perfect place for Rufus and Tim to live and work."

"And Clemons." The big boy had healed nicely after his injury, which turned out to be minor, and had been back at work within a few weeks. Bless the Guardians and their blessed existence.

"Most definitely Clemons."

She took a sip of coffee before she responded. "Then I don't think we have any choice."

Mercy turned serious. "I mean it, Aradia. I don't want to spend another day without you. I didn't realize until the day you showed up at my farm that I've been waiting for you my whole life."

Aradia set her mug on the rail, walked to Mercy, and took her hands to pull her to her feet. Then, she took off the necklace she'd worn since the day of her divorce and dropped it onto the deck, along with the gold band. It made a small clatter and slipped between the cracks to disappear in the darkness below.

Mercy smiled. "That's a really good start. Anything else?"

She wrapped her arms around Mercy in a tight hug. "What do you say we start forever right now?"

About the Author

Sheri Lewis Wohl grew up in northeast Washington State and though she always thought she'd move away, never has. Despite traveling throughout the United States, Sheri always finds her way back home. And so she lives, plays, and writes amidst mountains, evergreens, and abundant wildlife.

Sheri likes to write stories that typically include mystery, murder, and mayhem along with a bit of the strange and unusual. Always with a touch of romance. Multiple novels have been Golden Crown Literary Awards finalists, and her novel *Twisted Whispers* was a 2016 Golden Crown Literary Award winner for Paranormal/Horror. *The Talebearer* was a 2019 LAMBDA finalist.

A former nationally certified human remains detection K9 handler, Sheri and her German shepherd partner, Zoey, deployed throughout the Northwest. She continues to train with her youngest dog, Deuce, is working on running half marathons in all 50 states, and puts her acting chops to use every chance she gets. You can catch her in televisions shows such as *Z Nation*, *Grimm*, and *Going Home*.

Books Available from Bold Strokes Books

Close to Home by Allisa Bahney. Eli Thomas has to decide if avoiding her hometown forever is worth losing the people who used to mean the most to her, especially Aracely Hernandez, the girl who got away. (978-1-63679-661-1)

Golden Girl by Julie Tizard. In 1993, "Don't ask, don't tell" forces everyone to lie, but Air Force nurse Lt. Sofia Sanchez and injured instructor pilot Lt. Gillian Guthman have to risk telling each other the truth in order to fly and survive. (978-1-63679-751-9)

Innis Harbor by Patricia Evans. When Amir Farzaneh meets and falls in love with Loch, a dark secret lurking in her past reappears, threatening the happiness she'd just started to believe could be hers. (978-1-63679-781-6)

The Blessed by Anne Shade. Layla and Suri are brought together by fate to defeat the darkness threatening to tear their world apart. What they don't expect to discover is a love that might set them free. (978-1-63679-715-1)

The Guardians by Sheri Lewis Wohl. Dogs, devotion, and determination are all that stand between darkness and light. (978-1-63679-681-9)

The Mogul Meets Her Match by Julia Underwood. When CEO Claire Beauchamp goes undercover as a customer of Abby Pita's café to help seal a deal that will solidify her career, she doesn't expect to be so drawn to her. When the truth is revealed, will she break Abby's heart? (978-1-63679-784-7)

Trial Run by Carsen Taite. When Reggie Knoll and Brooke Dawson wind up serving on a jury together, their one task—reaching a unanimous verdict—is derailed by the fiery clash of their personalities, the intensity of their attraction, and a secret that could threaten Brooke's life. (978-1-63555-865-4)

Waterlogged by Nance Sparks. When conservation warden Jordan Pearce discovers a body floating in the flowage, the serenity of the Northwoods is rocked. (978-1-63679-699-4)

Accidentally in Love by Kimberly Cooper Griffin. Nic and Lee have good reasons for keeping their distance. So why does their growing attraction seem more like a love-hate relationship? (978-1-63679-759-5)

Fatal Foul Play by David S. Pederson. After eight friends are stranded in an old lodge by a blinding snowstorm, a brutal murder leaves Mark Maddox to solve the crime as he discovers deadly secrets about people he thought he knew. (978-1-63679-794-6)

Frosted by the Girl Next Door by Aurora Rey and Jaime Clevenger. When heartbroken Casey Stevens opens a sex shop next door to uptight cupcake baker Tara McCoy, things get a little frosty. (978-1-63679-723-6)

Ghost of the Heart by Catherine Friend. Being possessed by a ghost was not on Gwen's bucket list, but she must admit that ghosts might be real, and one is obviously trying to send her a message. (978-1-63555-112-9)

Hot Honey Love by Nan Campbell. When chef Stef Lombardozzi puts her cooking career into the hands of filmmaker Mallory Radowski—the pickiest eater alive—she doesn't anticipate how hard she falls for her. (978-1-63679-743-4)

London by Patricia Evans. Jaq's and Bronwyn's lives become entwined as dangerous secrets emerge and Bronwyn's seemingly perfect life starts to unravel. (978-1-63679-778-6)

This Christmas by Georgia Beers. When Sam's grandmother rigs the Christmas parade to make Sam and Keegan queen and queen, sparks fly, but they can't forget the Big Embarrassing Thing that makes romance a total nope. (978-1-63679-729-8)

Unwrapped by D. Jackson Leigh. Asia du Muir is not going to let some party girl actress ruin her best chance to get noticed by a Broadway critic. Everyone knows you should never mix business and pleasure. (978-1-63679-667-3)

Language Lessons by Sage Donnell. Grace and Lenka never expected to fall in love. Is home really where the heart is if it means giving up your dreams? (978-1-63679-725-0)

New Horizons by Shia Woods. When Quinn Collins meets Alex Anders, Horizon Theater's enigmatic managing director, a passionate connection ignites, but amidst the complex backdrop of theater politics, their budding romance faces a formidable challenge. (978-1-63679-683-3)

Scrambled: A Tuesday Night Book Club Mystery by Jaime Maddox. Avery Hutchins makes a discovery about her father's death that will force her to face an impossible choice between doing what is right and finally finding a way to regain a part of herself she had lost. (978-1-63679-703-8)

Stolen Hearts by Michele Castleman. Finding the thief who stole a precious heirloom will become Ella's first move in a dangerous game of wits that exposes family secrets and could lead to her family's financial ruin. (978-1-63679-733-5)

Synchronicity by J.J. Hale. Dance, destiny, and undeniable passion collide at a summer camp as Haley and Cal navigate a love story that intertwines past scars with present desires. (978-1-63679-677-2)

The First Kiss by Patricia Evans. As the intrigue surrounding her latest case spins dangerously out of control, military police detective Parker Haven must choose between her career and the woman she's falling in love with. (978-1-63679-775-5)

Wild Fire by Radclyffe & Julie Cannon. When Olivia returns to the Red Sky Ranch, Riley's carefully crafted safe world goes up in flames. Can they take a risk and cross the fire line to find love? (978-1-63679-727-4)

Writ of Love by Cassidy Crane. Kelly and Jillian struggle to navigate the ruthless battleground of Big Law, grappling with desire, ambition, and the thin line between success and surrender. (978-1-63679-738-0)

Back to Belfast by Emma L. McGeown. Two colleagues are asked to trade jobs. Claire moves to Vancouver and Stacie moves to Belfast, and though they've never met in person, they can't seem to escape a growing attraction from afar. (978-1-63679-731-1)

Exposure by Nicole Disney and Kimberly Cooper Griffin. For photographer Jax Bailey and delivery driver Trace Logan, keeping it casual is a matter of perspective. (978-1-63679-697-0)

Hunt of Her Own by Elena Abbott. Finding forever won't be easy, but together Danaan's and Ashly's paths lead back to the supernatural sanctuary of Terabend. (978-1-63679-685-7)

Perfect by Kris Bryant. They say opposites attract, but Alix and Marianna have totally different dreams. No Hollywood love story is perfect, right? (978-1-63679-601-7)

Royal Expectations by Jenny Frame. When childhood sweethearts Princess Teddy Buckingham and Summer Fisher reunite, their feelings resurface and so does the public scrutiny that tore them apart. (978-1-63679-591-1)

Shadow Rider by Gina L. Dartt. In the Shadows, one can easily find death, but can Shay and Keagan find love as they fight to save the Five Nations? (978-1-63679-691-8)

The Breakdown by Ronica Black. Vaughn and Natalie have chemistry, but the outside world keeps knocking at the door, threatening more trouble, making the love and the life they want together impossible. (978-1-63679-675-8)

Tribute by L.M. Rose. To save her people, Fiona will be the tribute in a treaty marriage to the Tipruii princess, Simaala, and spend the rest of her days on the other side of the wall between their races. (978-1-63679-693-2)

Wild Wales by Patricia Evans. When Finn and Aisling fall in love, they must decide whether to return to the safety of the lives they had, or take a chance on wild love in windswept Wales. (978-1-63679-771-7)